"Damn you," Kate muttered

"Sorry, but we have to talk." Matt glanced at the elevator numbers. "And nine floors simply isn't enough time."

"The combined floors of the Empire State Building and both World Trade Center Towers wouldn't give you enough time to apologize for what you've done!"

"Then I guess I have no choice." Matt pushed Stop, and with a bump and grind that would have made Gypsy Rose Lee envious, the elevator ground to a halt, trapping Kate with the most infuriatingly irresistible man she'd ever met.

"I thought we had a deal," she said breathlessly, as he came closer.

"We do," he assured her. "But this should seal the bargain." His mouth widened and his tongue began to gently probe her lips.

ABOUT THE AUTHOR

Connie is the author of eight contemporary and five historical romances, but she is especially proud of this, her first Harlequin American Romance, because it gave her a chance to write a romantic comedy romp and bring her favorite hero to life. "Every man should have a little Matt Gallagher in him," Connie says. "And every woman should be lucky enough to find him."

Connie loves to hear from her readers. Letters can be sent to:

Connie Bennett
P.O. Box 14
Dexter, Missouri 63841

Please feel free to send an SASE, for a response from Connie.

Books by Connie Bennett

HARLEQUIN SUPERROMANCE

CONNIE BENNETT

FIFTY WAYS TO BE YOUR LOVER

Harlequin Books

TORONTO • NEW YORK • LONDON
AMSTERDAM • PARIS • SYDNEY • HAMBURG
STOCKHOLM • ATHENS • TOKYO • MILAN
MADRID • WARSAW • BUDAPEST • AUCKLAND

This book is dedicated to Julianne, for a lot of reasons

ISBN 0-373-16547-1

FIFTY WAYS TO BE YOUR LOVER

This edition published by arrangement with Harlequin Enterprises B. V.

Printed in U.S.A.

Chapter One

"Oh, my God. He's gorgeous!"

Kate Franklyn heard the soft exclamation and glanced down at her petite blond friend. "Dee, are you at it again?" she asked with mock exasperation. "I can't take you anywhere."

"Oh, but it's worth it this time, I swear! This guy is a definite ten!"

Kate chuckled. Dee Angstrom had elevated the practice of man-watching to an art form. Wherever the two friends went, Dee was constantly on the lookout for handsome men, much to Kate's chagrin.

In this instance, though, Kate could hardly blame Dee for engaging in her favorite pastime. They were pressed into a corner of a crowded theater lobby, waiting for the box office to clear so they could get their tickets. They had already studied the cast photos on the wall beside them. They had cursed the rainy weather and discussed the day's problems at the newspaper where they both worked. Until the play began, there wasn't much else to occupy them.

Normally Kate didn't pay much attention to Dee's hunks, but then, Dee rarely gave any man a Perfect Ten. That alone was enough to spark Kate's curiosity, but before she could turn to judge for herself, Dee grabbed hold of her arm to restrain her. "No, don't look now. He's glancing this way."

Kate did as she had been told and resisted the urge to look. "Who is it?" she asked, thinking that Dee had spotted a movie star. "From the size of this reaction and rapturous look on your face it's got to be Tom Selleck or Mel Gibson," she said, though what either of those stars would be doing in one of Los Angeles's smallest theaters, Kate couldn't imagine.

"He's better."

"What could possibly be better than Tom or Mel?"

"How about a combination of both?"

"Impossible." Kate shook her head definitively. "Such a man does not exist. At least not on this planet."

"Yes, he does, and I'm looking directly at him out of the corner of my eye."

Rather than challenge the convoluted logic of that statement, Kate pressed, "Well, who is it? A movie star? Television?"

Dee shook her head. "No one famous—not yet, anyway. He's gotta be an actor, though."

"Deanna, you think every man you meet should be an actor," she teased, her curiosity abating now that she knew the man wasn't famous. Like everyone else in Hollywood, Kate was always excited about seeing a celebrity in person. In her capacity as an entertainment critic for the Los Angeles *Sentinel,* she had met more than her share, but there was still something that never failed to thrill her about stumbling into the path of Sylvester Stallone in a parking lot in Westwood or seeing Michelle Pfeiffer on the escalator at Neiman Marcus.

But unlike Deanna, who made man-watching a full time career, Kate was still in a state of hibernation from having recently ended a relationship that had lasted four years. The painful deterioration of her romance with superstar Dan McBride was still a fresh wound and Kate wasn't looking for a new involvement.

"But he *should* be a star," Deanna was saying. "You should see this guy!"

"How can I? You won't let me turn around!" Kate said with a laugh as she ran one hand absently through her long, sable-colored hair. It was still a little damp from the rain. "I swear, Dee, you are incorrigible. Are you ever going to stop man-hunting?"

"Not until I catch a good one. Anyway, this one's not for me. He's too tall."

"Speaking for all the women of the world five foot ten and over, Dee, I must remind you that no man is ever *too* tall."

The blonde cast an envious glance at her tall, willowy friend. "I meant he's too tall for me, but he's perfect for you."

"You forget, I'm unavailable just now. I'm here to review a play, not shop, and if I were, I wouldn't do it in a bargain basement like the Players Theater."

"Snob."

"No..." Kate corrected her lightly, "just not interested."

"Well, you should be." As though dangling a bone in front of a ravenous dog, Dee began a tantalizing description. "Black hair with a sexy beard and moustache cut real close—you know, like Richard Chamberlain's when he did *King Solomon's Mines.*"

"Find Richard Chamberlain for me and I'll be glad to look."

"Cute little dimples when he smiles," Dee continued, pointedly ignoring the interruption. "Great eyes that have *got* to be blue... broad shoulders..."

"What scent of cologne is he wearing?"

"Don't get cute, Kate, you're gonna flip when you see this guy."

"Okay, okay." She sighed with resignation as she checked her watch. They still had more than five minutes to curtain time. "Is the coast clear yet? When do I get to see Tall, Dark and Handsome?"

"Just a minute...." Dee paused until her quarry turned his head, then she gave the signal. "All right... *now.* Across the room in the opposite corner."

Casually Kate turned as though idly scanning the room. It didn't take any guesswork to figure out which man was the subject of Deanna's instant infatuation. To say that he was handsome was an understatement. Even gorgeous didn't come close. The man was just too stunning for words.

Nearly a full head taller than anyone around him, the dark-haired stranger stuck out like a sore thumb. Dee had drawn a very accurate picture of him physically, but what she had failed to mention was the magnetic confidence that fairly oozed from him. He seemed at ease and comfortable, a pleasant half smile on his face that bespoke his interest in everything going on around him, even though he seemed to be alone.

His date's in the powder room, Kate guessed. A man like this certainly didn't go anywhere without a beautiful woman on his arm.

Probably because Deanna had given this Adonis such a big buildup, Kate violated the first rule of man-watching her friend had taught her: Never focus on the subject too long when looking directly at him. As though sensing her stare, Tall, Dark and Handsome turned toward her. Their eyes met and held, his gaze pinning Kate like a butterfly to a board and setting off a flurry of flapping the likes of which her stomach had never felt before.

An intake of breath hitched in Kate's chest for a fraction of a second, but she attributed it to embarrassment for having been caught looking. Rather than admit her chagrin, she managed a polite, bemused smile that acknowledged her guilt without being a come-on. He returned the smile wholeheartedly, and Kate realized that Dee was right. His eyes *had* to be blue... Paul Newman sky-blue with a devilish twinkle.

Amused at her own thoughts, Kate allowed the moment to pass and looked casually away, breaking the contact. She turned back to Deanna and made an exaggerated effort to look normal. "You were right, he's gorgeous."

"Oh, how romantic." Dee sighed melodramatically. "That smile when he looked at you! The way your faces both lit up—I could feel the electricity pulsing across the room."

Kate laughed, probably a little louder than Deanna's performance deserved because she was certain that Tall, Dark and Handsome was still looking at her—a thought that made her suddenly feel very much alive. Still, she chided, "You've been reading too many romances. Smoldering glances across a crowded room and love at first sight don't exist."

"You mean your pulse isn't racing and your lips aren't trembling in anticipation?" Dee asked with mock innocence.

"My pulse is fine and my lips are as steady as a rock, thank you."

"Uh-huh.... I guess that's why your eyes are sparkling and you're more animated than I've seen you in ages. Take it from me, kid, even old Dandy Dan never made you light up like you did when that hunk looked at you."

Kate smiled, grateful that she had finally reached the point that hearing Dan's name no longer felt like a blow to her midsection. She still wasn't able to watch his movies or see a picture of him without resentment and regret flooding over her like a tidal wave, but after six months, speaking Dan McBride's name was no longer forbidden in Kate's presence.

In fact, she was finally able to joke about him to an extent, and she grinned wickedly. "Let's leave Dandy Dan out of this, okay? Have you forgotten that he's become the man every woman in America wants to be tucked in with at night?"

"That's right. And from what I hear, he's systematically 'tucking' his way through the population."

"Yes, ladies and gentlemen," Kate intoned in a quiet radio-announcer voice, "this is H&R Block with Reason Number Fourteen why Kate Franklyn dumped Dan McBride."

Dee smiled with admiration. "Have I told you lately that I'm proud of you, kiddo? It's so good to see you able to talk about that drunken Irish gigolo without that horrible look of pain in your eyes."

"Time heals all wounds. Or so they say."

"Now, if you'd only start dating again—"

"Oh, no, please!" Kate begged plaintively. "Not this again. I should have known you had an ulterior motive when you started all that flattery."

"No ulterior motive, Kate, just a friendly desire to see you get yourself back into circulation."

"When I'm ready, I will," she promised. "But not yet. Dan was my whole life for four years, and before he became a star I was never happier. I poured everything I had into making that relationship work, and I've got to recharge my batteries before I can afford to expend any energy on another man."

"You're just gun-shy."

"You bet your life I am. Listen, when a revolver explodes in your face, you learn to be a little more cautious about loading it the next time."

"Honey, I'm not suggesting you pull the trigger yet." Dee smiled slyly. "Just...fondle it a little. Get the feel of it again. No matter what you think, Dan McBride never was right for you, even *before* he went off the deep end with all that superstar business. Why don't you give Jack the Jock a try?"

Kate was mortified. Jack the Jock was the not-so-affectionate nickname Dee and her colleagues in advertising had given to one particularly obnoxious sports reporter who thought he was God's gift to women. "Are you kidding? Dee, the man has eight hands and more muscles than a seafood restaurant—and most of them are in his head!"

"Oh, come on, he's not that bad."

"Have you stood close to him lately? He wears a cologne called *Locker Room*. I'm not going to date someone who smells like dirty gym socks and thinks a theater is just a place to eat popcorn and watch Jean-Claude Van Damme movies."

"Those are only excuses and you know it."

"The man is not my type and I wouldn't date him even if I was ready, which I'm not, so could we drop it, please? The play will be starting in a few minutes."

"Okay. We can discuss this later—" Kate's razor-sharp glare stopped Dee in midsentence "—or maybe not."

Kate smiled. "Good choice. Now come on, let's get our tickets." She started across the room but couldn't resist one last covert glance toward Tall, Dark and Handsome's corner. He was still there, and he was still looking.

It was everything Kate could do to squelch the jolt of satisfaction that shot through her.

WILLPOWER HAD NEVER BEEN Matt Gallagher's strong suit, so he didn't even bother trying to take his eyes off the gorgeous brunette. She was just too stunning for words, and Matt liked the idea of being stunned. It had been a long time since a woman had knocked his socks off, and this one also got his shoes, his trousers and was doing interesting things to his Fruit of the Loom briefs.

Since moving to Los Angeles, Matt had discovered that the city contained more beautiful women per square inch than anywhere else in the world, but this one put the others to shame. She had shoulder-length sable hair that was tousled and windblown from her bout with the rain. Her features were elegant, even classic, with high cheekbones, a perfect patrician nose, soft, full lips and an oval face framed by her lustrous, silky hair. Her body was tall and willowy, and she moved with a natural grace that added an aura of elegance.

Her face and form were what one expected to see on a magazine cover or movie screen, yet here she was in the Players Theater doing her damnedest to pretend that she wasn't as aware of Matt as he was of her. That suggested a hint of shyness he found intriguing.

He had to meet her. He had to have a name to put to that gorgeous face—and a phone number wouldn't hurt, either.

Matt caught the covert glance she threw in his direction as she and her petite blond friend moved toward the box office, and he smiled. Yep. Phone number. Definitely.

He checked his watch. It was time to take his seat, but he still had a little leeway for a reconnaissance mission, so instead of circumventing the line at the box office, he moved toward it. He wouldn't be able to sleep tonight if he didn't at least find out what color those fabulous almond-shaped eyes were.

Before he had taken two steps, though, a booming voice brought him and everyone else in the lobby to a halt.

"Signorina Franklyn! *Mia bellissima, signorina!*"

The absurdly phony Italian accent filled the room, and Matt swiveled around to find a portly gentleman who was surrounded by an entourage that resembled a small army. The effusive little man rushed toward Matt's sable-haired goddess as though she were a fire in desperate need of extinguishing. In his right hand he waved an unlit cigarette, held in the European manner with the filter outermost, and his left he extended to her, nearly upsetting the delicate balance of the calf-length overcoat draped across his shoulders.

Matt glanced at his goddess and felt an automatic rush of sympathy. She looked as though she wished the ground would open up and swallow her whole, but when that didn't happen she plastered on a polite, reserved smile. Hesitantly she extended her hand, and endured the trial of having the phony Italian kiss it a bit too fervently.

Matt felt simultaneous surges of envy and dislike for the cartoonish gigolo. He edged closer to hear their conversation.

"Signor DeAngelo. It's a pleasure to see you again," the goddess said in a hushed voice.

If she was hoping the "Italian" would take the hint and lower his volume a decibel or two, she had to be disappointed because the subtlety was obviously lost on him.

"Signorina Franklyn, the pleasure is mine," he bellowed, glancing around, indicating to his entourage that he wanted them to gather closer. "My friends one and all, you musta meet this delightful lady. Signorina Katerina Franklyn. She is here to review my humble production for the mighty Los Angeles *Sentinel,* but her beauty alone gracing our theater is all the reward thata we need."

Right on cue the entourage burst into applause and every patron in the lobby swiveled around to look at the embarrassed Ms. Franklyn. She accepted the smattering of applause with a wan smile and a gracious nod.

"Thank you for your kind words, *signor,* but you'd best be careful or I will suspect you're trying to influence my review with flattery."

Oh, boy, Matt thought, his spirits sinking so low that he barely heard the rest of the couple's conversation. The "Italian" was the director of the play, and he was giving Matt's goddess an absurd line of garbage about levels of Freudian meaning in his production of Noel Coward's frothy comedy *Blithe Spirit.* Under other circumstances, Matt would have been listening—and laughing. But not just now. He had a name to go with his goddess's incredible face: she was Kate Franklyn, the theater critic.

Chapter Five

Matt leaned back at his desk, staring sightlessly at the stack of newspaper and magazine articles that littered his desk. It was Sunday, and the *Press-Enterprise* newsroom was as quiet as any newsroom ever got. He appreciated the near privacy, because his foray into the *Enterprise*'s morgue files had nothing to do with work. He'd come in this afternoon to do a little private research into the life of Kate Franklyn, and he'd gotten more than he bargained for.

Matt felt thoroughly disgusted, but not by Kate. For her, he felt nothing but a sympathy that was nearly as strong as his attraction. It had been clear to him yesterday that Kate's refusal to date him had little or nothing to do with the white lies he had told or the way he had pirated the lead of her review. Those stunts weren't his finest hour, but they weren't capital offenses, either. And since she had lied as well, Matt had figured they were just about even in the veracity department.

No, Kate's reticence was genuine enough to make her want to deny their astonishing attraction to each other, and it went a lot deeper than irritation over a practical joke. She had enjoyed their verbal sparring. She had been as stunned by the sensuality of their kiss as Matt

He turned toward the exit and was halfway across the lobby before Kate realized that his words weren't a casual goodbye. They were a promise.

He had to meet her. He had to have a name to put to that gorgeous face—and a phone number wouldn't hurt, either.

Matt caught the covert glance she threw in his direction as she and her petite blond friend moved toward the box office, and he smiled. Yep. Phone number. Definitely.

He checked his watch. It was time to take his seat, but he still had a little leeway for a reconnaissance mission, so instead of circumventing the line at the box office, he moved toward it. He wouldn't be able to sleep tonight if he didn't at least find out what color those fabulous almond-shaped eyes were.

Before he had taken two steps, though, a booming voice brought him and everyone else in the lobby to a halt.

"Signorina Franklyn! *Mia bellissima, signorina!*"

The absurdly phony Italian accent filled the room, and Matt swiveled around to find a portly gentleman who was surrounded by an entourage that resembled a small army. The effusive little man rushed toward Matt's sable-haired goddess as though she were a fire in desperate need of extinguishing. In his right hand he waved an unlit cigarette, held in the European manner with the filter outermost, and his left he extended to her, nearly upsetting the delicate balance of the calf-length overcoat draped across his shoulders.

Matt glanced at his goddess and felt an automatic rush of sympathy. She looked as though she wished the ground would open up and swallow her whole, but when that didn't happen she plastered on a polite, reserved smile. Hesitantly she extended her hand, and endured the trial of having the phony Italian kiss it a bit too fervently.

Matt felt simultaneous surges of envy and dislike for the cartoonish gigolo. He edged closer to hear their conversation.

"Signor DeAngelo. It's a pleasure to see you again," the goddess said in a hushed voice.

If she was hoping the "Italian" would take the hint and lower his volume a decibel or two, she had to be disappointed because the subtlety was obviously lost on him.

"Signorina Franklyn, the pleasure is mine," he bellowed, glancing around, indicating to his entourage that he wanted them to gather closer. "My friends one and all, you musta meet this delightful lady. Signorina Katerina Franklyn. She is here to review my humble production for the mighty Los Angeles *Sentinel,* but her beauty alone gracing our theater is all the reward thata we need."

Right on cue the entourage burst into applause and every patron in the lobby swiveled around to look at the embarrassed Ms. Franklyn. She accepted the smattering of applause with a wan smile and a gracious nod.

"Thank you for your kind words, *signor,* but you'd best be careful or I will suspect you're trying to influence my review with flattery."

Oh, boy, Matt thought, his spirits sinking so low that he barely heard the rest of the couple's conversation. The "Italian" was the director of the play, and he was giving Matt's goddess an absurd line of garbage about levels of Freudian meaning in his production of Noel Coward's frothy comedy *Blithe Spirit.* Under other circumstances, Matt would have been listening—and laughing. But not just now. He had a name to go with his goddess's incredible face: she was Kate Franklyn, the theater critic.

Obtaining her phone number was pretty pointless now, and entertaining fantasies about what was underneath her elegant facade would be nothing but an exercise in frustration. Once she heard his name, Matt wouldn't have a prayer of getting to know her. He'd been down this road before and knew exactly what to expect. Damn!

Swallowing his disappointment, he cast one last, longing, regretful glance at his goddess, then continued toward the theater, staying close to the wall to skirt DeAngelo's entourage.

"Oh, Signorina Franklyn, I cana see that you, like many others, have long been deluded," he heard the director saying. "Buta knowing how fair you are, I feel much reassured that you willa keep an open mind about my *produzione.*"

Before the critic could respond, a vapid-looking woman on DeAngelo's right tugged his arm, pulling his attention away, and Kate Franklyn bent toward her blond friend.

"I'll keep an open mind if he'll keep an open front door."

Matt heard the whisper just as he passed behind her, and he couldn't help but chuckle. She heard him, of course, and straightened guiltily, whirling around so abruptly that it set her off-balance. She bumped into Matt, and in reflex, he took hold of her arms to steady her as her startled gaze met his. Her eyes—an astonishing shade of violet—widened in recognition, and she blushed.

An honest-to-God blush! Matt hadn't seen one in ages. The color it added to her face only made her more entrancing, and Matt felt an overpowering surge of desire twisting and curling in his stomach. It lurched lower, startling him with its intensity, and suddenly Matt realized that it didn't matter who Kate Franklyn was. It didn't matter who *he* was, either. He was going to do whatever it took to get to know this woman.

Even if it meant telling a little white lie or two...or three.

Chapter Two

Kate couldn't catch her breath. There he was, Tall, Dark and Handsome, his strong hands relaxing their hold on her arms yet not quite releasing her. His eyes, every bit as blue as Kate had imagined them, were fixed steadily on hers, and for a brief moment she had difficulty drawing a breath. Deanna's quip about him making her pulse race certainly didn't seem as farfetched as it had a few minutes ago!

He *was* gorgeous. Simply phenomenal. The blue eyes twinkled with amusement, not only because of Kate's jest about DeAngelo, but as though he knew some secret that he shared with her and her alone. His full lips were drawn tight into a barely restrained grin that seemed ready to evolve into a laugh, and the dark line of his close-clipped beard accentuated deep dimples. Dozens of tiny lines around his eyes told Kate that this was a man whose devastating smile was never far from the surface.

Because of her height it was rare that Kate ever had to look up quite this far to catch a man's glance, but now she found herself nearly overpowered by his size. It was a thrilling feeling.

As though he read her thoughts, his grin widened into a teasing smile that displayed dazzling white teeth, perfectly arranged and aligned. Something about the smile seemed familiar to Kate and the thought flitted through her head that perhaps she'd seen him in a toothpaste commercial. He certainly was the commercial type.

That thought and DeAngelo's booming voice brought Kate back to reality. Finally she gathered her wits and muttered an apologetic, "Excuse me."

With apparent reluctance Tall, Dark and Handsome tore his eyes away from Kate to glance at the director. Then he focused on Kate again, winking subtly. "Hang in there, beautiful," he whispered conspiratorially in a voice so deep it must have originated somewhere around his knees. Releasing his light hold on her arms, he slipped past her to the box office window.

Unable to help herself, Kate watched him go, enjoying the casual way he moved. His tan jacket was stretched perfectly over his broad back, and even though he was wearing a darker-hued cashmere sweater beneath the coat she was certain the bulkiness of his clothes had nothing to do with the size of the man beneath. The broad shoulders tapered down to a slender waist, lean hips and long, powerful legs. He was as much a pleasure to look at from the back as he had been from the front. Almost.

He finished quickly at the box office window and hurried to the theater doors, where he turned back for a last glance at Kate. The look on his face told her he was undeniably pleased that she was still watching him.

Mortified by the blatant way she was staring at him, Kate blushed to the roots of her dark hair and jerked her head away—but not before she caught the full effect of his dazzling smile. The breathless moment was over in seconds, but Kate felt as though she had been hit by a truck.

DeAngelo called her name again and finally Kate managed to come back into the real world.

"I beg your pardon, *signor?*" It was an effort to focus on the little director.

"I was saying the play willa start soon. I shall detain you no longer."

The lobby was completely clear now except for DeAngelo and his entourage, who swept through the double doors and were lost from view. Kate moved to the box office and Deanna followed.

"Wow!" the blonde exclaimed softly.

Kate nodded abstractly, praying the flushed color in her cheeks had receded. "He does have some weird ideas. I'm afraid I've dragged you here for a night of torture."

"No, not DeAngelo. Him . . . Tall, Dark and Handsome. He's even better up close! I swear, Kate, when you turned around and looked up at him I thought for a second you were going to swoon."

"Don't be ridiculous," she scolded as she reached the window. To the clerk inside, she declared, "Franklyn, the *Sentinel*. I should have two tickets on reserve."

The young woman checked Kate's name off the complimentary ticket list. "Yes, ma'am, just a second." While she flipped through the seating chart, Kate took advantage of her upside-down view of the reservation list, scanning it quickly to see if anyone from the *Press-Enterprise* was here for the opening. Halfway down the page she spotted Al Rossner's name, but there was a line through it with "canc" immediately after it.

"Great."

"I beg your pardon?" the young woman questioned as she handed her the tickets.

Kate smiled apologetically. "Nothing. Thank you very much."

"Enjoy the show."

"Rossner canceled," she told Deanna as they moved toward the auditorium.

"You mean no one from the *Enterprise* is here?"

"Exactly. If I don't have to worry about competing with Rossner in tomorrow's paper I may be able to convince Griffith to hold my review for the big Sunday Entertainment edition," she said as they moved into the auditorium. They took their seats just as the houselights dimmed.

The play was a nightmare. As DeAngelo had indicated to her in the lobby, he had directed the comedy as a tragedy, and the audience grew increasingly restless as what should have been a witty, fast-paced first act plodded painfully forward. When it ended, a thin spattering of applause—prompted more from relief than enjoyment—sounded here and there, then everyone including DeAngelo and his entourage beat a hasty retreat.

By the time Kate and Dee reached the lobby it was virtually empty despite the fact that almost everyone had preceded them out the doors. The line of people in front of her kept moving toward the outer exit and Kate couldn't blame them. If it wasn't her job, she'd be on her way home, too.

Like pigeons returning to the roost, she and Deanna moved to the corner they had occupied earlier, but when Deanna caught a glimpse of her reflection in the shiny glass of one of the cast photos on the wall, she blanched.

"My God, I look like I've been electrocuted!" she cried, raking her hands through her short blond curls.

"You look fine," Kate reassured her. "That's the advantage of those curly hairdos. Who could possibly tell it's not deliberate?"

Dee looked at her friend suspiciously. "You're a fine one to talk. You could run around in sackcloth and ashes with your hair looking like the Bride of Frankenstein and still be gorgeous. We lesser mortals have to worry about spiked hair and smeared mascara. I'm going to the ladies' room." She looked at Kate expectantly. "Unless you need me to run interference, of course."

"No, you go on." She glanced around the nearly deserted lobby. "There's no one left to ask me for an advance review of the play."

Deanna took off and Kate discreetly turned her back to the center of the lobby, just to be sure no one would accost her. She directed her gaze at the cast photos, but unfortunately, her attempt to look inconspicuous didn't work. Behind her the dreaded voice, high-pitched and thickly laid with an Italian accent, hailed her.

"Signorina Franklyn, *mia bellissima signorina.* Whya do you standa here alonea?"

With a ragged sigh, Kate plastered on her polite smile and turned. She looked down at the little director and found herself staring at a cashmere sweater vest and tan jacket. Lifting her gaze slowly, she took in the widening expanse of chest, the shoulders that spanned two time zones, and above that, a bearded face with a beguiling, mischievous smile.

As though he'd known her for years, Tall, Dark and Handsome took Kate's hand and kissed it, then tucked it familiarly into the crook of his arm as he moved beside her. Through the layers of clothing, Kate felt the ripple of rock-hard muscle and her heart did a back flip.

"*Mia bellissima signorina,* havea you no words? Has my esplindido productione lefta you found-dumb?"

Warning bells sounded in the back of Kate's brain. During the dreadful first act she'd had plenty of time to convince herself that her childish reaction to this man had been nothing more than an aberration. She had also reinforced her decision to avoid all men in general in order to retain the emotional equilibrium she had worked so hard to achieve these past few months. Unfortunately the warning bells in her head were completely drowned out by the insistent drumming of her heartbeat.

Completely captivated, unable to help herself, Kate laughed aloud at the stranger's fractured impersonation of DeAngelo. "I have never been *found-dumb, signor....* I've been speechless on occasion, but never found-dumb." Without forcing him to withdraw his hand, which she found delightful on her arm, Kate leaned back slightly and eyed him up and down, one delicately sculpted eyebrow raised. "I hope you won't think me too presumptuous, *signor,* but I must say, you've changed. You're so much taller."

He nodded with sage seriousness. "It isa de length ofa de first act. One cana grow many inches in so long a time."

"How true," she agreed, swallowing her laughter and falling easily in with his routine since there was no one in the lobby to overhear them. "Why, when I last saw you this beard was little more than a five-o'clock shadow. However did you train it to grow so evenly?"

"Isa no great mystery," he declared with an arrogant toss of his head. "'Twas my barber who sat next to me ina de theater."

"He did a wonderful job of covering your gray hairs, too."

"You tink so?" he asked eagerly, releasing Kate's arm to glance anxiously in the reflective glass of one of the photos.

"Careful, *signor,* or you'll convince me you've grown vain."

With mock embarrassment he turned to her, lowering his voice to an intimate tone that worked in direct opposition to his comic words. "Forgive me, *signorina,* I woulda never have you think ill of me."

His blue eyes impaled her with sudden intimacy and Kate sobered as her heart fluttered in her chest. Suddenly nervous, she assumed a more distant demeanor. "We probably shouldn't be making fun of Mr. DeAngelo. He could come through here at any moment and I'd hate for him to overhear and get the wrong impression."

Matt realized instantly that he had made a mistake that had caused her to put up her guard. Still, this was nothing compared to the roadblocks she'd throw up once she learned his name. But she was so beautiful, intelligent and witty that he knew he was right to try to forestall that moment as long as possible. He dropped the DeAngelo impersonation and smiled. "You're right. I'm sorry, Miss Franklyn, but I couldn't resist. You just looked so forlorn standing here trying unsuccessfully to blend into the woodwork."

His voice had lowered more than an octave to a bass timbre that was as deep and smooth as silk. Kate ignored the tingling sensation that rippled down her spine and looked at him suspiciously. "How did you know my name?"

"Are you kidding? Thanks to DeAngelo everyone at the theater knows who you are and where you work."

Kate felt foolish. "Of course."

"So, you're a critic?" he asked casually, leaning against the wall as though he owned it.

"I am."

"Would you care to give me a preview of your review?"

Kate shook her head. "Sorry. You'll have to read it in the *Sentinel.*"

"Tomorrow?"

"Probably not. If I'm lucky it'll go into the Sunday edition, but you can never tell."

"Really? I thought you'd want to—what's the word? —*scoop* the competition."

"The critic from the *Press-Enterprise* didn't show, so I've got an extra day to get the review in." She tilted her head to one side and looked at him closely. "You're awfully curious about my work."

"No, actually I'm just looking for an excuse to stand here and talk to you." Matt pushed away from the wall and inched closer. "Of course, if you don't want to talk, I'll settle for just being able to stand here and *look* at you."

His voice had lowered again to a soft, seductive purr and it was an effort for Kate to keep her eyes locked with his. "I'm not an entertainer. I don't do impersonations and funny faces," she managed with a semblance of smoothness she scarcely felt.

"No problem. After sitting in there for an hour I don't think I could stand the sudden change if you made me laugh."

"You mean you didn't like the play?" she asked with wide-eyed seriousness.

"Come on, Miss Franklyn. You didn't like it, either, did you?"

It seemed to Kate that she was faced with two choices in dealing with the man who was playing havoc with her senses: she could break one of her cardinal rules and discuss the play or she could try to withstand come-on lines that should have been corny but simply weren't because he was so innately sexy and so damned charming. The former seemed the safest.

"You really want my opinion?"

"I do."

"You're not connected with anyone in the show, are you?"

Matt raised his right hand. "I have never seen any of the actors before tonight, your honor," he swore, choosing his words carefully to placate his conscience. So far, he hadn't had to tell a lie...exactly. This one was stretching the truth just short of the breaking point, but it wasn't a lie.

"All right. I can tell you this much. If I live to walk out of this theater when the play is over it will be conclusive proof that there really *is* life after death."

Matt chuckled. "That's good. I imagine you'll use that in your review. For the, uh, what's it called . . . you know, the first line of an article?"

"The lead."

"That's it. It'll make a great lead. It certainly suits the play."

Kate lowered her eyelids demurely. "Why, thank you. I'll use it just to please you." *My God, what am I doing?* she cried inwardly, but couldn't seem to stop.

"Just for me? Then I'll be sure to look for your review. While I'm lying in bed Sunday morning reading my paper, I promise I'll be thinking of nothing but you."

"Is that outrageously suggestive statement supposed to make me melt like warm gelatin?" she asked coyly.

"Putty in my hands is more what I had in mind," he admitted with a sheepish, beguiling smile.

"Oh, you're one of *those*—a lobby lizard who specializes in between-the-act romances."

He shrugged nonchalantly. "What can I say? I like one-intermission stands."

Kate laughed openly, unable to remember when she'd had so much fun sparring with anyone. It was exciting and refreshing... and what could possibly be dangerous about it? she asked herself, trying to justify the enjoyment she was getting from the innocent flirtation. After the intermission she'd never see him again, so what harm could it do? "You are completely outrageous. You know that, don't you?"

"True," he admitted readily. "But I have to do something to get your attention or you'll leave here tonight and walk out of my life forever."

Something about his tone told Kate he wasn't joking, but she chose to ignore the implication. "That's the way of the world, my friend. Ships that pass in the night, as they say."

Tall, Dark and Handsome suddenly grew serious. "Does that mean you won't have coffee with me after the play?"

Taken aback, Kate could only sputter, "I... uh..."

"Is that a yes or a no?"

"That's a...uh, no. I'm sorry. I don't even know your name, and—"

Before she could continue he snapped to attention and clicked his heels together, bowing at the waist. "Matthew McKenna, at your service." Matt heard the truth snap, break and shatter into a thousand pieces at his feet.

But what else was he to do? If he told her his *full* name she'd be out of his life in an instant, and he couldn't permit that.

But the lie hadn't been as safe as he'd expected, because Kate actually paled. For an instant, Matt thought he'd been caught; that she'd been playing with him and really knew who he was, but that wasn't the case.

"McKenna?" she murmured. "Good Lord, not another Irishman."

Matt forgot to feel guilty about his lie as he arched one eyebrow skeptically. "What is this? No Irish need apply? I thought that prejudice ended shortly after the potato famine."

Kate held up her hand apologetically, but without thinking she backed away from him as though distance would protect her. "Look, I'm sorry. I didn't mean to offend you—"

"No offense taken," he replied, all teasing gone, replaced by a sympathetic look that was as devastating as his smile. "Has one of my kinsmen been giving you a hard time?"

Nervously Kate looked at her watch. What on earth was keeping Deanna? "That's a little more personal than I care to get with a perfect stranger."

"Sorry." He grinned suddenly and Kate had to build a wall quickly to keep from falling under his charming spell again. "What if I change my name? Would you have coffee with me then?"

"Look—"

"Would you go out with a perfectly nonthreatening George Burns? Or how about a George Bush?"

"Please—"

"Oops, sorry. You're probably a Democrat. What about a Bill Clinton?"

"No—"

"Walter Mondale?"

"Would you stop!"

"Geraldine Ferraro? That's my final offer, take it or leave it."

Kate's hastily built wall cracked and she laughed despite herself. "Please don't make me laugh," she begged. "I'm trying not to like you."

"Because I'm Irish?" he asked incredulously.

"Because I'm *engaged.*"

"Oh."

He paused long enough for Kate to realize that she'd told an out-and-out lie, and she masked her discomfort carefully, hoping he wouldn't call her bluff. It was an easy slip of the tongue, one she'd used legitimately until six months ago, but it no longer applied.

Still, a simple lie about a nonexistent fiancé was probably the best course she could follow to defend herself against this attractive man. It was certainly a lot more effective than claiming to be recovering from a broken heart. More often than not, such an admission encouraged a man to try harder, and *this* man was entirely too devastating already. Kate couldn't afford to prod him into high gear.

Matt studied her, letting the pause grow into a long, uncomfortable silence before he finally narrowed his eyes suspiciously and asked, "Engaged in what?"

Fighting the urge to laugh, Kate maintained a serious expression and lied. "Engaged in a relationship with a very nice man."

"As nice as me?"

"I don't *know* you."

"Then have coffee with me and find out. Haven't you ever heard of comparison shopping?"

"I've already done my comparison shopping!" Kate cried in a voice that begged for mercy. "Look, Mr. McKenna—"

"Call me Geraldine."

Kate sighed wearily. "Aren't you ever serious?"

"All right, I'll be perfectly serious." He sobered and suddenly Kate wished she hadn't asked. All the playfulness left him and the look that came into his piercing blue eyes nearly unhinged her. "Sometime shortly before eight o'clock this evening I was standing in that corner minding my own business when the most beautiful woman I have ever seen dashed into the lobby. Her hair was tousled and laughter bubbled on her lips making her face so radiant that everything else in this room vanished.

"A few minutes later, she looked at me and smiled and I thought my heart was going to pound right out of my chest. I told myself, Matt, old boy, *this* is a woman you've got to meet—so I did. And what I found was an intelligent, witty, utterly captivating woman who seems to be fighting an attraction equal to what I feel for her."

Kate couldn't have found words to answer him if she'd wanted to, but it wasn't necessary, because Matt wasn't finished. "Now, I don't know about you," he continued softly, "but I don't believe in love at first sight. *Lust* at first sight definitely exists, though. I know, because I've got one of the world's worst cases right now. In fact, if I thought I could get away with it I'd gather you into my arms and kiss you until one of us did something that could get us arrested. But since such public displays are frowned upon I will be content with getting you to say yes to my invitation. You are charming, remarkably lovely and a great sport. I want to get to know you better."

Matt finally paused, letting his speech sink in before he asked her bluntly, "Now tell me, Ms. Franklyn, can you handle that much seriousness?"

Is this man for real? Kate wondered, startled speechless by his boldness and the flattering things he'd said about her. Most of all, she was bowled over by the sincerity in his face and voice. Her ego wanted to believe every word he'd said. Her badly broken heart warned her to run like hell.

This time the latter won out. She swallowed hard to steady her voice and issued a prayer that she would be forgiven for continuing her charade. "I'm very sorry, Mr. McKenna. Truly I am. You're a very attractive man and I'm quite flattered. But I really am engaged. This is my fault—when you approached me I should have discouraged you, but I didn't and I apologize. And I also apologize for pressing you into declaring yourself quite so openly. If I've caused you any embarrassment I'm—"

"Embarrassment?" Matt laughed easily and shook his head. "Why should I be embarrassed? I told a beautiful woman she's beautiful. Surely I'm not the first man who's expressed a desire to throw you onto the carpet and ravish you."

"No, and you probably won't be the last," she said with a chuckle, amazed that he was taking her rejection so good-naturedly. "But not many men have the charm to declare themselves quite so eloquently and get away with it."

Like an eager dog grabbing hold of a bone, he teased, "Then you think I'm charming?"

"And handsome."

"Hmm..." He stroked his beard thoughtfully. "Charming *and* handsome."

"And you have a delightful sense of humor." *God, I just turned him down and now I'm flirting again. What's wrong with me?*

"Charming, handsome and fun to be with." He sighed dramatically. "But you can still reject my invitation. This fiancé of yours must be Superman."

"No, I happen to favor the Clark Kent type."

"Oh. Then I guess it wouldn't do any good to tattoo a big red *S* on my chest?"

"Sorry."

He looked at her closely as he said with all seriousness, "So am I."

Since she'd been honest with him, Matt decided he'd better come clean. She was going to find out who he was sooner or later, anyway. If there really wasn't a chance for them to at least flirt with the possibility of a relationship, she might as well hear the truth from him.

But just as he opened his mouth, his eyes fell on her left hand. It was a beautiful, graceful hand, with long, elegant fingers, perfectly sculpted nails... and a noticeable absence of jewelry.

An engagement without a ring? It was possible, of course, though Matt couldn't imagine any man in his right mind committing such a careless breach of sanity. If this goddess was his, he'd hang a sign around her neck that said Keep Off; another one that said Taken would hang around his own. Maybe her fiancé didn't realize what a jewel he had. Or maybe it was possible that the "fiancé" didn't exist. It just could be that Ms. Franklyn, like Matt, was hiding behind a convenient falsehood.

The truth wouldn't be too hard to ferret out, and until he did, Matt decided to let his own fib stand—right alongside the hope that was bubbling up inside him again.

The lights blinked overhead announcing the beginning of act two and Matt smiled again. "I think that's our cue. May I escort you into the theater at least?"

Remembering Deanna, Kate frowned and looked around. "I'm waiting for my friend."

"The cute blonde?"

"Yes."

"She went into the theater five minutes ago. I guess she decided not to run interference for you."

"That traitor! This is the last time I get her complimentary theater tickets."

"After this fiasco I should think she'd be grateful for that." He extended his arm to Kate and she took it, allowing him to lead her toward the theater.

"I'm going back in there because it's my job and I have a personal commitment to never leaving a show before it's over. If you hate the show so much, why are you going back?"

They approached the double doors and Matt leaned close enough that Kate could feel the warmth of his breath on her cheek. She had the feeling that he was well aware that his innocent gesture was very erotic. "After another hour of this torture I'm willing to bet you'll submit to anything—even a date with me."

"That's not going to happen," she told him seriously, ignoring the heat in her stomach.

He shrugged. "Don't be so sure, Ms. Franklyn. You never can tell what surprises tomorrow may bring."

Before she could argue or even catch her breath, he disappeared into the theater.

Chapter Three

The offices of the Los Angeles *Sentinel* took up three floors of an aging high rise that had, at one time, been the tallest skyscraper in downtown L.A. Now it stood sedately between the shadows of the towering Arco Building, Bank of America and half a dozen others, dwarfed but still serviceable except for one infuriatingly undependable elevator.

On Saturday afternoon, the streets and sidewalks were far less congested than they were during the week, but inside the *Sentinel*'s Entertainment section things were as chaotic as ever. Desks were crowded so close together in the large, open room that privacy was impossible and sometimes even coherent thought was a hopeless dream.

The deadline for Saturday's paper had long since passed, but Sunday's deadline was looming close and Kate found herself pressed for time. Doing her best to ignore the chaos, she inserted a blank floppy disk into her terminal and entered the code that labeled the copy to follow as hers.

Paul Griffith, her editor, had been in a surly mood when Kate had approached him this morning about saving her *Blithe Spirit* review for Sunday. Her witty, scathing and justly deserved diatribe against the show was exactly the kind of attention-getting piece Griffith liked to use in the Entertainment section, but he was so fanatical about scooping his competition that he hadn't agreed to save her review for Sunday's paper until Kate assured him that the *Press-Enterprise* hadn't covered the opening.

"Coffee break!" From out of nowhere, Deanna appeared in front of Kate's desk and placed a cup of steaming black coffee on top of the copy of the review Kate was transcribing into her computer. Without looking up, Kate deftly moved the cup into an empty space on the cluttered desk and resumed her eighty-words-per-minute typing.

"Hang on a sec... I'm almost done."

The blonde pushed aside a stack of file folders and planted herself on the corner of the desk, craning to get a view of the monitor. "Is that the *Blithe Spirit* review?" she asked incredulously. "I thought you'd have finished that hours ago."

"Fielding had the terminal," Kate answered without breaking stride.

"All morning?"

"I'm typing."

"Sorry." She lapsed into silence until Kate punched the story into the file memory and extracted the disk. On a removable label she coded the disk and stood up.

"Jack!"

The harried copy boy's head swiveled as he flew through the busy room. Making a wide sweep around three desks, he swooped down on her, wordlessly plucked the disk from her hand and disappeared again into the mayhem.

"Being a copy boy around here has got to be the best aerobic exercise in the world," Dee observed as Kate reseated herself and took a sip of coffee. "And speaking of which, I'm on my way to the spa as soon as I can blow this joint. Wanna come?"

"No, thanks."

Dee frowned and leaned closer. "Listen, Kate, you're not upset with me about last night, are you? I was a little worried when you said you had to go straight home after the play."

"Of course I'm not upset with you," Kate reassured her.

"Then what is it? Did Tall, Dark and Handsome say something to upset you during that intermission?"

"No!" Kate snapped much more sharply than she intended.

"Well, what *did* he say?"

"It was nothing. He cracked a few jokes and asked me for a date. After I said no a few hundred times he finally got the message and was very nice about it. No big deal."

"You turned him down?" Dee asked incredulously. "I don't believe it. I suppose you didn't get his name and phone number, either."

"Phone number, no, but his name is Matt McKenna."

Dee cocked her head to one side and suspiciously looked at Kate, who was shuffling some files that didn't need shuffling. "You're acting very strange, you know that, don't you?"

"I am not! He was a nice guy, but I'm not interested."

"Sure.... Listen, sweetie, when I came back to the lobby last night and saw you two together your face was lit up like the Fourth of July. I haven't seen you that alive since—"

"Dee..."

Unfortunately the warning tone in her voice didn't stop her friend. "Kate, you need—"

"No, I don't *need,* nor do I *want* a man in my life right now. Particularly not one like Matt McKenna. He's dangerous!"

"Why? What did he say to you?"

"Nothing! He was very charming and funny. He did a great impersonation of DeAngelo and he flirted and teased..." Her voice trailed off as she remembered the intimacy of some of Matt's words.

"And what?" Dee demanded. "Don't leave me hanging."

Kate shrugged offhandedly. "He made some comment about wanting to throw me on the carpet and ravish me."

"I love it!" Dee threw back her head and laughed with sheer delight. "Why didn't you take him up on it?"

"Oh, come on. He was just joking," Kate insisted despite the clear memory she had of his intense look of sincerity that still had the ability to rock her to the very core of her carefully constructed composure. "And besides, I don't need that kind of aggravation in my life right now."

"Aggravation? Sweetie, when are you going to learn that the *aggravation* you try so hard to avoid is what life's all about! You know, man-woman, me Tarzan, you Jane—let's go back to the tree house and—"

"Deanna!" Kate glanced around frantically to be sure no one was eavesdropping. "Look, could we drop this? I'm happy with my life as it is right now and I certainly don't need some caveman to drag me back to the tree house to... *what*ever."

"But—"

"No buts! Okay? Just drop it."

"Okay, okay." She sighed reluctantly and reached for the typewritten copy of Kate's review. "Can I read this? After all, I did invest two and a half of the worst hours of my life on that play."

"Sure, go ahead," Kate consented, relieved that Dee had dropped her questioning. Kate had done enough thinking about Matt without her best friend badgering her to death. When she'd gotten home from the theater last night she'd spent three hours at her home computer trying to write a review that should have taken fifteen minutes. But every time she'd tried to visualize her words on paper that bearded Irishman had burst into her thoughts.

It had been a maddening experience for someone like Kate, who was so accustomed to controlling her thoughts and emotions. Yet the man just wouldn't go away. Each time he swept into her thoughts she remembered some new detail about him, as though the impression he'd made had been carefully stored for future reference . . . the handsome face, the dazzling smile, the attractive crinkles at the corners of his eyes.

She'd remembered, too, the solidity of his body when she'd taken his arm. That memory had prompted several hot minutes as she tried to decide what that body would be like without his clothes. Would his chest be smooth and hard or matted with crisp black hair over the muscled expanse? Unable to stop herself, Kate had mentally undressed him and the exercise had left her as frustrated and depressed as she had been lying beside Dan McBride on the many occasions when he'd rolled away from her and fallen into a sated sleep, leaving Kate to wonder if there was something wrong with her as a woman.

Her experience with men wasn't extensive but as nearly as Kate could tell, women made a lot of fuss over something that was infinitely more exciting to think about than to participate in. The pleasure she'd taken from Dan was in knowing that she was pleasing him. Despite what the books and Dr. Ruth said, Kate was convinced that sex was only the smallest part of the many lovely things that went on between a man and a woman.

Not that Kate had never been sexually satisfied, of course. She had been. A number of times, in fact, and it was nice. She couldn't deny it. But bells didn't go off in her head, waves didn't crash onto the shore, and her toes had never once curled, not with Dan or either of the two men she'd been involved with before him.

Getting herself all hot and bothered over Matt McKenna was just a waste of time, she'd finally convinced herself.

"It's great!" Dee tossed the sheath of papers onto the desk and smiled. "I loved the lead about conclusive proof of life after death and all the burial puns you used. They're dead on the money, if you'll pardon the expression."

"Thanks."

"Kate Franklyn?"

Kate turned toward the voice and saw a florist's messenger looking totally lost as the newsroom whizzed around him.

"Over here!" She stood and almost laughed at the look of relief on the man's face. "I'm Kate Franklyn."

"These are for you, ma'am. Sorry, but I'm a little late. They were supposed to be delivered exactly at 1:00 p.m." He smiled and apologetically offered her a bud vase wrapped in green paper.

"Thank you." She fished in her desk for some spare change and dropped several coins in the delivery boy's hand.

Puzzled, Kate turned the wrapped vase in her hands, inspecting it from all angles until Deanna rasped out irritably, "For God's sake, it's just green florist's paper. It won't bite you. Open it up and see what's inside. And more importantly, who it's from!"

"I can't imagine..." Kate frowned as she ripped away the paper to expose a delicate, cut crystal vase with one red rosebud, a profusion of baby's breath, and delicate fern. "No one has sent me flowers in years. Even *Dan* never sent me flowers, so this couldn't be a sneak attack from him after all these months." She plucked the card from the plastic pitchfork and fell silent as she looked curiously at the card.

"What does it say?"

"I'll forgive you, if you'll forgive me."

"That's all?"

Kate nodded, unable to imagine what it meant. "It's unsigned. But what—"

"Franklynnnn!"

The whole room seemed to shudder and everyone within earshot of the blistering bellow froze as though startled by a California earthquake.

"Four point one on the Richter scale," Dee muttered, sliding off the desk as Paul Griffith barreled down on them with murder in his eye.

"Maybe so, but I don't think he believes that this is San Andreas's fault—whatever *it* is," Kate muttered as two hundred and forty pounds of ill-tempered editor thundered across the room brandishing a folded newspaper in her direction. Like the Red Sea parting, the crowd melted aside, then business as usual resumed in his wake.

Paul Griffith, fiftyish, balding and paunchy, stormed to the desk and waved the folded newspaper in front of Kate's nose. He paused a moment as though letting the full impact of his anger sink in, then spat out in crisp measured tones, "You'd better have a good explanation, lady, because I'm about this—" he snapped his fingers "—close to firing you."

"Why am I being fired this time? Sir?"

"Damn it, Franklyn, I trusted you! You've always been straight with me... no tricks to con me into letting you into the Sunday edition. But this! I could sack you for a lot less!"

Griffith's tantrums were something Kate rarely took seriously, but today his tone was different. He was genuinely disappointed in her, which distressed Kate deeply because his respect and belief in her integrity were very important to her. "Mr. Griffith, I honestly don't know what's wrong."

"This!" He waved the paper in her face again and Kate realized it was the morning edition of the *Press-Enterprise* that hit the stands at 12:30. "You told me the *Enterprise* didn't have a critic at the play last night."

"They didn't! I saw the reservation list myself. Al Rossner's name had been crossed out with 'Cancel' penciled in beside it."

"Rossner? Good God, what planet are you living on? Rossner gave his notice two weeks ago! He's gone!" Griffith slammed the paper on the desk.

"Oh, no," Kate groaned, slouching back in her seat. Obviously, someone from the *Enterprise* had been at the Players last night—someone she'd been too preoccupied to notice, thanks to Matt McKenna. All Kate's energy drained away. "I'm sorry, Mr. Griffith. Honestly I didn't know."

"Obviously!" He leaned on the desk, towering over her menacingly. "Tell me, Kate, haven't you been around long enough to know that you keep your reviews to yourself until you get your copy in to me? What the hell did you do, hold a press conference in the lobby?"

Totally confused, Kate could only stare at him. Briskly Griffith picked up the newspaper and read aloud with great fanfare, "Dear Los Angeles: As a newcomer to the L.A. theater scene I had hoped that my first review for you would be great news of a resounding theatrical success. Unfortunately that is not the case. Instead it is with mixed feelings that this critic must announce to you that he has obtained conclusive proof that there really is life after death. I know, because I somehow managed to survive last night's opening of Howard DeAngelo's hopelessly misguided interpretation of *Blithe Spirit,* a production that should have been buried before it ever began."

Griffith glared at Kate. "Shall I read more?"

Aghast, she grabbed the paper. "That's not possible! I didn't—" As she spoke her eyes scanned the quarter page of the folded paper for the review, but finding the actual words was unnecessary. The reviewer's photo did the trick.

Hanging there, just below the small headline Views and Reviews, was a handsome, bearded face with twinkling eyes that laughed mockingly up at Kate with alarming life. She didn't need to read the byline next to the photo to know that she'd been had by a scoundrel who'd called himself Matt McKenna!

"I see you recognize the hotshot critic the *Enterprise* hired last week," Griffith observed, somewhat mollified by Kate's expression, which was quickly boiling into anger. "He's a writer from somewhere back East."

"I'll kill him," she murmured with quiet intensity.

"Be my guest," the editor chirped. "We'll get someone from the city room to cover the murder and you just might make it into the Sunday edition after all. As it is, I'm killing your review. Write another one and have it on my desk in time for Monday's paper."

Kate heard Griffith with only one part of her brain and she had the presence of mind to nod her assent, which sent the editor huffing off to find someone else to harass.

"Kate? Kate?" Deanna's voice penetrated the red fog clouding Kate's mind and she finally tore herself from the photo. "It's Matt McKenna, right?" she guessed.

"No, Matt *Gallagher.*" Kate ground out the name between gritted teeth. "The bastard even lied about his name, damn him!" She hurled the newspaper toward Deanna, who eagerly scooped it up and scanned the article.

"Well, you've got to admit it's a good picture. Usually these things look like mug shots—as though the guy ought to have one of those little license plates hanging around his neck. That's why I've always been glad the *Sentinel* doesn't run reviewer photos with—"

"Will you knock it off!" Kate snapped irritably as she coded a fresh disk and began rewriting her review. "I can't believe I actually fell for that creep's line of garbage!"

"Oh, come on, it's not so bad. You and Al Rossner have played a hundred little dirty tricks on each other over the years. Rivalries between critics and reporters are an integral part of the newspaper business."

"Don't tell me you're going to stand up for Gallagher?"

"Come on, Kate, it's a joke. Don't you get it? He's flirting with you in print. You turned him down last night and this is just his way of saying he hasn't given up."

Kate glared at her, unable to believe what she was hearing. "Are you saying I should be flattered because he conned me into giving him my lead for the review?"

"No, but don't make a federal case out of it. We're talking about one little review of a very bad Equity-waiver production. This isn't the L.A. premiere of *Phantom of the Opera,* for heaven's sake. You know that and Gallagher knows it. Take it for the practical joke it is."

Kate knew Dee was right. Rivalries between critics were a fact of life, and she had personally played professional tricks on her competition that made this stunt look tame, but Kate was too furious to relent. Rather than continue the argument, though, she tightened her jaw and glared at her friend. "Could we drop this? I've got a review to write. Again."

"Okay." Dee slid off the desk. "Listen...call me if you change your mind about going to the spa this afternoon. You could stand to burn off a little excess energy."

Kate shook her head. "No, thanks. I've got more creative things to do with my time—like thinking up a way to make Matt Gallagher pay for tricking me into spilling my guts."

Dee shook her head. "Get a grip, girl. Casually discussing a theatrical production is not exactly divulging military secrets."

"It is to a theater critic," Kate replied with a don't-get-mad-get-even gleam in her eyes. "And I'm going to make Gallagher regret this, big time."

Dee smiled. "All right. Go ahead and plot something devious and I'll help you refine it later. I've got to run."

Kate gave her an absentminded wave goodbye, then shoved aside her thoughts about Gallagher's treachery and went to work revising her review. Thirty minutes later she had finished. It wasn't as clever as her original, but at least it was accurate and honest.

Honest.

That was something Matt Gallagher obviously knew nothing about, Kate mused, her anger building once again as she tried to make sense of what her rival critic had done. What point had the whole charade served? He had lied about his name, presumably because he figured she would recognize his real one, and he had pretended to know nothing about the newspaper business. He had flirted outrageously with her and had convinced Kate that he was genuinely attracted to her—just so that he could get the upper hand in a childish game of one-upmanship.

As much as she hated to admit it, that's what bothered Kate the most. Gallagher had made her feel good about herself as a woman for the first time in months—no, years—and then he'd slapped her flat. It was a blow to her ego that she didn't need right now.

With her work finished for the day, Kate made a halfhearted attempt to straighten the clutter on her desk, but she was interrupted by a sudden ripple of silence that flowed through the room, followed by a few titters of laughter. She looked up, but several reporters blocked her view of the swinging double doors that led to the corridor, so she stood, slipping into her jacket as she craned her neck to see what was drawing everyone's attention.

There, across the room, receiving directions from a stunned secretary, was a tall bearded figure dressed outlandishly in a black trench coat with the collar turned up. Dark sunglasses and a brown, low-brimmed hat shaded the man's face, but Kate didn't need to see behind the ridiculous disguise to know that it was Matt Gallagher. He was headed toward her, his movements comically furtive as though he was being extraordinarily subtle when, in fact, he was quite obviously—and deliberately—calling a great deal of attention to himself.

With quick, darting glances he checked beside and behind him, evidently to ascertain if he was being followed. Despite her anger with him, Kate had to force back laughter at his performance. The man was outrageous!

Willing herself not to be amused, she looked down at her desk to regain control. Matt's photo in the *Enterprise* was staring up at her, and that's all it took. The black-and-white newsprint turned vivid red and by the time Gallagher reached her desk she was boiling mad again.

"What the hell are you doing here?" she asked, forcing her anger to a fever pitch to counteract the effect of his comical appearance.

As though she hadn't spoken, Matt sidled up to her desk and slipped the sunglasses down the bridge of his nose, "allowing" her to penetrate his disguise. "It's me...Matt. I don't think I was tailed here, but you never can tell. Just act casual."

"Will you stop that? Take off those glasses and that ridiculous hat."

"I can't do that!" he cried softly, his tone desperate. "Do you realize how much danger I've put myself into by coming here? Why, if someone recognizes me I could be drawn and quartered for infiltrating the enemy camp. You wouldn't want that, would you?"

Kate laughed humorlessly. "Oh, I can think of a number of things a great deal *worse* that I'd like to see happen to you."

Matt clutched his chest as though wounded. "Is that any way to talk to me after what I've risked to see you?"

"Gallagher, the way I feel about you, your greatest risk *is* seeing me!"

He plunked down on Kate's desk and sighed dis-hearteningly. "Obviously you saw my column."

"Of course I did!"

"Did you like it?" He grinned hopefully, infuriating Kate with his abrupt change in moods.

"Was I supposed to?" she practically shouted. The gall of this man!

"I don't know. I thought it had its good points."

"Points stolen from me!"

"Picky, picky, picky."

"You are impossible! You are also the lowest, most disgusting excuse for a life-form I've ever met."

"Last night you thought I was charming," Matt reminded her calmly.

"Last night I didn't know you were a lying con artist!"

"I don't suppose it would change your opinion if I apologized, would it?"

"Not a bit."

"Won't you at least hear me out?"

"I think we've said everything there is to say, Gallagher. I have no interest in this comic opera or in your apologies. I have a hearty dislike of liars."

"Kate..."

"Goodbye, Mr. Gallagher," she said firmly, snatching up her purse. She came around the desk, but when she spotted the mysterious flowers she'd received, Kate froze. They were to have been delivered precisely at one o'clock—thirty minutes after the *Enterprise* hit the newsstands!

"You!" Kate snatched up the vase. "You sent this!"

"Guilty as charged."

With a calm she scarcely felt, she started to throw the flowers—vase and all—into her trash can, but Matt reached across the desk and stayed her arm.

"Don't do that!" he cried with alarm. "Do you have any idea how much a dozen roses cost these day?"

Stunned, Kate jerked her arm away and glared from the bud vase to Gallagher. "This isn't a dozen roses!"

"Of course not. Do you have any idea how much a dozen roses cost these days?"

"Cheapskate," she muttered, stiffening her jaw against the smile that threatened to overpower her anger.

"My mother always taught me it's the thought that counts."

"You should have remembered your mother's axiom before you stole my review. Personally I've always been fond of 'do unto others...'"

A quick suggestive smile brought out Matt's dimples as he purposely misinterpreted Kate's clipped message. "That's always been one of my favorites, too," he crooned silkily.

"Well, here's another favorite of mine. Get lost, bozo." She dumped the flowers into the trash can and flew around her desk toward the exit.

Trailing doggedly behind her, Matt picked his way across the room, blithely bestowing his dazzling smile on the astonished reporters who'd witnessed their argument and were now following their progress all the way to the door.

There, Kate hit one of the swinging doors with all the force she could muster. As she breezed through, Matt turned back to their stunned, amused audience. "Thank you, ladies and gentlemen, for your kind attention. The next floor show will begin in fifteen minutes." With a jaunty wave, he turned just as the door snapped back in his face with an embarrassing plop.

The room exploded into thunderous applause, and Matt turned to acknowledged their accolade with a bow before beating a hasty retreat.

The comical gesture cost him too much time. By the time he emerged from the newsroom, he could hear the distinctive clatter of the elevator door.

"Whoa! Hold the elevator!" he called, dashing down the hall.

But Kate didn't pause. She stepped into the empty carriage and threw a killing glance at Gallagher when he appeared at the door. "If you press that little button on the wall out there another elevator will arrive shortly," she told him. "I don't feel disposed to riding downstairs with liars."

Imperiously she pressed the Lobby button and prayed that he wouldn't defy her.

But Matt wasn't about to let her escape so easily. "Sorry," he said as he flung himself into the elevator a fraction of a second before the doors slid closed.

"Damn you!" Kate muttered as Gallagher righted himself. "Leave me alone!"

"Sorry, but we really do have to talk."

"No, we don't." She glanced at him and wished she hadn't. "Take off that stupid hat and those sunglasses. And while you're at it, get rid of that lopsided grin."

"The smile gets to you, huh?" Matt's grin widened and Kate's stomach did a back flip.

"You are impossible!" She glanced at the flashing numbers over the elevator door. Fourteen floors to the lobby. Unwilling to wait that long, she stepped across the narrow space intending to press the button for the thirteenth floor and make a speedy escape, but Gallagher read her intention and blocked the control panel.

"No, no, not until we talk," he told her.

"Get out of my way!"

"Only if you promise not to push that button."

Kate glanced up again. They had already passed the tenth floor. At this rate they'd be at the lobby in a few seconds anyway, so she backed off. "I promise."

Matt glanced at the numbers that were ticking away his time to apologize. "It's a short ride to the lobby," he observed.

"Thank heaven for small favors."

Regretfully he shook his head. "Nine floors is simply not enough time for an apology."

"The combined floors of the Empire State Building and both towers of the World Trade Center wouldn't give you enough time to apologize for what you've done!"

"Then I guess I have no choice."

Before Kate could anticipate his next move, Matt reached out to the control panel and pushed the red toggle switch Stop.

"No, don't!" Kate shouted in genuine alarm.

With a bump and grind that would have made Gypsy Rose Lee envious, the aging elevator ground to a halt between the second and third floors, trapping Kate alone with the most infuriatingly irresistible man she'd ever met.

Chapter Four

Gasping for air, Kate tried to control her anger. When she addressed Gallagher her voice was gravelly with controlled rage. "You idiot. Do you know what you've done?"

"Correct me if I'm wrong, but I think I stopped the elevator."

"You stopped *this* elevator, known with great disaffection as Old Faithful because it has a habit of stranding passengers for *hours* at a time."

"You mean I didn't have to play the villain and make you even madder? I could have just waited and Old Faithful would have stopped all by itself?"

"With my luck, yes!"

Matt leaned against the wall, eyeing her nonchalantly as he grinned. "You know, you're even more beautiful when you're angry."

Kate groaned and turned away. "You must be from Iowa, 'cause corn don't grow that tall around here."

"Actually I was born and raised in Minnesota, but until recently I've been living in—"

"I don't want your résumé! I don't want to know anything about you except how you plan to start this elevator again!"

"—New York," he concluded as though she hadn't interrupted. "And as for restarting Old Faithful, I have no immediate plans to that effect."

"Well, I do." Throwing him a stormy glance that threatened violence if he interfered, Kate crossed the scant distance to his side of the room and reversed the position of the Stop button. As she had feared, nothing happened. Ferociously she jabbed the switch up and down. Nothing. She punched the Lobby button then pressed several more for good measure.

"With a button punching technique like that you could make big bucks on a game show."

"Don't talk to me."

Matt smiled wryly. "After all the trouble I've gone to to strand us in an elevator so we *can* talk, I think it would be pretty silly of me not to at least—"

Kate's desperate fingers found the alarm bell and Matt grimaced as the piercing sound bounced loud and long off the metal walls.

When the ringing finally stopped, he informed her, "I think they got the message."

"Now if only you would!" She moved back to the safety of her side of the elevator.

"Kate—" A shrill ringing made him stop and frown. "I think your bell permanently damaged my eardrums."

"It's the emergency telephone, you idiot." She moved toward the control panel again, but Matt beat her to it.

"I'll handle this one." He opened the small door above the control panel and pulled out the receiver. "Marty's Delicatessen. We deliva," he announced proudly in a convincing Brooklyn dialect. "Can I take youse orda, please?"

"Give me that phone!" Kate made a lunge toward him, but Matt imperturbably held out one arm to keep her at bay. "No, I'm sorry. You musta got the wrong numba. We ain't got no elevator here. Dis is a one story buildin'."

Insufferably pleased with himself, Matt returned the receiver to its nest and clicked the door shut.

"You are insane!" she shouted, then went very still as her words belatedly reached her brain. Genuine fear dawned in her eyes and she began backing away from him. Until a moment ago, Matt Gallagher had been nothing more than an irritating liar, but now that she was alone with him, completely isolated from the rest of the world, it occurred to Kate that she really knew nothing about him. He could be a mass murderer escaped from a lunatic asylum for all she knew!

Forcing herself to be calm, she unconsciously shifted her grip on her purse, ready to use it as a weapon. "They know we're in here," she said quietly. "You realize that, don't you? That telephone is a one-way line to the maintenance department. You can't possibly believe that you could try something in here and escape."

Matt's smugness vanished. "Oh, great! Now you think I'm an ax murderer. I really have botched this one, haven't I?" With a resigned sigh, he slipped his dark glasses off and dropped them into the pocket of his trench coat. "Excuse me a moment." He reached for the phone, this time pressing the button on the red receiver until someone at the other end picked up.

Kate breathed a sigh of relief as she listened to Matt's end of the conversation.

"Hello, sir...yes, this is the party trapped in Old Faithful.... No, sir, I'm sorry about before. I got carried away by the absurdity of the situation."

Blinking in surprise, Matt jerked the phone away from his ear as the gruff voice bellowed a reply Kate couldn't quite make out. "That's right, sir," he finally agreed when the yelling stopped. "I was just trying to be funny.... Yes, I *do* appreciate that you have a difficult job.... Thank you, sir, I'd be grateful. Before you go, sir, could you please write this information down? My name is Matthew McKenna—" he threw a meaningful glance at Kate "—Gallagher. I work for the Los Angeles *Press-Enterprise* and I am trapped in here alone with a very nervous Kate Franklyn. If you don't mind, would you please speak with her so that you can testify that at the time of this conversation Ms. Franklyn was alive and unharmed?"

Matt raised his eyebrows and held out the phone to Kate. The cord was short and she had to move all the way across the elevator to take it from him. With a gracious bow that made Kate feel all the more foolish, Matt stepped back to give her room.

"This is Kate Franklyn."

"Ms. Franklyn? This is George, the maintenance supervisor. You okay in there with that nut?"

"I'm fine, George. Just get me out of here."

"Sure thing. I'll have you out in a jiffy."

"That's great, George. How long is a jiffy?" she asked dryly, then ignored the snort of laughter behind her. George, however, did not see the humor of the question and Kate could almost imagine the frown on the super's gruff, wizened face.

"Oh, I don't know. Ten, maybe twenty minutes at the most. I already got Billingsly working on the box. Just hang on and if that fruitcake from the *Enterprise* gives you any trouble, press the alarm and I'll call the cops."

"Thanks, George."

The line went dead and Kate replaced the receiver.

"Well?" Matt prompted as Kate crossed the elevator again. "Did you find out how many minutes constitute a jiffy?"

"Ten or twenty."

He nodded in apparent relief. "Great. You're safe. I generally like at least thirty minutes to toy with my victims before I close in for the kill."

Kate eyed him intensely. "You mean the way you toyed with me last night?"

"Touché. I deserved that one." He leaned negligently against the wall and Kate glanced away in self-defense. Without the ridiculous sunglasses he looked rakishly handsome with his turned up collar and low-brimmed hat framing those twinkling blue eyes.

The elevator car fell silent until Matt finally asked, "Well, are you ready to listen to my apology, since we have a jiffy to kill?"

Kate ran her hand nervously across her forehead to hide the smile tugging at her lips. She was *not* going to give in to this man's charm! "I am not interested in anything you have to say to me, Gallagher."

"In that case, I'll talk to myself and you can hum the 'Battle Hymn of the Republic' or something." He straightened and though Kate refused to look at him she could imagine the same startling look of honesty she'd seen in his face last night. "Look, Kate, I'm genuinely sorry for what I did. After I had the chance to think about it I realized—"

"'Mine eyes have seen the glory of—'"

"You're not going to make this easy, are you?" Gallagher said over her soft soprano voice.

Angrily Kate whirled on him. "Easy? You want easy? My God, I should think you are the master of *ease.* Last night was easy for you, wasn't it? Smile, crack a few jokes and suddenly ol' Kate Franklyn is eating out of the palm of your hand!"

"Is that how it looked from your side?" Matt asked in gentle disbelief. "What I saw was a beautiful woman rejecting me."

"Oh, so you ripped off my review to get even! How noble!"

"That's not what happened."

Furious, Kate jabbed a finger in Gallagher's direction. "You lied to me, buster. No amount of apologizing can worm your way out of that."

"I didn't lie to you."

"Oh, excuse me. You just neglected to tell me your full name and mention that you were a critic from my rival newspaper."

"Those are omissions, not lies," he pointed out wisely. "*You* are the one who lied."

"I? What lie did I tell?"

"You said you were engaged, which I have to tell you I found a bit suspicious, since you weren't wearing a ring. When I asked around this morning I was told that you had recently broken up with some movie star. Ergo, you lied to me last night, and in my book a lie beats an error of omission any day."

"Ah! But you omitted and you stole," Kate pointed out smugly, too angry to be embarrassed about having been caught in a lie. Or maybe she was just having too much fun. "Where I come from omission and theft top a lie."

"Fine. I'll see your accusation of omission and theft and raise you a *pair* of lies."

Kate gasped. "A pair? Where do you come up with a pair?"

Matt leaned against the wall casually. "You lied about being engaged *and* you lied about not wanting to go out with me."

Hotly Kate snapped, "I never said I didn't *want* to, I just said I wouldn't!"

"Aha! Then you admit that you want to have dinner with me!"

"After what you've done? You've got to be kidding!"

The absurdity of their heated exchange finally caught up with both of them and when Matt started laughing, Kate's anger crumbled. Ruefully she laughed with him, enjoying the deep resonant sound of his laugh that enfolded her in warmth.

"Can we start again?" Matt asked, bringing his mirth under control.

Kate's own laugh ended in a weary, drawn out sigh. "No. I'm still mad as hell at you. Why in God's name did you pirate my lead for the review? And why didn't you tell me who you were last night?"

"The last half is easier to answer than the first, so I'll start there," he told her. "It was fear, pure and simple. You see, when I worked as a critic in New York there was intense, petty rivalry between the theater staffs of all the major papers. I wasn't joking when I said I wanted to get to know you the minute you walked through the door. I was standing in that corner trying to come up with some brilliant, creative way to sweep you off your feet, and then DeAngelo made his announcement about who you were. I knew that once you found out I was from the *Enterprise* I wouldn't stand a chance."

"But you deliberately played ignorant and led me into talking about my review!"

"It was the only thing I could think of to get you talking, and I played dumb because I didn't want to arouse your suspicions. I was hoping to convince you to like me before I hit you with the bad news over a cup of coffee after the play."

"And when that didn't work, you stole my review because you thought *that* would make me like you?" Kate's raised eyebrows conveyed her skepticism.

"Not exactly. I wrote my own review after the show last night, but when I asked around this morning and discovered that you weren't engaged, I made a few changes to pay you back for lying to me."

"Well, that's typical. It's okay for you to bend the truth, but heaven forbid that a woman be anything but totally honest."

At least he had the courtesy to look sheepish. "Pretty chauvinistic, huh?"

"That's putting it mildly."

"But it got your attention, didn't it?"

Kate shook her head wearily. "I don't know how they do things back East, Gallagher, but out here we're a little more straightforward. Usually a gentleman who wants a lady to find favor with him just sends her flowers or something."

"But I did," he protested.

She shot him a killing glance. "That was a little after the fact, wouldn't you say?"

"Better late than never."

Kate groaned. "Don't you ever run out of platitudes?"

"I rent them by the hour. That one's due back at four."

"Do you have a snappy comeback for everything?"

"Everything, it would seem, except how to convince you to forgive me. I'd give anything if we could just start all over—with a little more honesty on *both* sides."

Kate thought it over. "I'm sorry I lied about being engaged. It just slipped out. Force of habit, I guess. But after I'd said it, it seemed easier and safer to keep up the charade than to explain that I'm not dating because I recently broke up with someone."

"Dan McBride?"

"That's right. You did your homework very well."

Matt cocked his head to one side. "Why was lying safer than telling the truth?"

"Most men think a woman on the rebound is an easy target."

He shook his head. "Only an unprincipled cad would think that. Of course, I realize that you have no reason to think that I'm anything other than that right now."

Kate sighed with exasperation. "I must be nuts, but despite direct evidence to the contrary, I have a feeling you're probably a nice man." His dimple deepened above his beard and Kate rushed on, "But that doesn't mean I'll go out with you. I'm not ready yet."

"Oh, I think you're more ready than you want to admit, even to yourself."

Kate frowned. "How dare you! You don't know me. You don't know how I feel or what I went through with Dan McBride."

Matt sobered. "That's true. But I know you're just as excited by the chemistry between us as I am. You can't deny that."

Kate opened her mouth to contradict him but found she couldn't. The butterfly churning in her stomach and her heightened sense of being alive were too strong to allow her to lie to him again. But she didn't want to date him. She wasn't ready to open the door to her heart yet, and even if she had been, Matt Gallagher wasn't the man she'd want to invite in. He was too glib. Too charming. Too damned charismatic. A man like that, one who'd been willing to stoop to a little creative lying to impress a woman, was certainly capable of perpetrating deeper, far more painful deceits . . . just like Dan McBride.

"Sorry, Gallagher. I'm not going to go out with you, and that's final."

He paused thoughtfully, then asked, "Sort of final, or absolutely final?"

Kate stiffened her jaw. He wasn't going to make her laugh again. "Absolutely, positively final."

"All right. Let it be on your head," he said with a sad, resigned sigh.

Kate frowned. "Let what be on my head? What is that, some kind of Gaelic curse?" she asked irritably.

He turned toward the elevator doors, planting his back to her. "Just wait. You'll see."

"I don't want to see anything! That's the whole point. I want you to leave me alone!"

"Sometimes we don't get everything we want in this life." He glanced at her over his shoulder and flashed a wicked grin. "And sometimes we do."

"Damn it, Gallagher—" Furious and frustrated, she plucked at his arm, forcing him to turn toward her. "What's it going to take to convince you to leave me alone?"

He thought it over a second. "Cash?" he suggested hopefully.

Kate nipped her lower lip to keep from smiling. How could she maintain her anger at a man who made her want to laugh all the time. "How much cash?" she asked, unable to keep herself from falling into the game of teasing banter that they played so well.

This time it was Matt who laughed. "How much have you got?"

"How much will it take?"

"Fifty thousand," he announced.

Kate's mouth flew open. "That's all I'm worth? A lousy fifty thou?"

"All right. Make it a hundred."

"It's a deal," she replied. "Can we work out an installment plan?"

"Well, sure, but if your salary as a critic is anything like mine, that's going to bind us together for a long time." He grinned. "It would be cheaper if you'd just take me out to dinner."

"Now I'm supposed to take you to dinner? Not on your life."

He shrugged. "Have it your way."

Kate shook her head and leaned wearily against the wall. "That's the problem in a nutshell, Gallagher. I haven't had *anything* my way since I met you. Can we get serious for a minute?"

"I'd rather not. You have no idea how beautiful you are when you're sparring like this."

Kate's brow furrowed into a frown again. "Don't."

"What? Tell you you're beautiful? You are, you know."

She eyed him frostily. "That's what you said last night—just before you tricked me into giving you the lead for my review."

Matt sobered, too. "I've apologized for that, Kate."

"I know. And I will accept your apology on one condition."

"What?"

"*You* accept the fact that we're never going to be anything more than two people who share a common occupation. We're bound to run into each other from time to time, so maybe we'll even become friends. But we're not going to date." She looked at him seriously. "I'm not ready for a relationship, and if you're really the decent sort of fellow you'd have me believe, you'll respect that."

Kate examined the sober look on his face and concluded, "Now, do we have a deal or not?"

Matt studied her closely, wondering what Dan McBride had done to this beautiful woman to make her so guarded. It was obvious she'd been hurt and was afraid of a repeat performance. He certainly couldn't blame her for that, and he was equally certain that he couldn't *force* her to give him a chance to prove that something very special was happening between them. It didn't seem that he had any choice but to accept her terms—for the time being.

Slowly, his eyes never leaving hers, Matt extended his right hand. "All right. It's a deal."

"Good." Trying to be businesslike, Kate accepted his handshake. All the power and energy bundled up in Gallagher's tall frame flowed into his warm, firm grip, and Kate felt a jolt of excitement at his touch.

Matt felt it, too, but he didn't find it nearly as surprising as Kate did. She tried to retract her hand, but Matt didn't let go. "Tell me something, Kate. Have I at least convinced you that I'm not a dangerous serial killer?"

The intensity of his look made Kate swallow hard. "Yes."

"Good."

"Why?"

"Because—" it took only half a step to close the distance between them "—I'm going to kiss you, and *fear* is not the emotion I want you to feel."

Kate's breath hitched in her throat as he lowered his face toward hers. She could have stopped him, of course. She knew instinctively that if she turned her head or jerked away, he wouldn't pursue her. His arms weren't around her. Only his hand was touching hers. She could avoid the kiss quite easily. But she didn't. She waited with expectation hammering in her heart until his lips met hers.

Nice, she thought, her mind strangely disconnected from her body as his lips plied hers. It wasn't a stormtrooper kiss, at all. It was warm and gentle, but just insistent enough to demand a response. And Kate gave him one. She couldn't help herself. Somehow, her arms had found their way around his shoulders, her body was pressed against his, her breathing was nonexistent and her heartbeat was hammering in her ears. What else could she do but respond?

When his mouth widened and his tongue gently probed her lips, she opened to him eagerly, slanting her head to receive him, straining toward the intimacy of that caress. His tongue mated and danced with hers, sending fiery shafts of longing through her and bringing a soft moan into her throat. Every one of her senses came to vibrant life, making her ache for more.

Matt's hands slipped under her jacket and roved insistently over her back, then one hand moved lower, lightly brushing her hip. That single, feathery contact was enough to send a shaft of fire coursing through her and settling in the pit of her stomach.

Kate's body had never betrayed her so completely. She'd never been so consumed by a single kiss, and when

Matt's lips finally left hers, she felt bereft. She found herself staring up into blue eyes that had darkened to the color of midnight and seemed almost as overwhelmed as she was by the intensity of what had transpired.

It was a struggle, but Kate finally managed to pull her scattered senses together. She couldn't muster any indignation, though, because she had contributed just as much to the kiss as he had. "I thought we had a deal," she said breathlessly as she slipped out of his arms.

Matt was more than a little breathless, himself. Though his instincts had told him Kate was a passionate woman, he hadn't expected to find such a deep well of desire in her. But his instincts also told him that she was afraid of that well, and he knew he was going to have to tread very carefully or he'd lose any slim chance he had with her.

He summoned a smile that he hoped was genial and nonthreatening. "We do have a deal," he assured her, wondering if she noticed that his voice was hoarse. "That was just a friendly kiss to seal our bargain. Consider it a gesture of goodwill from one critic to another."

Kate didn't trust his sudden congeniality any more than she trusted herself at the moment. "Funny, it didn't feel very friendly to me."

"No, it didn't, did it?" His voice was a gentle caress that touched Kate as tangibly as if he had enfolded her in his arms again.

Before she could come up with a suitable response, Old Faithful finally sprang to life. Kate almost exclaimed with relief, but Matt looked surprised, as though he'd forgotten where they were.

Kate collected herself, doing her best to pretend that their earth-shattering kiss had been nothing more than the friendly gesture Matt claimed it was. She turned toward the doors when the elevator glided to a halt, and Matt did likewise.

Because she'd pushed so many buttons on the panel, the elevator automatically stopped at the next floor, but after what had just happened, Kate wasn't about to trust the unreliable conveyance again. She held out her hand to keep the doors from closing.

"This is the second floor," she announced, grateful that her voice seemed steady. "This is also the second time this week I've been trapped in here, so I'm sure you'll understand if I opt for taking the stairs down to the lobby."

Matt accompanied her into the brightly lit hall. "I'll go with you. You never can tell, there might be muggers on the stairwell."

She felt enough in control to shoot him a teasing, sidelong glance. "And you're going to protect me? I don't know about that. Where I come from, a mugger on a stairwell is better than an ax murderer in the elevator any day."

Matt laughed. "Very funny." They reached the windowed door to the emergency stairs. "Allow me." He pulled open the door and turned furtively to Kate, admonishing, "Wait here."

Checking to see that the coast was clear, he stepped to the landing rail where the stairs spiraled up and down. "Excuse, please, this is warning to muggers," he called out, using another of his apparently endless dialects. "This is a wrestler coming down the stairs with a deadly KGB agent. Better stay clear."

Right on cue a stone faced business executive appeared at the bottom on the landing, looking up at the bearded lunatic above him.

Completely nonplussed, Gallagher asked, "Excuse me, sir. Are you a mugger?"

"No." With a disgusted look the businessman started up the stairs and Matt moved back to Kate. "It's okay, dear. The coast is clear," he informed her, gently placing a protective arm at her back to usher her down the stairs. The unamused businessman slipped past them and Matt leaned toward Kate. "Really, honey, you must stop practicing your Rich Little impersonations in public," he said in a stage whisper. "It's getting embarrassing."

"You are incorrigible!" Despite herself, Kate laughed as she quickened her step and reached the lobby just ahead of him.

"I know. But if you can't laugh at yourself, Kate, you might as well find a hole to hide in and pull a rock over the top. There's too much pain in this world, and laughter is one of the two best medicines known to modern man."

Unable to resist, Kate stopped and looked at him. What she found in his eyes left her with barely enough breath to ask, "What's the other?"

"Love," he replied softly. Matt raised his hand to her face, lightly tracing the line of her brow, the high cheekbones, the gentle hollow of her cheek.

Kate's heart tripped like a jackhammer. "Are you for real, Gallagher?" she found herself asking breathlessly. "Or are you just another Irishman who kissed the Blarney stone one too many times?"

Matt didn't look at all offended. "That's something you'll have to decide for yourself, Kate. I just hope you'll do us both the favor of giving me a fair trial." His hand fell away from her face. "I'll be seeing you, Kate."

had been. Despite that, though, she'd said she wasn't ready to date again, and Matt had decided he'd better find out why.

Now, he knew. Dan McBride had put her through hell. Even if only a fraction of the articles Matt had just read contained a grain of truth, the actor was a thoughtless, childish, womanizing jerk who believed that his stardom gave him license to do anything he damned well pleased—no matter who it hurt. And in McBride's case, the victim had been his fiancée.

Kate had been publicly humiliated by rumors of McBride's many affairs—the last of which had been confirmed in scintillating full-color photographs taken by a tabloid photographer. The pictures of McBride and actress Sandra Berringer making love on the deck of Sandra's Malibu home made Matt physically ill. He could only imagine what they had done to Kate.

How could any man betray a woman that way? Particularly a woman like Kate, whose beauty was enough to captivate anyone. Her sparkling wit would keep even the sharpest man on his toes for a lifetime. A man could spend eternity relishing her intelligence and plumbing the depths of her passionate nature, so what possible need would there be to even look at another woman, let alone risk losing Kate because of one?

McBride was a gold-plated, card-carrying fool, and the evidence in front of Matt suggested that the actor had hurt Kate so badly that it was going to take more than patience, persistence and tender-loving care to convince her to trust again. It was going to take a Sir Galahad in full armor on a white horse. Maybe even a pure-of-heart, infallible saint.

Unfortunately Matt had never been a saint, and the only time he'd ever mounted a horse he'd promptly fallen off.

But that didn't mean he was going to give up on Kate Franklyn. Someone had to prove to her that not all men were unfaithful louts. Someone had to show her that love, compassion and good old-fashioned romance still existed.

For that, Matt was imminently qualified, and he had a shelf full of books at home to prove it. He didn't know Kate well enough to promise happily ever after, of course, but he believed in the premise—and his gut instinct told him that Kate Franklyn was the woman he'd been waiting for all his life.

All he had to do was make her believe it.

Smiling thoughtfully, he began mentally polishing his suit of shining armor and started planning an all-out assault on Castle Franklyn.

THE TREE SEEMED to be moving across the newsroom floor all by itself. It towered over the heads of a half-dozen gawkers, tottering precariously as it lumbered toward Kate's desk. The halting movements and the titters of laughter those movements aroused reminded Kate of Saturday's debacle with Matt Gallagher.

Twin shafts of dread and excitement coursed through her. Kate had used the last forty-eight hours to convince herself that refusing to date Gallagher had been the right decision. Her reaction to his kiss was disturbing but understandable; after all, she had been feeling a little lonely recently and there was no denying she was still vulnerable because of Dan McBride. Her love for him had died a violent death, but the trauma and turmoil that surrounded their breakup had left her with wounds that were only now healing over. She just wasn't ready to risk that kind of pain again.

She didn't need another charming, insincere scoundrel in her life. She didn't want to experience the excitement and expectation that went hand in hand with falling in love. Most of all, she couldn't afford the risk of losing her heart to a man who'd already proven he couldn't be trusted.

But like it or not, Gallagher was back, just as she'd feared he would be. Kate was ready for him this time, though. She wasn't going to let him make her laugh. She wasn't going to find him charming. She was going to be firm, even businesslike with him, and under no circumstances whatsoever would she allow herself to be alone with him, even if it meant confronting him in front of the entire newsroom.

Strengthening that resolve, she watched as the tree pitched toward her, completely obscuring the man carrying it. When it reached her desk, the enormous planter hit the floor with a thud, and a large, strong hand tenuously parted the foliage. The handsome face that had haunted Kate all weekend peered through the greenery.

"Hi. It's me," Matt whispered conspiratorially.

Kate stiffened her jaw against an overpowering desire to laugh. "Now, I wonder why I couldn't guess that?" she asked sarcastically.

"Probably because my disguise is so good."

Kate summoned a look of disgust and gave it to the tree. "What is this thing?"

"A philodendron with a thyroid problem."

"Well, get it out of here. This is a newsroom, not a greenhouse."

"I can't," Matt replied, abandoning his hiding place to sit on Kate's desk. "It's for you. A gift."

"We had a deal, Gallagher," she reminded him sternly. "I thought we settled this in the elevator last Saturday."

"Was that what you thought?" he asked softly, his voice a husky whisper that made Kate's pulse quicken. "I didn't get that impression at all. In fact, I found what happened in the elevator particularly *un*settling."

Somehow, Kate managed to ignore the physical and mental flashback his words evoked. "That's your problem."

Matt looked surprised. "You didn't find it unsettling?"

"No. I didn't."

Matt put his fingertips lightly under Kate's chin and turned her head so that he could examine her profile. His touch brought a tantalizing warmth to her skin and Kate jerked her head away with a gasp. "What are you doing?"

"Checking to see if your nose is growing."

"Well, it's not."

"No, but you are lying. I can tell." He leaned forward and grinned. "You spent the whole weekend thinking about me, didn't you?"

"No."

That seemed to set him back a bit. "Part of the weekend?" he asked hopefully.

She shook her head.

"Two minutes Saturday night while you were washing your hair?"

She swallowed the urge to smile. "Not even that much."

"Riiiight," he said with a knowing wink. "And Santa Claus is just a figment of R. H. Macy's imagination."

"I wish you were a figment of *my* imagination so I could make you—" she pointed to the tree "—and your greenery go away."

"Sorry, but this is just the beginning. You've heard of the Twelve Days of Christmas? This is the Twelve Apologies of Gallagher."

Kate groaned. She didn't need this and she wasn't sure how much of Gallagher's peculiar brand of persuasion she could handle before she caved in. But letting him know that would be the worst mistake she could make. "I don't want your gifts, Gallagher."

Matt shrugged. "Then feel free to ignore them." He flashed her a devilish grin. "If you can."

Kate stiffened her jaw and looked away, trying to conquer the melting sensation that his smile always gave her. "If that's the pear tree, where's the partridge?"

He pointed. "It's right—" He stopped and frowned, then began searching the branches.

"Your bird flew the coop?" Kate asked lightly.

"Apparently so," Matt muttered.

"Any chance you'll take that as a sign and follow suit?"

"No. Ah, here it is!" Triumphantly he bent over to retrieve the elusive bird from the planter where it had fallen, and held it out toward Kate.

She stared. It wasn't a partridge...it was a fuzzy stuffed replica of one of Kate's favorite cartoon characters. Matt squeezed the lemon-yellow tummy and the little bird squawked, "I tawt I taw a puddy tat."

Kate bit the underside of her lip to keep from smiling. "Tweetybird?"

Matt shrugged. "Partridges are hard to come by in L.A." He held the fuzzy toy out to her.

If Kate hadn't known that every eye in the newsroom was on her she might have refused to take Tweety from him. As it was, though, she hoped to get out of this with as much dignity as possible. She took the bird. "Are you trying to draw a parallel between the cat and the canary?" she asked archly.

Matt stroked his beard thoughtfully. "I hadn't thought of it that way, but it's an appropriate analogy."

She gave him a smug smile. "Good. That means I'm safe, because Sylvester never caught Tweety."

"True. But he never stopped trying, did he?"

His sexy look and even sexier voice nearly undid Kate and she slapped a bandage on her weakening defenses. "Look, Gallagher, you can send me all the gifts you like, but that still won't change my mind," she said firmly. "I'm not going out to dinner with you."

Matt frowned. "I don't recall asking you out to dinner today. We had a deal, remember?"

For the first time, Kate was truly surprised. If he wasn't here to ask her for a date, what was his game? "B-but you . . . I thought . . . I mean, I assumed . . ."

"You're lucky I'm a sucker for an articulate woman," he said with a grin. "Never assume anything, Kate. You made yourself quite clear on Saturday. You don't want to go out with me, and I wouldn't dream of trying to coerce you into changing your mind. This is just a friendly gesture of goodwill. It's the least I owe you after the way I swiped your review."

Kate remembered his last goodwill offering only too well. Sometimes she even thought she could still taste him on her lips, and the thrilling feeling of being in his arms was a memory that wouldn't go away. Still, she managed to find the willpower to tell him, "You don't owe me anything, Gallagher. If you recall, I've already accepted your apology."

"No, you haven't. If you really had forgiven me, you wouldn't still be calling me Gallagher and treating me as though I had a virulent case of chicken pox."

"Don't be silly," she countered with a frosty smile. "I'm not worried about you being contagious because I've already been thoroughly immunized against charming scoundrels."

Matt winced. "Ooh. Direct hit. Though I can't say that I like being lumped into the same category as Dan McBride just because we share an ethnic heritage."

Kate met his gaze evenly. "Your family tree had nothing to do with the criteria I established for making that determination," she assured him. "This was strictly a behavioral judgment."

Matt's smile faded. "Kate, I'm not Dan McBride," he told her seriously. "I bent the truth a little last Friday night because I wanted a chance to get to know you better before our positions as rival critics put a wall between us. That doesn't make me a lying, womanizing jerk. Unlike Dan McBride, I believe in things like loyalty and fidelity, so don't judge me by his standards, okay?"

Kate knew that was exactly what she was doing, but it was the only defense she had against the way Gallagher made her feel. She wasn't about to let go of it. "It seems that you've done a little more research," she commented mildly.

Matt nodded. "You accused me of not knowing what McBride had put you through, so I took a look at his file in the *Enterprise* morgue."

Kate knew what he'd found in that file and she felt a flush of humiliation that was almost as fresh as it had been in the days right after the Dan McBride/Sandra Berringer scandal broke. "Then you should know why I'm not anxious to jump back into the dating game."

"I know that Dan McBride should be shot for what he did to you," Matt replied, unable to keep the anger he felt toward the actor from showing. "He couldn't see what an incredible treasure he had."

"You mean me?" Kate scoffed, dismissing what she assumed was blatant, insincere flattery.

"No, I mean love," Matt replied forcefully. "*That's* the treasure, and it's more precious than gold no matter what form it takes."

He spoke with such sincerity that it frightened Kate. No one believed in that kind of romantic claptrap anymore, yet Gallagher sounded so convincing. But he'd made other things sound convincing, too. Kate knew she didn't dare trust him, no matter how much she wanted to.

"You really are something, you know that, Gallagher," she said as she rose. "You're a throwback to the days when women were stupid enough to be seduced by romantic drivel, but those days are long gone, and I'm not impressed."

Matt folded his arms over his chest and smiled. "If you're trying to make me angry, that won't do it," he informed her pleasantly. "I've been called a sentimental, romantic fool more than once, and it doesn't bother me a bit because, you see—" he leaned forward and whispered conspiratorially "—it's true."

Kate felt her defenses crumbling and she tried desperately to shore them up. "I don't care what you are, Gallagher."

"No, you don't *want* to care," he replied easily. "But you do, because the chemistry between us is unlike anything you've ever felt before."

Kate squirmed. How could she deny something that was so obviously true? "I don't believe in chemistry."

"No? Then what do you believe in?"

Kate raised her chin defiantly. "Honesty."

"I have been honest with you, Kate. About everything that's important, like how exciting you are and wonderful you make me feel. We got off on the wrong foot and that's my fault, but now I'm trying to rectify that."

"You can't," she insisted.

"Yes, I can. You see, you're not mad at me about the review or anything I did Friday night. You're mad at Dan McBride for betraying you, and you're afraid of being hurt again."

"Can you blame me?"

"No," he replied gently. "But I can't let you get away with using what *he* did as an excuse to reject me." Matt stood. "And that means you're going to have to see me for who I am—not who he was."

His voice was as soft as a caress that wound itself around Kate's heart. "And just how do you intend to accomplish that?" she asked without much force.

Matt grinned as he lightly fingered a branch of his First Day of Gallagher offering. "Just wait. You'll see," he said, then all hints of teasing left his eyes as he told her, "Dan McBride was a fool to let you get away, Kate. I don't intend to make the same mistake."

Without giving her a chance to protest, he turned away and sauntered across the room, softly whistling the tune to "The Twelve Days of Christmas" as he went.

THE THICK MANILA ENVELOPE lying on Kate's oak coffee table looked innocuous enough. She had seen thousands of them in her lifetime. She had opened hundreds of them.

This was the first time she'd ever been afraid of one. It had arrived via messenger service shortly after Matt had left her office this afternoon. She had tried to accept his dare and ignore the envelope completely. She'd even thrown it into her trash can once in a gesture of defiance, but when it came time for her to leave work she had rescued it, reasoning that she simply didn't want to give any of her curious co-workers an excuse to snoop through her trash.

Now, it was just sitting on the table, silently mocking her feeble attempts to work up the resolve to destroy it without looking at the contents Matt had placed inside for her.

She couldn't do it, of course. Even in absentia, Matt Gallagher worked a magical spell on her. She had to know what lame, manipulative trick he was trying on her this time. The only reason she was delaying at all was that she needed time to work up some more of the righteous indignation she'd used this afternoon to hold him at bay.

Not that her indignation had worked, of course. He had knocked gaping holes in her defenses and she couldn't seem to find a way to plug them. Finally she gave up trying altogether. Her curiosity got the better of her and she settled onto the sofa, opened the envelope and spilled the contents onto the table.

A dozen or more pictures—some in color, some in black-and-white—fell out first; then a few newspaper clippings floated out; and finally, a thick sheath of white paper held together by a paper clip plopped onto the table. The top sheet appeared to be a fax, and she glanced through it quickly.

Kate had thought she was ready for anything, but she'd been wrong. Nothing could have prepared her for that first page. Despite herself, she laughed out loud as she read the "To Whom it May Concern" letter of recommendation from Matt's mother!

Half apology and half glowing praise, the letter recounted a humorous litany of Matt's faults and virtues. "Heaven knows he's not perfect," Maureen Gallagher wrote near the end. "I've told him more than once that his warped sense of humor will be the death of him—and me—but since he acquired it honestly from his father I can't be too critical. Despite his irreverent view of the world, though, he's a fine man. Ted and I tried to instill a sense of responsibility and honor in him, and I think it took.

"If he has a serious fault, I suppose it's that he's a hopeless romantic. He genuinely believes that there is one woman out there who was meant for him and him alone. He hasn't found her yet, but I do keep hoping. Our daughters have provided us with seven lovely grandchildren, but Ted is anxiously awaiting one that bears the Gallagher family name."

The letter was absolutely charming. Of course, it flitted through Kate's mind that Matt had written it himself, but she really didn't think that was the case. Having his mother write a letter on his behalf was just the sort of off-center stunt Gallagher would pull, and he could be fairly confident that his own mother wouldn't say anything too damaging to his case.

What ultimately convinced Kate of the letter's validity, though, were the pages that followed the fax. *Those* were from Matt himself, but they contained no ham-handed manipulation, no insincere declarations of attraction or affection for Kate. He had written, instead, a charming narrative résumé.

It was by far the most entertaining and compelling reading Kate had done in ages. She learned, for example, that Matt was the oldest of six children, and his five siblings were all girls who had done their best to drive their big brother insane. His parents were retired and still lived in the rambling old Victorian farmhouse where they'd raised their children.

He was a thirty-seven-year-old graduate of the University of Minnesota, where he had taken a double major in theater and journalism. He liked children and animals, and they—he claimed—liked him back. He'd never been arrested, he loved to read and he had a yen to travel extensively in Europe. His first girlfriend had been a blue-eyed, freckle-faced beauty named Penny, with whom he had fallen madly in love in the second grade. He'd once received a black eye defending Penny's honor, yet despite his devotion she had dumped him for a third-grader who had a ten-speed racing bike.

There were stories about his sisters, accompanied by carefully labeled photos so that Kate could put faces to the family members Matt wrote about with such humor and affection. The youngest was Andie, a raven-haired siren who was dating a member of a motorcycle gang, much to Maureen's dismay. The oldest, Lorna, was a lawyer who had her mother's fair complexion. Tish shared Matt's sense of humor; Terry was painfully shy; Collie was an earth mother with three children and a degree in horticulture.

By the time Kate finished the letter, she was exhausted from laughing. She also felt she knew more about Matt than she did about some of the people she'd worked with for years. It was a strange, intimate feeling, yet nothing about his letter suggested intimacy. It was just a simple, lay-it-on-the-line narrative explaining who Matt Gallagher was—take it or leave it.

He had done exactly what he promised to do. He was making her see him for who he was—a nice man with a wicked sense of humor and a romantic streak a mile wide.

He was a charming, relentless bulldozer, and despite herself, Kate found that she was beginning to like the idea of being dozed.

Chapter Six

The Friday evening traffic around the Music Center was atrocious. Limousines were backed up for nearly a mile on the Hollywood Freeway and the surface roads weren't much better. Even using shortcuts, it took Kate forty minutes just to reach the parking garage and find a space for her sporty little Mustang. Fortunately she had anticipated the crowd and had allowed plenty of extra time.

This particular opening night was a charity affair, so nearly every star in Hollywood had turned out for the photo op—hence the limousines. That also accounted for the legion of reporters, photographers and TV news crews that was camped alongside the red carpet in the concrete courtyard.

Since Kate had no desire to run the gauntlet of reporters, she skirted them, heading straight for the box office. She picked up her on-call ticket and went into the crowded lobby, where champagne was flowing freely and elbow-rubbing with the stars was being elevated to a science.

Kate had no desire to rub elbows. She'd done enough of that to last a lifetime while she was living with Dan. But neither was she ready to take her seat. It was still twenty minutes before the curtain went up, and excitement was bubbling inside her like uncorked champagne. She tried to tamp it down, but it wouldn't stay quiet because she knew that Matt would be here to review the play, as well.

It had been nearly two weeks since he launched his Twelve Apologies attack, and Kate thought she knew how Custer must have felt at the Little Bighorn: outnumbered, outgunned and hopelessly surrounded. But the funny thing was, she hadn't actually seen Gallagher again. He had laid siege to her via long distance. Every day she received at least one remembrance from him, each in keeping with his "Twelve Days" theme—Gallagher style, of course.

On the morning after his Monday visit, she had received two personally autographed copies of Andrea Mathers's wildly romantic, scintillatingly sexy novel, *White Dove.* Wednesday morning, a trio of musicians carrying three French *horns* instead of three French *hens* had followed her from the parking garage to the office, serenading her with a rousing rendition of the torch song "I'm Sorry." Thursday's gift had been a quartet of crystal parakeets in a delicate, bird cage music box. Friday a local catering service had spread a lunch buffet on her desk; five golden onion rings were included in the menu, naturally.

Somehow, Matt had learned her home address and the gifts had continued through the weekend and the following week. Kate now had stuffed geese and origami swans in her apartment. She had been serenaded down Wilshire Boulevard by a drum and fife corps. She had a certificate from a cleaning service that called itself "Maid to Order."

In all, eleven clever gifts—each accompanied by another of Matt's charming, chatty letters—had been delivered to her. But so far today there had been nothing, and that worried Kate. Something was going to happen at the theater tonight because a nut like Gallagher couldn't possibly resist the inherent similarities between Twelve Lords a-Leaping and a performance of *A Chorus Line*. The question was: How outrageous would his gift be this time? He was capable of anything, but surely he wouldn't embarrass her in front of hundreds of Hollywood celebrities and the news media. Would he?

And an even bigger question: Would Kate really mind if he did?

"Kate? Over here!"

She turned toward the familiar voice and found Rolf Lundon, the *Drama Review* critic, motioning to her with his champagne glass. Thomas Hampton, a columnist/critic for the *Hollywood Weekly*, was beside him. Kate liked both of them, but they had nothing to do with the flush of excitement that brought color to her cheeks. Matt was responsible for that. He was standing with them, looking like he just stepped out of a tuxedo ad.

Kate swallowed hard, gathered her composure and joined them. "Hello, Rolf. Thomas. What are you two reprobates cooking up? You're not trying to stuff the ballot box for the Critics' Choice Awards, are you?"

Rolf feigned shock. "Me, cheat? Heaven forfend!" He took Kate's hand and she leaned over slightly so that the diminutive gentleman could kiss her cheek. "You look ravishing, my dear. Burgundy is definitely your color."

"Thank you, Rolf," Kate answered. She had dressed carefully tonight in a simple silk suit, hoping to look elegant and restrained without being flashy. Apparently she had succeeded, because she was vividly aware that Matt hadn't taken his eyes off her. She hadn't looked at him again, though, because she was afraid he'd see how happy she was to see him. "Hello, Thomas."

Hampton's greeting was cordial but more restrained. "Good to see you, Kate. It's been a while," he said as he shook her hand. "I enjoyed your review of *Swing Time* last month."

She smiled at him. "That's because you agreed with me."

"For once," Rolf added.

"Well, it had to happen eventually," Kate replied philosophically.

"Yes, but I never thought I'd live to see the day you two would agree on anything," Rolf replied ruefully. "Have you met Matt Gallagher yet?"

Kate finally turned her attention to Matt. He was searching her face, somewhat anxiously, Kate thought. Probably looking for some clue about how she felt toward him now, after two weeks of his siege tactics. She wanted to give him a frosty, imperious stare to keep him guessing, but she wasn't that good an actress. "Hello, Gallagher."

"Hello, Kate. You look exquisite," Matt said, drinking in the sight of her like a thirsty man at an oasis. He hadn't imagined that it was possible to miss anyone as much as he'd missed her these past two weeks, but if the sparkle in her violet eyes was any indication, she had missed him, too.

He didn't quite believe it. He sensed no tension in her—save for the acute awareness they always generated. He saw no hint of the barriers she had thrown up during their last meeting. In fact, she actually seemed pleased to see him. Maybe, just maybe, the Twelve Days of Gallagher had worked.

Rolf's curious gaze moved back and forth between them. "Hmm. It appears that you two already know each other."

Thomas's wicked chuckle answered him. "Where have you been, Rolf?" the tall, thin critic asked. "Kate was introduced to the new kid on the block the hard way. Rumor has it that Gallagher conned her into giving away the lead of her review for that dreadful DeAngelo production a few weeks back."

Rolf's eyes grew round and large as he looked at Matt. "Is that true? Did you really put one over on Kate?"

Oh, brother. Some mistakes were just impossible to live down. Matt could envision two weeks of hard work being shot to hell, but when he looked at Kate, she seemed entirely calm. "Actually rumors of my coup have been greatly exaggerated," he told the men.

"Don't be so modest, Gallagher," Kate said pleasantly, enjoying the way Matt was squirming. "It was a masterful stroke. And you shouldn't be so surprised, Rolf. Just because you've never trapped me in a practical joke doesn't mean it can't be done. I'm not easy, but I can be had."

All three men laughed, but Matt's was more relief than humor. Obviously Kate wasn't mad at him any longer—unless she was just trying to save face in front of her colleagues.

"You must be shaking in your boots, Gallagher," Thomas commented. "Kate doesn't get mad, she gets even. She has quite a reputation for retribution."

"Really?"

Rolf nodded. "If anyone should know, it's Thomas. He made the mistake of taking a swipe at her in his column once. The next morning when he came to work he discovered that the lock on his office door had been changed."

Matt looked at Kate in surprise. "You did that?"

She gave him an aloof, Mona Lisa smile. "Yes."

"Should I be worried?"

Her smile didn't change. "Yes."

"In that case, I'll be on my guard."

"It won't help," she assured him. "I always strike when it's least expected."

Her eyes were locked on his, and Matt felt the sizzle of sexual sparks all the way to his toes. This was the same Kate who'd knocked his socks off at the Players Theater—charming, mischievous and so beautiful that it almost hurt to look at her.

"Thomas, I don't know about you, but I feel a bit like excess baggage," Rolf said as he looked back and forth between the rival critics who were generating enough electricity to power the chandelier overhead. "I wish *I'd* tricked Kate into giving me her DeAngelo review."

Kate felt a familiar blush creeping into her cheeks and she reclaimed her gaze from Matt's possession. "No, you don't, Rolf. You don't want to be on the receiving end of my wrath."

The diminutive critic took her hand and darted a quick look toward Matt. "Darling, if this is wrath, I'm Tom Cruise." He kissed her hand, then dropped it reluctantly. "Come on, Thomas. We have a juicy rumor to start spreading."

Rolf nodded to Kate and Matt. Thomas did the same, then they disappeared into the crowd.

Kate watched them go because it was safer than looking at Matt. "Oh, joy. More rumors about me. Just what I need," she murmured.

"Do you want me to find a creative way to silence them?" Matt offered. "Thumb screws? The rack? Bamboo shoots?"

"You've got your torture devices mixed up, Gallagher," Kate replied, turning to him. "Those are for making people talk, not vice versa. Besides, it wouldn't do any good. The damage is already done. Our courtship hasn't exactly been subtle so far."

Matt felt a shard of excitement pierce his chest before it moved south. "Are we courting?"

"No. You're courting. I'm playing hard to get."

Matt grinned. "For how much longer?"

That was a question Kate couldn't answer. Matt's siege had forced her to deal with emotions she didn't want to be having; things like anticipation, excitement and a sensation of having finally awakened from a long, deep slumber—not unlike Snow White, she had thought more than once during the past two weeks. A handsome prince had kissed her, and she had started believing in fairy tales again.

It was a scary feeling, because sensitive, intelligent, romantic men didn't exist. But every time Kate had managed to convince herself of that, another silly note had arrived and she'd found herself a little more captivated by the man who had sworn he wasn't foolish enough to let her go.

And now, for better or worse, she was hooked. "I don't know," she replied seriously. "In two weeks you've inserted yourself into my life very efficiently and made it pretty clear you're not going to go away."

"Is that bad?" he asked as he searched her face.

"I wish I knew. It's like a book I can't seem to put down because I want to know how it ends."

"A good book?"

"That depends a lot on what happens tonight," she said ruefully. "The Twelfth Day of Gallagher has been conspicuously peaceful, but I have a sneaking suspicion that won't last much longer. You're not planning something totally humiliating for me, are you?"

Matt's blue eyes widened in an innocent "Who, me?" look. "Kate. Would I humiliate you?"

"If it suited your purpose."

"What, exactly, are you expecting?"

"Oh, I don't know. Chippendale dancers during intermission? Someone skywriting 'Surrender Katherine' over Beverly Boulevard?"

His eyes lit up. "What a great idea! I'm sorry I didn't think of that one myself."

"Don't you dare," she warned him.

"No promises. In case you hadn't noticed, I have a penchant for stealing great ideas."

"Don't remind me."

He held up his right hand. "All right. If it will put your mind at ease I'll promise you—no skywriting tonight."

"Then what are you planning, Matt? Seriously."

He shook his head. "You'll see," he replied cryptically.

That helped a whole lot. "Should I be worried?"

Matt leaned close enough that Kate could feel the warmth of his breath on her cheek. "That depends on how many defenses you have erected against me," he said softly.

Something inside her melted into a pool of longing and she realized that it would be incredibly easy to get lost in the blue of his eyes. "Obviously not nearly enough," she replied unsteadily.

"Good." The sweet, subtle scent of her perfume numbed his senses and filled him with an overpowering desire to take her in his arms and kiss her in front of several hundred witnesses. Only the sure and certain knowledge that such a display would anger her kept him from matching the thought with the deed.

Kate had never been a mind reader, but it didn't take psychic powers to tell what Matt was thinking. Since her own thoughts were headed in the same direction, she took a step back just to make sure that neither of them gave in to temptation. "Don't even think about it, Gallagher," she warned him quietly. "Couldn't we just do this normally?"

Matt conceded the distance between them because he needed it as much as she did. "Do what?"

"Get to know each other the way ordinary people do."

"There's nothing ordinary about you, Kate, but I won't argue the point if it means you'll consider having dinner with me tonight."

Kate chuckled. "Slow down, Tex. You're getting the cart before the horse. We have a play to review, remember?"

Matt glanced around the crowded, noisy room as though he'd just realized where he was. "I guess you have a point," he admitted reluctantly. "For all I know, you snore through the intermission."

"Is that what it would take to get you to leave me alone?" The question was out before Kate could censor it.

Matt's handsome features melted into a disappointed frown. "Kate, if all this is a joke building up to a punch line where you tell me to get lost, then we can cut this short. I've given you my best shot. I've tried to let you get to know me in the most nonthreatening way I could think of. If I've failed, tell me now and I won't bother you again."

He was completely serious. Kate knew she should jump at it his offer, but she couldn't. "Gee, thanks."

"What's wrong? Isn't that fair?"

"No, it's not," she replied. "For better or worse, I'm hooked now. I've got origami swans hanging from my ceiling at home. I've got a goose named Esmerelda on my bed and I gained two pounds because of your stupid Lady Godiva chocolates. Plus that, I have no idea whether or not your little sister Andie married What's his name from the motorcycle gang."

Matt was laughing. "No, she didn't."

"Well, good. He wasn't right for her," Kate said, smiling because Matt's laughter was infectious.

"What are you trying to tell me, Kate?"

"That you hoodwinked me into getting on this roller coaster and I can't seem to find a way to get off," she replied.

Matt nodded, and Kate realized that he understood exactly what she was telling him: she wasn't committing to a relationship but she wasn't asking him to get lost, either.

"Then what do you say we take this slow," he suggested.

"Something tells me Matt Gallagher doesn't have a slow gear," she replied wryly. "You've been running full steam ahead since the moment we met."

"You're mixing your metaphors, but that's okay. And I do have a slow gear," he told her. "As you suggested earlier, let's just get to know each other."

Kate wasn't sure anything could be that simple with a man like Matt, but she was willing to give him the benefit of the doubt. "Good. We're in agreement, then. No shenanigans."

He frowned doubtfully. "I kinda like shenanigans."

"Matt..." Her eyes made her warning very clear, and Matt relented.

"All right. I'll behave myself and be content with the two major victories I've won tonight."

She looked at him questioningly. "Two victories?"

"We're talking, and you've stopped calling me Gallagher. That's definitely a step in the right direction."

"One that you engineered quite skillfully, I might add," she complimented him. "It's hard to be formal with someone after you've seen a picture of him naked on a bearskin rug."

A statuesque blonde in a sequined evening gown happened to be strolling past them, but when she overheard Kate's comment she stopped dead still and gave Matt a thorough once-over. When Matt became aware of her scrutiny, he explained sheepishly, "I was only two months old."

"What a pity," the sequined beauty said, then moved on.

Kate laughed and Matt scowled at her. "You did that on purpose, didn't you?"

"No, but I can't say I'm disappointed with the results. It's nice to have the shoe of embarrassment on your foot instead of mine."

"Rolf was right. You are vindictive," he said without any rancor.

"I believe in an eye for an eye."

"Really? Does that mean you'll be sending me some presents?" he asked hopefully.

"I may plan a surprise or two," she answered cryptically.

"But no shenanigans?"

"Not a one," she promised.

Matt thought that over. "Will I like your surprises?"

"As I said, I believe in an eye for an eye," she repeated.

"Ah. Then the real question is, what did you think of my gifts—aside from the weight you gained due to your lack of self-control?"

She let that pass. "I liked the crystal music box, but I could have done without the drum and fife corps that chased me down Wilshire playing 'Love is a Many Splendored Thing.'"

Her sparkling eyes and her subtle body language told Matt that every one of her senses was tuned on him like radar. He understood that feeling very well, because his own radar was working overtime, too. "What about *White Dove?*" he asked a lot more casually than he felt. "Have you read the Mathers book yet?"

"I'm about half way through. I gave the second copy to Dee, who finished it in a night. She's a big Andrea Mathers fan."

"And you're not?"

"I'm not much of a romance reader," she told him. "Are you?"

"Of course. A life without romance is like dinner without a fine wine."

Kate grinned. "Thank you, Ernest Gallo, for that gem of thought-provoking philosophy."

"You're making fun of me," Matt claimed with a touch of petulance. "If you don't stop, I'll tell my mother."

"Something tells me Maureen would be on my side. How did you get her to write that letter for you, anyway?"

"I told her the truth."

Kate's dark, sculpted eyebrows went up in feigned surprise. "The truth! What an original idea!"

"I do have one from time to time," he assured her with a barely restrained grin.

At his mention of time, Kate became aware that the flow of elegantly dressed celebrities coming through the doors had slowed to a trickle and the lobby had begun to clear. She checked her watch. "Oh. It's five minutes to curtain," she informed him. "We'd better take our seats."

"That's probably a good idea," Matt replied.

Kate looked at him, waiting for him to make some suggestion that they rendezvous during intermission, or after the play. When it didn't seem that he was going to do either, Kate quelled her disappointment and dug into her evening bag for her ticket. "Well... It was nice seeing you, Matt." The instant the words were out, she knew they sounded lame considering the intensity of their conversation, but what else was she supposed to say? She certainly wasn't going to make either of those suggestions herself.

Matt just nodded, as though he didn't think her comment was odd at all. "Yes. It was. Though I do recall that you said we'd probably bump into each other from time to time."

"And I was right." They were making inane small talk, now! Wonderful. Kate supposed that was what sexual tension did to people—reduced them to babbling idiots.

"Well... you were sort of right, Kate," he told her.

Kate frowned as she tried to catch up on the thread of their conversation. Maybe it wasn't as inane as she had thought. "What does that mean?"

"We did run into each other here . . . now. Before the play, I mean. *That* was pretty much of an accident."

Kate suddenly realized that the twelfth shoe was about to drop. "And what *wasn't* an accident?"

Matt pulled his own theater ticket from the inside pocket of his coat and held it up for Kate to read. Same section, same row, the seat next to hers. "The twelfth day of Gallagher," he explained. "I called the box office last week and told them we'd be attending together."

Kate was too relieved to be even mildly irritated. "That's it?" she asked with a laugh. "No skywriting? No Chippendale hunks? Just you?"

Her throaty laugh turned Matt's body temperature up a degree. "Just me. Sitting next to you," he replied softly. "Whenever I go to the theater, I always make it a point to get the best seat in the house."

His soft, seductive purr made Kate catch her breath, and when he held out his arm to escort her into the theater, she didn't hesitate to take it. A glorious smile that started deep inside her worked its way out, making her feel good every inch of the way, and Kate realized with some surprise that she had forgotten what it felt like to be this happy.

She just didn't want to have to remember what it was like to be miserable.

Chapter Seven

"Well, Kate, do you have any thoughts you'd like to share?"

The last-act applause was just fading and the houselights were coming up. Kate looked at Matt as though he were a bug that had just landed on her shoulder. "You've got to be joking. I may be a pushover for babies on bearskin rugs, but I never make the same mistake twice," she told him. "What about you? Got your review written yet?"

He grinned at her. "Only the lead. But I think I'll keep that to myself."

"Smart move."

"Kate, a good critic never talks about a production until his—or her—review is in," he informed her. "Haven't you learned that yet?"

Kate's eyes narrowed dangerously. "Don't push your luck, Gallagher," she replied, barely managing to overcome the urge to swat him with her beaded evening bag.

"Yes, ma'am," he said with a laugh as they stood up and joined the queue headed toward the lobby.

The jostling crowd made conversation difficult, so they didn't even attempt it until they reached the staircase overlooking the glass-walled lobby rotunda.

"What do you think of your first big Hollywood theatrical premiere, Matt? Not the musical—just the experience as a whole," Kate asked as they moved down the stairs side by side.

"Unusual. Almost disorienting, in fact." Matt looked out over the sea of faces below them. "There are more stars here than I've ever seen without the aid of a telescope. It's strange seeing them in person when I'm so accustomed to seeing them bigger than life on a movie screen. Did I tell you I bumped into Charlton Heston just outside the box office tonight—I mean, *literally* bumped into him. And he said, 'excuse me.'"

Matt sounded so amazed that someone of Heston's stature would have manners that Kate had to laugh at him. "What did you expect him to say? 'Out of my way, you peasant!'?"

"It was my fault. The least he could have done is challenge me to chariots at fifty paces."

Kate chuckled. "If you can find him down there, call him over and see if he can do anything about parting this crowd. We seem to be stalled."

A camera flash drew her attention to the bottom of the stairs and she realized what the problem was. Somehow, an uninvited photographer had crashed the reception that was already getting underway in the lobby. Apparently he had taken a picture of a rock star who was well-known for her aversion to the press. The lady's bodyguards were taking exception to it and trying to hustle him to the exit without doing anything that would generate a lawsuit. Unfazed, the photographer was shouting questions at his quarry and snapping away like mad even as he was dragged away.

Kate shuddered as she remembered similar scenes she had experienced before and after her breakup with Dan.

"Is this what they do for an encore out here?" Matt asked lightly, but when he looked at Kate he discovered that all the animation had left her face. "Kate? Are you all right?"

"I'm fine. I just want to get out of here."

"All right." The crowd started moving again, and Matt placed his hand solicitously at Kate's back as they continued down the stairs.

"You don't have to leave if you don't want to, Matt," she told him, trying to smile. "You should stay for the reception and collect a few autographs."

"I'd rather be with you, if you don't mind," he replied, sliding his hand into hers. "Coffee? Someplace quiet?"

His comforting touch helped her shake off the lingering effects of her ugly flashback. "Considering what happened the last time I refused to have coffee with you, I don't think I have much choice."

"I knew you were a fast learner," he said with a grin that displayed his dimples at their very best. "Let's go."

With Kate leading the way, they inched through the crowd toward the exit. It was less congested near the glass doors, but just as Kate thought they were in the clear, she was pulled up short by the sight of the man lounging casually against the glass. When he caught sight of her, he straightened and eased into her path.

"Hello, Kate."

It was such a shock that it took a moment for Kate to collect herself. "Hello, Dan."

"You're looking as gorgeous as ever."

"So are you."

He mistook the comment for a compliment and laughed, displaying the set of dazzling white-capped, perfectly aligned teeth that Kate had helped him pay for.

"Thanks for noticing," he replied, then glanced at the man who was standing behind her. "Who's this?"

"Matt Gallagher," she said, fighting the urge to tell him it was none of his business. "Matt, this is Dan McBride."

"Nice to meet you, Gallagher," Dan said tonelessly without making any effort to shake hands.

Matt didn't, either. This was the man whose betrayal had hurt Kate so terribly. He didn't feel inclined to make friends, or even polite conversation.

Kate sensed the tension in Matt and prayed that he wouldn't say or do anything to ignite Dan's short fuse. The last thing she wanted was to be at the center of a scene. "I thought you were on location in Rio," she said to distract her former fiancé.

"I just got back," he told her, turning his attention away from Matt. "It's gonna be a good film."

"Congratulations," she said.

"The conditions were terrible, though. Bugs, heat—"

Kate didn't want to hear it. "Excuse me, Dan, but I think we're holding up traffic," she said, gesturing toward a cluster of people behind them who were trying to get to the door. "Matt and I were on our way out."

"Oh. Right. I'm waiting for Corinne. Lawrence," he added as an afterthought.

He looked as though he expected a response, but Kate didn't give him one. She couldn't have cared less whether or not he was dating the costar of his last picture. If he thought she'd be jealous, he was sadly mistaken.

"Well, listen. I'll give you a call," he said when she didn't react to his announcement.

Kate shook her head. "Don't."

For a moment he looked as though he might argue with her, but then he glanced at Matt. "Right," he said again. "Well . . . see you, Kate."

"Goodbye, Dan." She moved forward and McBride had no choice but to give ground. He edged aside and Kate slipped past him, but she knew that he was watching her. She could feel his eyes on her until she reached the door, and then she heard an excited female voice say, "Dan McBride? Oh, I'm your biggest fan. I just loved you in *Dangerous Loyalties.*"

Kate didn't look back to see how Dan reacted to the fawning young woman. It wasn't her problem anymore, thank God.

She made it outside to the courtyard and stopped, not to wait for Matt, but to take stock of what had just happened. It was odd, but she felt curiously detached, as though she had just been looking at an old photograph of someone she could barely remember. It wasn't what she had expected from her first encounter with Dan since their breakup. That deep well of hurt didn't bubble up and spill over, it just sort of stayed quietly inside her feeling more like sadness than pain.

What an incredible relief.

"Kate?"

She looked up, but it took a moment to focus. "Matt." She had forgotten all about him. "I'm sorry about what happened in there."

"Why? It was all very civilized," he replied. "I'd even say that he still has feelings for you. Not that I feel sorry for him, of course."

Kate shook her head. "Dan's like a spoiled little boy. He only wants the toy he can't have."

Crystal globed lamps illuminated the courtyard, and Matt studied her face in the light. "Could he have you back if he worked at it?"

She met his gaze evenly. "Never in a million years."

The answer seemed to please him. "Come on. Let's get out of here. My car is in the lot next door."

They started across the courtyard, but neither of them noticed the man who had been lounging by the entrance until they turned and were blinded by the flash that went off in their faces.

"Damn," Kate muttered, trying to blink away the spots in front of her eyes.

"Kate Franklyn, right?" the man said, stepping in front of them. "It took me a minute to recognize you. You changed your hair."

Kate recognized the voice even before her vision returned. Her assailant was Harry Townsend, a free-lance photographer who made his living selling celebrity photos to any rag that would buy them. Kate's sense of panic tripled, and she fought to remain calm. "Hello, Harry. Goodbye, Harry," she said tersely.

Matt had his arm at her waist and he tried to spirit her around the photographer, but Townsend wasn't cooperative. He cut them off and raised his camera again. Kate had just enough time to shield her eyes before the flash could blind her. "Tell me, Kate, what do you think of Dan's new girlfriend? Are you upset by his affair with Corinne Lawrence?"

Kate knew better than to comment. Townsend probably didn't have a lick of proof that Dan was involved with the actress. If Kate protested, it would be grist for a story about Dan's jealous, vindictive former lover. If she didn't protest, Townsend would use her as a source, claiming that she had verified his supposition.

"I have no comment on Dan McBride," she replied noncommittally, trying to skirt him again. "I told you that six months ago, and it still stands."

"Are you still seeing him?"

"No comment."

"Is it true that you made threats against Sandra Berringer after her affair with McBride became public?"

"No comment!"

"Do you—"

"The lady said she doesn't want to talk about it," Matt said angrily as he stepped forward, inserting himself between Kate and the photographer.

"Who are you?"

Kate grabbed Matt's arm. She knew too well how quickly a situation like this could get out of control. "He's a colleague, Harry. Just a plain, ordinary journalist. Not an actor. Not a studio head. He's a nobody, just like me. Now, leave us alone, okay? There's no story here."

With Matt in tow, she hurried around the photographer. She didn't look back until they were out of the courtyard and halfway to the parking lot. It didn't appear that Townsend had followed them, and for good reason. There were too many big fish still inside the theater for him to prey on.

"Jeez, the nerve of that guy," Matt said irritably, looking over his shoulder, too. When he saw that the coast was clear he glanced at Kate and his frown deepened. He touched her arm, stopping her. "You're shaking," he said, his eyes filled with concern.

Kate clasped her hands, but the trembling wouldn't stop, not even when Matt gently took her hands in his. "It's posttraumatic stress syndrome," she said, trying to make a joke of it, but her voice was as shaky as the rest of her. "You know, like war veterans who have flashbacks." A knot of emotion welled up in her throat and she suddenly found that she was fighting back tears. "Damn! Sometimes I hate this town."

Matt gently placed his hands on her shoulders and tried to pull her into his arms, but Kate rejected the offer of comfort. She wasn't news anymore, but people like Harry Townsend could make news out of nothing. She didn't want anyone to open a tabloid next week and see a picture of her and Matt embracing in a parking lot next to the inevitable photo of Dan and Corinne Lawrence. "Just get us out of here, Matt, please," she begged. "Where's your car?"

"Over here. Come on."

They were safely settled in Matt's car and a full six blocks away from the theater before Kate finally began to calm down. It took her just about as long to realize that Matt was driving with one hand and holding hers with the other. She gave a shaky laugh. "I'm sorry, Matt. You must think I'm a real fruitcake."

"Why would I think that? Kate, that photographer was way out of line. No one should have to be subjected to that kind of torture."

She let her head fall back against the headrest. "Torture. That's exactly what it is. Slow, insidious and painful." She blinked back tears again. "You wouldn't believe how many scenes I went through like that because of Dan."

"While you were dating him?"

"And after we broke up," she said with a nod. "Townsend and a half dozen just like him followed me for weeks after I called off the engagement."

Matt had seen the pictures of Dan and Sandra Berringer. He'd also seen pictures of Kate, but he hadn't really considered it from this point of view before. "Why did they hound you?"

"Because they were hoping to catch me arguing with Dan, or even better, confronting Sandra. They trailed me to work, cornered me at theaters. One of them even tried to break into my apartment."

Matt felt sick. "Oh, Kate... I can't imagine how horrible that must have been for you."

"Believe me, you don't want to," she said bitterly. All the emotions she hadn't felt at seeing Dan finally made an appearance as a flood of ugly memories assaulted her. "Being involved with a celebrity made my life a living hell."

Matt squeezed her hand gently. "You want to talk about it?"

"What's there to talk about? You told me that you read Dan's morgue file. You already know all there is to know."

"I don't know what you went through."

"Yes, you do. You just got a dose of it. From the moment Dan's first big movie role made him a star, I lived with a notoriety I didn't want. I tried to stay in the background, but the press wouldn't let me."

"Didn't Dan try to shield you from it?"

"Are you kidding? He ate it up like candy. It never mattered to him why his picture was in the paper or what they said about him. He didn't care that our complete lack of privacy was eating me alive. The publicity made him feel important, and that's all that counted."

Matt fell silent for a moment, but finally he couldn't keep from asking, "Did he really have as many affairs as the tabloids claimed?"

"No one could have that many affairs," she replied sarcastically. "After he made it big, the tabloids started claiming that he was sleeping with just about every woman in the Screen Actor's Guild directory. Their claims were so outrageous that I knew they couldn't possibly have been true, so I ignored the rumors."

She laughed humorlessly. "That was my first mistake. The tabloids had some of the names and the number of affairs wrong, but there were plenty of them, just the same. It turned out that he was fooling around with just about anyone who'd look at him twice—and believe me, there were a lot of women who were looking. Sandra Berringer was just the first one he got caught with. Townsend got pictures of them in a highly compromising position on the deck of Sandra's house at Malibu."

She shot him an embarrassed glance. "But you know all about that."

Matt's thumb grazed the back of her hand lightly. "How did you find out? Did you see the pictures in the paper?"

A wave of nausea rolled over Kate. "I wish it had been that easy. Dan had just wrapped the picture he and Sandra had done together, and he insisted that I go to the cast party with him. Townsend wormed his way onto the soundstage and presented me with copies of the pictures while Sandra, Dan and I were having drinks."

"God..." Matt was silent for a moment. "What did you do?"

"I ran out. Dan followed me. Townsend followed me. Every reporter in the place followed me. Actually I think the only person there who *didn't* follow me was Sandra. Dan very stupidly tried to force a confrontation in the parking lot, and Townsend got some more juicy pictures and a couple of great quotes. Months later, someone told me he got nearly twenty thousand dollars for the full set of pictures and the story."

"I guess I missed that particular photo spread," Matt said tersely, trying to keep his anger in check. "Who said being sleazy doesn't have its rewards?"

"Oh, Townsend doesn't see anything wrong with what he does. Public figures are fair game in any season, and nothing is sacred. The only problem is, *I'm* not a public figure. I never wanted to be famous. I didn't ask for any of it, but I certainly got the fallout."

"How did Dan take your decision to call off the engagement?"

"Not very well. He didn't see what the big deal was. Sandra didn't mean anything to him. It was me he loved." Kate looked at Matt. "That's a direct quote, by the way. His words, not mine. Turns out my definition of love was very different from his. He begged and pleaded for another chance, but the longer he carried on, the worse he made it. He thought confessing to all his indiscretions would prove his sincerity, so he told me about the other women—none of whom meant anything to him, of course."

All the bitterness Kate thought she had left behind welled inside her and it was everything she could do to keep from crying. "It made me sick, Matt. Physically ill. Thinking of Dan and all those women.... I had known for a long time that our relationship was falling apart, but I hadn't imagined that Dan was capable of that kind of betrayal."

She sighed and looked at Matt's profile in the patchwork of light and shadow cast by the street lamps they passed. "I'm really sorry, Matt. This was a perfect evening until we ran into Dan."

Matt glanced at her and smiled. "What are the chances that we can still salvage some of it? You promised to have coffee with me, remember?" He could see her hesitancy and quickly added, "If you don't want to talk, there's still time to catch a late movie."

Kate didn't want to go for coffee or a movie. She wanted to crawl into a hole and hide. But that's exactly what she'd been doing for the past six months, she reminded herself. It would be stupid to let a chance encounter with Dan and his leechlike tabloid photographer send her back into that pit of loneliness she had been wallowing in. Matt had just started making her feel alive again, and she didn't want to let go of the sensation.

"All right," she answered with a smile.

Matt had been holding his breath while she decided, but now he let go of it with relief. Kate was okay. The night was still salvageable. "What kind of a film are you in the mood for?"

She thought it over. "I don't know. Is there anything playing right now about a reporter who gets chopped into bloody little pieces and fed to lions?"

"Not that I'm aware of," Matt said, chuckling.

"Too bad," Kate quipped. "In that case, I'll settle for a cup of coffee and a slice of cheesecake."

"Hmm. I don't think I'm familiar with that film," he said doubtfully. "Where's it playing?"

She had walked neatly into that one. "You know, Matt, I don't think you're looking for a girlfriend. You just want a good straight man."

He grinned at her. "And you do it so well."

"Thanks."

"All right. I'll be serious. Where's the best coffee and cheesecake in town?"

"Canters. On Fairfax," she told him.

"Consider it done, milady. Your wish is my command," he said gallantly. "How do I get there from here?"

Kate glanced around to get her bearings. They had been driving aimlessly, but they weren't lost. "Turn left at the next light and go up to Wilshire."

"All right." He changed lanes and stopped to wait for the light to turn green. "Listen, Kate..." He turned to her, and he suddenly sounded so serious that Kate tensed. "I don't want to upset you, but there's just one more thing about what happened with that reporter...."

"What?" she asked, dreading whatever he was going to say.

"I know you were just trying to get rid of him as quickly as possible, but—" he flashed her a wicked grin "—did you really have to tell him I was a nobody?"

Chapter Eight

Kate lost all track of time as Matt worked his peculiar kind of magic on her. In one of the back booths at Canters, they talked and laughed over cup after cup of coffee. By mutual but unspoken consent, they stayed on safe, unemotional topics like their mutual love of the theater. Kate discovered they were both rabid fans of Stephen Sondheim musicals and they agreed that Neil Simon was a comedic genius but that none of his work had ever surpassed the brilliance of *The Odd Couple* in the late sixties. They both loved movies and were violently opposed to the colorization of black-and-white classics.

Matt encouraged her to talk about her family since she already knew so much about his own, and they laughed over the similarities and differences in their rural upbringings. Like Matt's parents, Kate's still lived in the home where they'd raised their family. Kate's father was a banker in Ojai, several hours north of Los Angeles; her mother, a professional fund-raiser. Her older sister, Paulette, was a lawyer.

When they finally noticed the time, it was well after two in the morning. Since they both had reviews to present to their respective employers the next morning, they decided to call it a night.

"Are you sure you don't want me to pick you up on my way to work?" Matt asked as he turned off Beverly into Kate's quiet Larchmont neighborhood. They had agreed that it was too late to go all the way back downtown.

"No, it's not necessary," she assured him. "Dee lives right around the corner from me. I'll call her in the morning and have her drop me off at the Music Center so I can pick up my car." She pointed to the street ahead of them. "Turn left there."

A moment later, Matt pulled into the driveway that led to an underground parking garage. He stopped short of the iron gate and turned off the engine. The silence of the deserted street introduced an intimacy that hadn't been in the car a moment ago, and the easy camaraderie they'd shared all night vanished in the silence. The tension suddenly became so thick that the air nearly crackled with electricity.

"Thank you for a wonderful evening, Matt."

"It was my pleasure." He unbuckled his seat belt and turned toward her. "But I should be thanking you. After the rocky way we started, it's a miracle you're even speaking to me."

"Oh, but you've handled everything very expertly since then."

Her tone was pleasant, but the undercurrent he heard in it worried him. "Handled?"

"The gifts, letters . . . leading up to an almost casual meeting at the theater," she explained. "If you had stormed into my office again I probably would have resisted you out of sheer stubbornness. But then, you knew that, didn't you?"

That was exactly what he had done—and why he had done it this way—but he didn't like the inference. "Kate, you make it sound like coldhearted manipulation."

"It was. But it worked, didn't it? We had a wonderful time together tonight. Isn't this what you intended?"

"It's what I *hoped* for," he replied, still not certain what she was getting at. She didn't sound angry. More like . . . resigned.

"Then it's not inaccurate of me to say you handled it well."

His brow furrowed into a frown. "If you think I'm such a calculating manipulator, why didn't you just go home after the play? I thought we settled all this earlier."

Kate had thought the same thing herself, but that was before a chance encounter with Dan had reminded her of that devastating relationship. "Matt, two weeks ago, you told me you wanted me to see you for who you are. That's what I'm doing. Only I'm trying to be realistic about it. You're funny and charming. You make me feel good about myself, and it's been so long since I've felt that way that I'd almost forgotten what it's like. But you're also a man who is single-mindedly determined to get his own way, and I have to wonder just how far you're willing to go to get what you want."

"Oh, I see. You're afraid I'm just in this for the chase, and that once I've . . . obtained my objective, I'll move on to the next challenge. Does that about sum it up?"

Kate reached out and touched his hand. "Don't be angry, Matt. I'm not trying to insult you."

"No, you're trying to throw up a roadblock because you're worried about what's going to happen when I kiss you again."

He was only half right. Maybe even three-quarters. Part of Kate wanted to embrace all the tantalizing possibilities Matt had dangled in front of her. The sensible side of her knew it would lead to nothing but disappointment. "Matt, I'm just trying to give myself an emotional cushion so that when I fall, I won't break anything—especially my heart."

After what he'd learned tonight, Matt couldn't really blame her for trying to protect herself. "Kate, I promised we'd take this slow, and I meant it. In exchange, I wish you'd stop assuming that I'm going to hurt you."

"I like you, Matt. A lot," she told him. "But I'm a long way from trusting you." *Or myself,* she added mentally.

He couldn't blame her for that, either, Matt reflected as he rested his elbow on the steering wheel and stroked his beard. Trust wasn't something to be given freely. It had to be earned. "All right. Have it your way."

He turned abruptly and got out of the car. When he opened Kate's door, she looked up at him in confusion. "Matt, please don't be angry."

"I'm not angry," he assured her, holding out his hand to her. "I'm being chivalrous, and like any good knight errant, I can embrace the concept of chastity."

Kate did her best to hide a smile. She had accidentally prodded him into his playful mode again, but that didn't make her one bit safer from him. If anything, it was worse. "You're going to be chaste?" she said doubtfully, placing her hand in his.

"Absolutely." He helped her to her feet, but didn't step back, which trapped Kate in a tight triangle between the car, the door and him. "If you're afraid of what my kiss will do to you, I won't kiss you, Kate."

"Ah. Now we're using reverse psychology," she said, hoping her voice sounded steadier than she felt, because Matt's proximity was having its usual debilitating effect on her senses—and her good sense. "You think that accusing me of being afraid will force me to prove you wrong."

He cocked his head to one side. "Did it work?"

"No."

"Oh." He thought a moment. "How about this?" He slid one hand around her waist and let the other brush lightly up her arm until his hand was cradling the back of her neck.

"What about your vow of chastity?" she reminded him breathlessly.

"This is chaste," he assured her as he wove his fingers into her silky hair.

"Funny...it doesn't feel that way to me."

"Oh, but it is. I'm not touching one single erogenous zone."

Kate could have argued with him about that. Any spot he touched became an erogenous zone simply because Matt seemed to have more control of her body than she did. "But you are *touching* me," she pointed out, trying unsuccessfully to ignore the ache that was blossoming inside her.

"Chastely," he replied. "Now *this,* on the other hand, wouldn't be chaste." He lowered his lips to her throat and allowed his tongue to glide lightly along her pulse point and Kate's head fell back, giving him complete access. He stopped long enough to nibble at her earlobe, then raised his head.

"See the difference?" he asked, his voice a husky whisper.

Kate met his eyes and the hunger in his gaze nearly undid her. "Not quite."

"Would another demonstration help?"

"Maybe."

"Okay." He brought one hand to her face and traced the contours of her brow with gentle fingertips, then ran the back of his hand along her cheek. His thumb lightly brushed her lips and Kate's sharp intake of breath forced them to open. "Now that's chaste. Almost reverent, even," he told her without taking his eyes off her parted lips. "That is a knight paying homage to his lady's exquisite beauty. But this..."

The hand at her waist pulled her inexorably closer until her body was nestled snugly against his. The hardness of his chest was a perfect counterpoint to the softness of Kate's breasts pressed against it. "This is most decidedly not chaste..." His mouth covered hers and his teeth nipped lightly at her lips before he plunged his tongue into her mouth. Both arms went around her, pulling her up, almost off her feet, until Kate had no choice but to wrap her arms around his neck and hold on for dear life.

Her fingers wove through his hair and a heavy ache of desire settled in her loins as Matt's tongue teased and caressed hers. She willed herself not to respond, but that was impossible. Matt was in charge now, as he had been from the moment they met. She had tried to resist him then and had only barely succeeded. Every day for the past two weeks she'd thought of a dozen reasons why she should keep her distance.

But there was no distance between them now, and Kate found she didn't want any. If anything, she wanted *less.* She wanted to do away with the restrictions between them and find out if Matt could satisfy the ache he was so skillfully creating. She wanted his hand at her waist to work its way between them, unfasten the buttons of her jacket and touch her through the sheer fabric of her chemise.

As though he'd read her thoughts, Matt did exactly that, and Kate moaned softly, moving restlessly in his arms as his hand curled around her breast. His thumb made tiny, dizzying circles on the hardening crest. His agonized moan echoed Kate's, and suddenly she found herself being lifted and pinned against the car. Matt tore his mouth from hers and moved it to her breast, lathing and teasing her through the lacy chemise until Kate thought she was going to die from the heat of her own need. Her hands cradled his head and she buried her lips in his hair.

"This is definitely...not...chaste," she moaned hoarsely.

Her words introduced a semblance of sanity into Matt's consciousness. Never in his life had he gotten so carried away. No woman had every created this kind of hunger in him. What had started as a joke had become mind-numbing passion in the space of a heartbeat.

With painful reluctance, he eased Kate's feet to the ground and took a step back. It was the hardest thing he'd ever done. Not pulling Kate back into his arms was the second hardest. She leaned against the car for support, looking as thoroughly stunned as he felt.

"I'm sorry, Kate," he said, trying to get hold of his senses again.

"Why? You did it very well," Kate replied, her voice soft and shaky.

He looked into her eyes and nearly pulled her into his arms again. "I didn't mean to get carried away," he explained.

Now *that* was amusing. "Since when?" she asked, a smile tugging at her well-kissed lips.

"Believe it or not, even I have my limits. And I very nearly just reached one. I'm sorry. I promised we'd take this slow."

Kate reached for his hand, and Matt almost groaned with need when her fingers laced with his. "You're not here alone. I could have stopped it before it started."

"Why didn't you?"

She released his hand and fumbled with the buttons of her jacket. "Because there's a big gulf between what my heart wants and what my head thinks is good for me," she said, suddenly unable to look at him.

"Then trust me, Kate," he pleaded.

She lifted her gaze to his. "Make me."

It was a heartfelt dare and Matt was only too happy to accept the challenge. "All right. Let's start tomorrow night with dinner."

Kate just nodded in agreement, and Matt bent down to retrieve the evening bag she'd dropped sometime during their heated kiss. He handed it to her, escorted her politely to her door, said a gentlemanly good-night, then drove home and took the coldest shower he'd ever taken in his life.

"IS THERE a Matt Gallagher here?"

Deeply immersed in the article he was writing, it took Matt a moment to realize he was being summoned. Even before he looked up from his computer screen, though, he became aware of the titters of laughter around the newsroom.

What is it today? he wondered gleefully as he whirled to find a delivery boy coming toward him with a huge bouquet of Happy Anniversary balloons tied to a small package.

"I'm Gallagher," Matt said, grinning like an idiot as he stood to accept the latest of Kate's gifts. Last week at the theater, she had promised him an eye for an eye, and she was living up to her word, much to Matt's delight. The delivery boy handed over the package and left with a generous tip.

"Gee, Gallagher, I wish I had a secret admirer," Todd Burkette called out from his desk across the room.

"So do I," Matt called back good-naturedly as he sat. "Then you wouldn't be so curious about mine."

"What is it this time?" someone else asked.

"Who cares?" Todd said. "What's important is who sent it. Come on, Gallagher. 'Fess up. Who is she?"

Another of Matt's colleagues jumped into the conversation. "I told you yesterday, Todd, it's Rita down in composing."

"No, it's not. It's a girlfriend from back East," someone else said. "She's pining away and wants to lure him back."

"Nah. I think he scored big with Kate Franklyn," Todd said. "I heard that she got a bunch of dopey gifts, too. What about it, Matt? Are you consorting with the enemy?"

Matt couldn't blame them for being curious, but he wasn't about to broadcast his new and tenuous relationship with Kate. It was too fragile and too precious. "Keep guessing, Todd. You can use all the mental stimulation you can get," Matt joked.

Todd took the jibe in the spirit it was intended. "You know, what I don't understand is how you got her to forgive you for pirating her review."

Naturally the story of that escapade had spread through both newspapers like wildfire—fueled, without a doubt, by Matt's comical raids on Kate at the *Sentinel.* It did surprise him, though, that no one in this roomful of reporters had been able to ferret out the fact that Matt and Kate had actually gone on a date. Nor did they know that it had been the most wonderful evening of Matt's life. Rumors were flying, but no one had any facts, and Matt wanted to keep it that way for a while.

When he didn't comment on Todd's statement, the others went on speculating around him while he opened the gift. The balloons were, of course, in deference to their third anniversary. It was Friday, exactly three weeks since they had met. All week long, Kate had been sending him gifts—an exotic plant on Monday. Tuesday, he received a copy of *Bartlett's Familiar Quotations* along with a note that read, "If you're going to steal, at least steal from the best."

Wednesday, he received a selection of low-calorie cookies from a health food bakery. Thursday, the gift was a gigantic stuffed replica of Tweety's nemesis, Sylvester.

And today? With mounting excitement, he opened Kate's anniversary gift and found two passes to Disneyland nestled in a bed of baby-blue tissue paper.

Matt smiled happily. Disneyland! What could possibly be better than that?

Matt hadn't spoken to Kate all week, not even to confirm their tentative plans for a date this weekend. When Kate had surprised him by taking the initiative, he had happily let her call the shots. He had been more than content with the gifts she sent and the funny newspaper clippings, cartoons and notes that appeared on his desk every day.

This, however, required a response, and he grabbed the phone. But when he realized every eye in the room was on him, he smiled graciously at his colleagues and stood.

"Well, what is it?" Todd asked.

"Something that requires my immediate and personal attention," he replied enigmatically. "If you'll excuse me...."

Amid a chorus of curious speculations and grumblings, Matt hurried through the newsroom and down the hall to a pay phone. He dialed the *Sentinel* number and waited for the switchboard to patch him through.

"Kate Franklyn."

"Hello, Kate. This is Matt."

There was a brief pause. "Matt who?"

He chuckled. "How quickly they forget. Matt Gallagher. You know, the tall, nutty guy who thinks you're the most beautiful woman on the face of the earth."

"If he thinks that, he *must* be nuts," she replied, but Matt could tell she was smiling. He could imagine only too well what that smile looked like, and his pulse sped up. "What can I do for you, Mr. Gallagher?"

"Well, it seems that I have just become the proud recipient of two passes to Disneyland, dated for this Sunday," he said casually.

"Really? How nice."

"I thought so. That's why I'm calling, actually," he said, adopting the amused formality of Kate's tone. "I know you and I had made tentative plans to do something on Sunday, but I really can't pass up a chance to go to Disneyland. Could we get together some other time?"

Kate laughed. "This serves me right for playing hard to get. The tickets are from me, you dolt. We thought it might be fun to play tourists, remember?"

"Uh, that does seem to ring a bell now that you mention it," he replied, though he remembered very vividly everything that had taken place on their date last Saturday. He was keenly aware, too, of what hadn't happened. Somehow he'd managed to keep his desire for Kate under control and hold to the vow of chastity he'd made. They had already proven that the passion between them could get quickly out of control, but Matt didn't want a union with Kate if there was even the slightest chance that she might regret it afterward. When they finally made love, he wanted her heart and soul, too, not just her body.

He was pretty sure he'd be taking a lot of cold showers before Kate finally allowed herself to trust him, but the price would be worth it.

"Is Disneyland okay with you?" she asked him.

"I would enjoy that more than anything I can possibly imagine," he said warmly. "Well...almost anything."

Kate cleared her throat and ignored the innuendo. "Since this was my bright idea, why don't I pick you up Sunday morning about eight?"

"Make it seven-thirty and I'll fix breakfast for us," he replied. If they were going to switch roles, they might as well go all the way.

"Done. I'll see you then."

Matt gave her his address. "I can't wait to see you again, Kate," he said as sincerely and seriously as he knew how, because it was absolutely true. "I haven't thought about anything but you all week long."

"That's called poetic justice," she replied softly. "I'll see you Sunday morning, Matt."

She hung up, and Matt stood for a long time mulling over what she'd said. Poetic justice. She'd been thinking about him, too. Well, of course she had. Planning all those gifts had taken a great deal of thought, naturally. Was that all she had meant? Or was there more to it than that?

"Slow down, Gallagher," he muttered to himself as he replaced the receiver of the pay phone. *Kate is still a long way away from being ready for a relationship. Don't go off the deep end just yet.*

It was good advice, but it wasn't going to be easy to take because Matt knew he'd stepped into water over his head the moment he'd first kissed Kate Franklyn. He'd been treading water ever since, struggling to keep afloat in a sea of excitement and expectation. He knew he was losing the battle, drowning inch by torturous inch....

But what a way to go.

Chapter Nine

Matt's house wasn't hard for Kate to find. It sat in a quiet, residential neighborhood near the border of Beverly Hills and West Hollywood, where the real estate values were outrageous. His place was small and modest compared to some of the homes surrounding it, but Kate was still impressed. She was also curious about how he could afford such an expensive address. Despite all the disclosures he had made about his life, there were obviously things Matt hadn't told her yet.

She let that knowledge settle in as a reminder that she shouldn't take this man at face value, no matter how much she wanted to.

Kate was still surprised by her behavior this past week. She hadn't really intended to barrage Matt with gifts, it just sort of happened. One would have done it, but planning, plotting and selecting the presents had been such fun that she hadn't wanted to stop. It had also seemed like a good way to let Matt know she wasn't still pining over Dan McBride. After what had happened at the theater, he was bound to be wondering about that, despite her denials. She wanted Matt to know that wasn't the case. Whatever reluctance she still maintained had nothing to do with Dan.

Of course, she wasn't exhibiting her reluctance very well, but she couldn't help it. Matt had dangled hope in front of her and she had latched on to it like a drowning woman with a life preserver.

She was either being very stupid or very smart, but frankly, as she walked up to Matt's front door, she really didn't care. She was going to have fun today. Tomorrow could take care of itself for a change.

When he answered the doorbell, Matt was dressed in loose-fitting white cotton slacks and a baby-blue pullover shirt. He looked casual, comfortable and every bit as sexy as he had in a tuxedo. He also looked very happy to see her.

"Good morning, Madam Tour Guide. Welcome to Casa Gallagher," he said formally, but his eyes were twinkling merrily. He bowed slightly as he stepped back to admit her, and Kate noticed that he had a white tea towel draped over one arm like an ultraproper British butler. "Breakfast is almost ready, madam. Would you care for coffee to begin?"

"Thank you, Jeeves," Kate said as she stepped into a slate-floored foyer that opened into a sparsely furnished living room. A wall of windows overlooking a beautifully landscaped patio and pool made the small room seem positively palatial. "Coffee would be lovely."

"Very good, madam." He escorted her through the foyer and kept moving toward the patio. "We will be dining alfresco if that suits the madam's taste. The smog seems to be at a minimum this morning, so it should be quite safe. If you are worried, though, Casa Gallagher has an excellent selection of gas masks."

Kate did her best to suppress a smile. "I'm sure that won't be necessary, Jeeves."

"As you wish, madam." He led her out to a glass-topped poolside table and held out a chair. Kate sat, and couldn't hold back a laugh any longer. The table was laid quite formally, but none of the dishes, glasses or silverware matched, and as a centerpiece, Matt had cut a photograph of a bouquet of flowers from a magazine and propped it in the middle of the table.

Matt appeared to be highly offended by her chuckles. "Is something wrong, madam?" he asked haughtily.

"No, Jeeves," she said, trying to be serious, but failing. "Everything is quite . . . lovely."

That seemed to mollify him. "We do strive for excellence." He adjourned to a serving table near the living room door and returned with a pot of coffee, which he poured into a *Phantom of the Opera* coffee mug. Kate declined cream and sugar, then Matt recited the menu, which consisted of fresh melon, freshly thawed frozen Belgian waffles and blueberry syrup.

Kate's choice of melon, waffles and blueberry syrup seemed to please him, and he promptly disappeared with a promise to return shortly with her meal.

Kate sat on the patio and laughed with the sheer joy of being alive. Matt Gallagher was a certified nut! What would he do next? she wondered. Take a pratfall into the pool? Try out another goofy dialect? Kiss her?

That was the most appealing possibility of all. No man's kiss had ever made her feel as breathless with excitement as Matt's. No lips had ever been as warm or tender—or as passionately demanding. Not even Dan, in the early days of their relationship, had made Kate want as much as she wanted from Matt Gallagher.

That knowledge still frightened her a little. She wasn't quite sure she trusted his charm or his often-touted romantic streak. But that didn't change the fact that she was falling for him like a house of cards. That's why she knew she had to maintain at least enough emotional distance from him to break her fall—if Matt would permit it.

She had no idea what to expect from him when he returned, but she got her answer when he reappeared, dropping his waiter persona to imitate a normal person. Well, almost normal.

"Kate! Good morning. Did you meet Jeeves?" he asked ebulliently as he bounded onto the patio carrying a large serving tray.

"Yes," she replied. "He seemed a trifle stuffy, but otherwise he was very efficient."

This time it was Matt who laughed as he placed their breakfast on the table. "You're really a good sport, Kate. I do believe you would have gone along with that stupid impersonation for hours."

"I just wanted to see how far you would carry it. I should warn you, though, I'm not a big tipper."

"I'll remember that," he said, setting plates at their respective places.

"I love the centerpiece," she commented mildly.

"Oh, thank you. I thought it went well with my fine china service." He sat across the table from her and grinned. "I hope you like frozen waffles."

"Is this your way of telling me you're not a gourmet cook?"

Matt spread his hands. "With a mother who loved cooking and five sisters, I never had to learn. If the microwave oven had never been invented, I'd starve to death."

"Obviously your family spoiled you rotten."

"Of course. It was my only reward for playing big-brother-to-the-rescue every other day."

They chatted through breakfast, and the conversation was so amiable that Kate barely noticed that her waffle was still half-frozen and about as tasty as cardboard. Matt wasn't a good cook, but he was a delightful companion. When they finished eating, Kate helped him clear the dishes and followed him into the kitchen. On the way, she got a better look at his house. It was only half furnished, but that didn't take away from the fact that it was very impressive.

"Matt, either you have an independent income or I'm working for the wrong newspaper," she told him as she set the dishes in the sink.

"I, um, do a little free-lance writing," he replied.

His voice sounded strange and when Kate glanced at him she found that he looked a little embarrassed. "So do I, but I don't live in Beverly Hills," she said mildly.

Matt scratched his beard thoughtfully. "Actually, Kate, I was hoping you might put it together for yourself," he said sheepishly.

"Put what together?"

"Did you ever finish *White Dove?*"

"Yes. It was wonderful," Kate said, frowning. "Why do I feel like I missed a step in this conversation?"

He sighed. This was the one area of his life he'd been careful to omit from his letters because a revelation like this required face-to-face contact. He hadn't found an opening for telling her when they went to dinner at Emilio's last week, either. Maybe he'd just wanted to show her instead of telling her, but either way the moment of truth was at hand.

"Come on." He took Kate's hand and led her through the living room down a hall and into a bright, window-lined office that overlooked the pool.

"Welcome to my inner sanctum," he said, stepping back so that she could look around.

What she found was surprising. The bookcases, desk, computer and sofa were unremarkable. What caught her attention were the framed posters that covered the walls. They weren't posters of musicals or plays or even movies. They were book posters. Some were outrageously sexy scenes of couples in a clinch, some were beautifully tasteful, even artistic, portraits, but every single one was for a book by Andrea Mathers.

Kate didn't get it. "You're a big fan of the author?" she asked, turning toward him.

"Kate... I *am* the author."

That took a moment to digest. "You're a romance writer?"

"Yes."

"Andrea Mathers?"

"That's right."

Kate looked at the posters and started to laugh. "I don't believe it."

"Believe it, Kate. It's true."

"Well, that certainly explains how you got those personally autographed books for me," she said wryly. "I assumed you found them at a bookstore where *Ms.* Mathers was having a signing."

Matt shook his head. "Actually that book hasn't been released yet. That's what I meant when I said I thought you might figure it out for yourself. *White Dove* hits the racks nationwide next week. What I sent you were advance copies from the publisher."

Kate had to take a moment to decide how she felt about his revelation. Matt Gallagher was a romance writer—and a very good one, if the book she had read were any indication. No wonder he'd said he didn't mind being called a romantic fool; that's how he made his living. "How many have you written?"

Matt stepped to the bookcase and gestured to the middle row. "Eight," he replied. "The first five were paperbacks. It took a while to build up a following, but when the fifth one hit the *Times* mass market bestseller list my publisher decided it was time to put me into hard cover. *White Dove* is my third hardback."

Kate wasn't a big romance reader, but she had heard of Andrea Mathers even before Matt had sent her the book. The author wasn't on the household-word level of Danielle Steele or Janet Dailey, but she—make that *he*—was a modestly popular author.

Once the shock finally wore off, Kate realized that she was very proud of Matt. Nearly every journalist she knew longed to be a novelist, but he was one of the rare ones who had made the dream a reality. "This is wonderful," she said, looking at the posters again. "But how in heaven's name did a would-be New York playwright become a romance novelist?"

"It's a long story," he warned her.

Kate sat on the sofa. This she had to hear. "Disneyland isn't going anywhere."

"All right, I'll tell you all about it," he said as he sat next to her. "But if I don't get to ride on the Teacups I'm going to be a very grumpy date."

"We'll do the Teacups first," she promised. "Now, explain."

"It was sort of an accident," he explained. "My first few years in New York I had a couple of plays produced way Off Broadway, and that was enough to get me a good agent. Beverly Carter is her name, and she's a jewel. We worked at it for years, but my career as a playwright never got very far off the ground."

"So you went to work as a critic for the *Times,*" Kate said, remembering the letter he had written her about it.

"That's right. I kept on writing, of course, but finally about seven years ago I got very frustrated and just for the heck of it, I turned one of my plays into a novel. Beverly thought it was a very promising piece of work, but it wasn't esoteric and expansive enough to be considered 'literary,' it didn't have the hard-hitting appeal of mainstream fiction and it didn't fit into any category.

"What it did have, she claimed, was a great heroine. It was Beverly's idea to turn it into a romance. She gave me a half-dozen novels to read and told me to start rewriting mine for the women's market."

Matt chuckled at the memory. "I thought she was crazy, of course, but I read the books and realized that Beverly was right. The novel I had written was a romance and I just didn't know it. I made the changes she suggested, adopted the pseudonym Andrea Mathers and the rest is history."

Kate was impressed. *White Dove* had been a wonderful, insightful novel about the inner workings of a Hollywood movie studio, but what she had liked most about it were the characters. They had become real to Kate. She had related to some of them, she had detested others, but at the bottom line, they had all moved her deeply. Andrea Mathers understood human nature and the feminine mind. Which meant, of course, that it was really Matt Gallagher who possessed the sensitivity and insight that had been so prevalent in that book.

That alone was enough to force Kate to look at him in a whole new light.

"Why didn't you tell me this before, Matt?" she asked.

"I don't know. It's not a deep dark secret, but it's not something I broadcast, either. With the exception of my boss who's an old friend from New York, no one at the *Enterprise* knows about my alter ego. Frankly most people think it's a little odd for a man to be writing romance."

"Does that bother you?"

Matt chuckled. "Do you mean, has it damaged my masculine ego? No. Being able to write from a woman's viewpoint doesn't have anything to do with my own sexual identity. The only thing I plead guilty to is being an incurable romantic."

Kate understood now how Matt had been able to bowl her over with his gifts and letters. But that realization made her a little suspicious. "Tell me something, Matt. Have any of your heroes ever wooed the heroine with a flood of gifts?"

Matt grinned. "Uh, no. But the idea is not new to the annals of romantic literature."

"You mean you stole it from someone else? How typical," she said dryly, but she was smiling, too.

"The gifts were original, if not the actual idea," he told her. "And I didn't invent my family or any of the things I told you about them."

Kate finally realized something she should have picked up on before. "Andie!" she exclaimed. "Your youngest sister's name is Andrea. That's where you got the pseudonym."

"It was a birthday present," he admitted. "And Mathers was supposed to be Matthews originally, but there's another popular author with that surname. Now, have I answered all your questions?"

"Most of them," she replied. "Unless you have any more secrets you should share with me."

"Not a one."

Kate wished she could believe that. "Then I have no more questions."

"Good, because I have a date with a teacup," he said as he stood and held out his hand to her. "Come on."

"All right." She gave him her hand and he pulled her to her feet. "A romance novelist," she muttered, shaking her head.

"Do you mind?" he asked, growing serious.

"Why should I?" she asked.

He studied her for a moment, then smiled. "No reason, I guess. Come on."

As he led her out of the office, though, Kate realized what he had been getting at, and a warning bell went off in her head. It was only a small bell, though, and it was easy to ignore. In a way, Matt was a celebrity of sorts. But he was an anonymous one. The pseudonym Andrea Mathers gave him anonymity, and even without it he couldn't really be considered famous by Hollywood standards. Fans didn't mob writers in restaurants. The press didn't follow them into their bedrooms. Unlike acting, writing was a solitary business and a man would really have to go out of his way to find the kind of temptations that had destroyed Kate's last relationship.

No, this wasn't the same at all. Kate shut off the warning bell and followed Matt out of his poster-filled office.

THEIR TRIP through Disneyland was an exercise in controlled insanity. Matt attacked his first-ever visit to the park with the innocence of a child, finding wonder and delight in absolutely everything, and he took Kate along for the ride. All day long, they assumed silly roles—like spies from Russia who were impersonating tourists in order to steal the technological secrets of Space Mountain in Tomorrowland.

They played Jane and Tarzan having a lovers' spat on the Jungle River cruise. They huddled close together in the black shell-like carriage that took them through the Haunted House, and freely shared their critical opinions of the rip-roaring musical revue at the Golden Horseshoe. And of course, they rode the Teacups in Fantasyland. Three times, in fact; but Kate put her foot down when he tried to coax her into riding Dumbo, the flying elephant.

"All right. We'll save that one for when we come back here with our children," he told her in a manner so offhanded that it left Kate with her mouth hanging open as he headed off in search of their next adventure.

By the time they stopped for lunch at the Blue Bayou and ate clam chowder amid a forest of sparkling fireflies, Kate had decided that his comment about children was just another of his many jokes. He certainly couldn't have been serious about it. Heaven knows, she didn't *want* him to be serious. Did she?

Of course not. It was ridiculous. Preposterous. Unthinkable. But it was also just tantalizing enough to make Kate feel a warm constriction in the vicinity of her heart as she thought of Matt guiding a little carbon copy of himself through the delights of Disneyland. She saw flashes of a wide-eyed toddler walking down Main Street of the Magic Kingdom with one tiny hand in Matt's . . . and the other in her own.

But he'd only been joking, Kate had to remind herself sternly every time the image returned. Assuming the temporary role of a happy parent would be just as effortless for him as being a Russian spy; and knowing

Matt, he'd probably hire a child actor to play the role of Matt, Junior.

A ride through the Matterhorn finally eradicated the Gallagher and Son image altogether, and Kate returned to enjoying herself. Determined to see everything, Matt dragged her from one attraction to the next until she was nearly exhausted. They finally rode one ride too many, though.

"I swear, Matt, if you sing one more chorus of 'It's a Small, Small World' I'll push you into the castle moat!" Kate threatened as they crossed the drawbridge of Sleeping Beauty's fortress.

Matt eyed the swans in the green water below them. They were lovely creatures, but he didn't think they needed his company. "All right. No more singing," he promised, but the insidious little ditty wouldn't stop running through his head. They had barely made it into the castle mall before he was humming again. "It's a world of—"

Kate stopped dead still. "Matt..."

"I'm sorry. I can't help it," he protested. "It won't go away."

"Then you shouldn't have insisted we go on that ride."

"Now wait a minute. You're the tour guide," he argued. "You could have warned me."

"Don't blame me. I haven't been to the Small World since I was six. I probably thought it was cute back then."

Matt shook his head, but the tune remained. "I can't imagine why our government never thought of using this as psychological warfare against the Russians. We could have piped it in via satellite and driven the entire country mad within a matter of hours."

"Think of something else," Kate suggested.

"I'll try. Where's the map?" he asked.

Kate dug into her shoulder bag and pulled out the much-creased guide to attractions. Matt moved back outside into the sunlight and spread the map on the ledge of the drawbridge. "What next? The Big Thunder Railroad or another ride through the Pirates of the Caribbean?"

Kate looked at him in disbelief. "The Pirates, again?"

"I love those guys!" he exclaimed. "And besides that, their 'Yo, Ho, Ho' song is probably the only thing in the park that can wipe out this stupid Small World ditty."

Kate patted his shoulder sympathetically. "If that's what it takes, we'll do it." She started folding the map again, but stopped abruptly when a five-foot-tall caricature of a mouse joined them on the drawbridge. "Oh, Matt, look! It's Mickey!"

"What? Where?" He whirled around, took one look at the kid in the mouse suit and threw himself dramatically between Mickey and Kate with his arms outflung. "Careful, Fair Damsel! Yonder blackguard is merely disguised as a mild-mannered rodent. But fear not! I shall protect you from this rascally knave," he swore melodramatically as he drew an imaginary sword.

The perpetually smiling, white-gloved cartoon character jumped back in surprise, but since the customer was always right, "Mickey" quickly recovered and drew his own invisible weapon. Matt lunged at him. Mickey danced and parried, which couldn't have been easy considering the size of large mouse feet, and a crowd quickly gathered to laugh and cheer the combatants on. They jockeyed back and forth on the drawbridge until Matt feigned a mighty blow that sent Mickey stumbling off, vanquished.

The audience applauded as Matt sheathed his sword. "There, Fair Damsel! You are safe. Distress yourself no more!" He whirled toward Kate, but she had vanished.

Frowning, Matt looked at the crowd, who seemed to be waiting for the show to continue. Kate wasn't among them. "Fair Damsel?" he called out. "Yo! Fair Damsel! Where hast thou gone?"

A community chuckle rippled through the crowd. "Excuse me, lovely young princess," he said, kneeling down in front of an adorable little girl with dark brown hair and wide eyes. "I seem to have lost my damsel. Did you see where the pretty lady in the flowery shirt went?"

With a shy giggle, she pointed toward the mall that ran through the castle.

"Thank you, lovely princess." Matt rose, then thought better of it and stooped to her level again. "If I can't find her, may I come back and rescue you?"

The little girl nodded eagerly and the woman holding her hand laughed. "If they're not paying you to entertain here, they should be," the child's mother told him.

"Thanks," Matt said, then took off in search of Kate. "Oh, Damsel?" he called out repeatedly as he went through the tunnel without spotting hide nor hair of Kate. She wasn't in the crowd gathered in the glass blowers' shop or the candy boutique or any of the other shops. He emerged on the other side in Fantasyland, but he didn't see her on any of the benches, either.

Frowning, he went back through the mall to the drawbridge wondering how one went about reporting a missing damsel in distress to security.

"Oh, woe is me."

Matt heard Kate's soft voice and whirled toward it, but she wasn't anywhere to be seen. Then he spotted the archway tucked just inside the mouth of the tunnel and the chase was on again. "Fear not! I'm coming, Fair Damsel!" He hurried through the archway into a stone passage that wound through the innards of the castle. He heard a footstep just around the bend and charged ahead in time to catch Kate fleeing down the hall.

"Wait, Fair Damsel! You have nothing to fear from me!" he called out, and Kate stopped. She turned timidly toward him.

"Hast thou slain yon dragon?" she asked, feigning a high, breathless pitch.

Matt did his best heroic march toward her. "Thou mayest count on it, Fair Damsel. The blackguard has been vanquished."

Kate batted her eyelashes ferociously. "Oh, my hero! What wouldst thou claim as a reward?"

He reached for her hand and brought it to his chest. "Only your lips, my beloved, in a kiss."

Kate's mouth formed a tiny pout. "Well . . . I supposest one kiss would not be amiss. And 'tis certain that thy lips art far more comely than the last I kissed."

Matt's eyes narrowed dangerously. "And whose lips were those, my beloved? Tell me now, so that I might slay him for his effrontery."

"Do not concern thyself with it, sir. 'Twas only a frog who deceived me into believing he was a handsome prince who had been bewitched."

"He lied to you!" Matt roared. "How dare he!"

"Calm yourself, my lord. 'Twas not the first time, nor shall it be the last. Thou hast no idea how hard honest frogs are to come by."

Kate saw Matt's jaw stiffen as he tried to hold back a laugh and she wanted to shout in triumph. It was the first time all day that she had come close to making him break character. He conquered the urge, though, and surprised Kate by pulling her into his arms. "Thou must trust me, my beloved. I wouldst never lie to you like that rascally frog."

She caught her breath and tried to maintain her own character, but it was suddenly very difficult. "Thou hast saved me, sir. What else can I do but trust you?" She didn't have to feign breathlessness this time.

"Thou canst give me my reward."

"Thy kiss?"

He nodded. "If thou wouldst."

Kate sighed. "Very well, then. Claim your reward. Take my lips." Matt's head dipped toward her, but Kate stayed him by placing her fingertips against his mouth. "But do not take them too far."

Matt's heroic facade cracked and he couldn't hold back a laugh. "You are wonderful, Kate," he murmured as his lips lightly touched hers. "I love you."

Kate heard the words and felt a stirring of alarm. She drew back and looked up at him, trying to discern if the words had been spoken in character or in truth. He seemed almost as surprised as she was. "Take care what you say, Sir Knight... damsels are easily distressed by foolishly spoken endearments," she said uneasily.

"Only fools speak foolishly, Fair Lady," he replied softly. "There are no fools in this enchanted castle. Only enchantment."

His head dipped toward hers again.

"Hey, Mom! Look in here! It's the guy who fought with Mickey!"

The young boy's voice echoed through the passageway startling them both, and Matt took a step back. With a shaky laugh, Kate ran one hand nervously through her hair and turned toward the exit. "Come on, Lochinvar. The spell is broken," she told him.

"Uh, not quite," Matt contradicted her, taking hold of her hand and sweeping her up into his arms in one grand, breathtaking gesture.

"Wow!" the kid in the passage exclaimed.

"This is your first lesson, son," Matt said as he swept past the boy. "Damsel Rescue 101."

"Cool!"

They left him behind and emerged into the sun in Fantasyland. A totally appropriate place to be, Kate thought.

"You can put me down now, Lochinvar. We're out of the castle and the Pirates of the Caribbean are waiting," she informed him.

"So they are." He complied with her wishes, took hold of her hand and led her through Adventureland to New Orleans Square. There, a ten-minute ride through a pirate's den finally eradicated the irritating song that had been plaguing Matt, but it took much longer to wipe his quietly spoken "I love you" from Kate's mind.

But like his children comment, she finally convinced herself it had been nothing more than a line of dialogue spoken by a character in one his many roles. Kate believed that miracles could happen in the Magic Kingdom, but this wasn't one of them. Matt wasn't in love with her. She wasn't in love with him.

Believing otherwise could only lead her down the road to Fantasyland . . . and a broken heart.

Chapter Ten

"Hello, gorgeous," Matt said when Kate threw open the door to admit him.

She smiled happily. "Hi there."

He stepped inside and automatically swept her into his arms for a long, lingering kiss. "God, I have been dying to do that all day," he told her warmly when he finally released her.

It took a fraction of a second for Kate to recover her senses. "I'm glad it wasn't a terminal illness."

"Me, too." He craned his neck to look into the living room. "Am I the last to arrive?"

Kate nodded. "Dee came early to help me move the furniture and fix supper, but her new beau, Collin Abbey, just got here."

Matt's dark eyebrows went up. "Collin Abbey? Sounds like a church in England."

"He is English," Kate warned him. "And I want you to be on your best behavior tonight. No Monty Python dialects, all right?"

Matt looked offended. "Would I insult one of your guests?"

Kate laughed. "I never know what you're going to do, Matt. It's one of the things that makes being with you so much fun. Usually," she added as an afterthought. "But try to behave yourself just this once."

"I will," he promised.

Kate wasn't sure she believed him, but she let it pass. "They were just asking what movies we're going to see tonight, but I could only tell them what I brought. What's yours?"

"My contribution to the Double Date Double Feature is *Tentation,*" he said in flawless French as he handed her a sack containing the videotape and a bottle of wine. "It's that foreign film Siskel and Ebert raved about."

Kate had heard of it. It had been highly praised for its sensitivity and insight into mother-daughter relationships. Kate had to laugh as she told him, "I picked *Firepower.*"

"The action film?"

She nodded and slipped her arm around his waist as they moved toward the living room. "Would you say that's an indication that there is something intrinsically wrong with our relationship?"

He thought about it. "Could be. If it will make you feel better, I can start watching football on Sundays and belch a lot," he offered.

"Don't you dare," Kate warned him. "I like things just the way they are."

"Do you?"

He sounded so serious that Kate looked up at him questioningly. "Of course. I'm very happy, Matt. Aren't you?"

It seemed to Kate that he was wrestling with something, but after a second the small cloud that had passed over his face moved on. "Yes, Kate. I'm very happy. Now, come on. Introduce me to Mr. Church."

"Abbey," she reminded him sternly. And just to cut him off at the pass, she added, "Not Church, not Cathedral, not Shrine, or Temple. Abbey."

"Got it. Cotswold Abbey."

Kate groaned. "You're absolutely hopeless. I give up."

They moved into the living room and Kate introduced him to Collin, but her mind kept flitting back to that momentary cloud that had marred Matt's features. Was he upset about something? she wondered. It had been three weeks since they had taken Disneyland by storm, and since then they had become virtually inseparable. They had covered theater premieres together—each jealously guarding their notes and opinions until after their respective reviews appeared. They had gone to movies, walked on the beach, shopped together at Farmer's Market, played miniature golf and taken long, leisurely drives up the Coast Highway.

Matt made every date seem like a trip to Disneyland; an exhilarating excursion into a wonderland of romance, as thrilling as a roller coaster ride—and just as scary. He seemed determined to prove to her that the fantasy was real, and he was succeeding. Every day it became a little harder for Kate to hold on to her conviction that his brand of romantic fantasy was just a fairy tale.

Now, though, she had to wonder if Matt was beginning to tire of his own illusion.

As her guests chatted amiably, Kate finally managed to shake off her concern. She joined in the conversation, and when it seemed obvious that Matt and Collin were going to hit it off, Kate and Dee adjourned to the kitchen to lay out the cold supper Kate had planned and prepared.

"I don't believe it," Kate muttered, throwing one last glance over her shoulder at the men before moving into the kitchen. "Matt's actually doing his normal person routine tonight."

They served supper buffet style and the foursome ate informally in the living room. Matt and Collin dominated the conversation with a rousing debate on foreign affairs and the international political situation.

Kate was content to sit back and let the discussion flow around her, commenting only occasionally, because she was seeing a whole new side to Matt. She had known he could be serious when the occasion called for it, she just hadn't realized how adaptable he was. He could fit in anywhere, with anyone, and be accepted.

He didn't entirely abandon his trademark humor or charm, though, and by the time they finished eating, the atmosphere was relaxed and congenial, as though they'd all known each other for years.

Kate and Dee cleared away the dishes and when they returned to the living room, Matt took Kate's hand as she passed him and gently pulled her onto the arm of his chair. It was a very proprietary move, but Kate didn't mind in the least. She leaned back with her arm around his shoulder, feeling completely content.

"Oh, Matt, I haven't congratulated you yet," Dee said as she sat next to Collin on the sofa. "I understand that *White Dove* hit the *Times* Bestseller list in its first week of release."

"White Dove?" Collin questioned in his ultraproper British accent.

Dee nodded. "It's a novel Matt wrote about Hollywood."

"How nice. Is it an exposé?" Collin asked.

"No, a glitz and glamour romance," Matt told him.

Collin seemed surprised and began asking questions, but Matt didn't appear to be the least bit disturbed that Deanna had placed him in the position of revealing his "secret" identity. But, of course, it wasn't really a secret, Kate reminded herself. It was just something he didn't advertise from the rooftops.

"What I don't understand is how you could write so accurately about the movie industry," Dee said. "I would have sworn the author of that book knew Hollywood intimately."

"It's called research," Matt replied. "I read every book about this town I could get my hands on and my agent pulled a few strings to get me on the set of a couple of films. One was out here and the other was being shot in New York."

"You've been to L.A. before?" Dee asked in surprise.

"Oh, sure. I spent several months out here doing research and interviews. I found that I really liked L.A., which is why I jumped at the chance to move out here when my friend from the *Enterprise* called with a job offer. I am heartily sick of winter."

"Would you believe, he let me play tour guide for a week before he confessed that he knew L.A. very well," Kate told them.

"But I didn't do touristy stuff when I was here before," he claimed, looking up at her. "It was all work, work, work."

"Sure," Kate said with a skeptical grin.

"You know, *White Dove* would make a great movie," Dee said enthusiastically.

"Thank you, Dee. I think so, too, but I'm not holding my breath. Amity's option expires in a month or so, but we haven't heard so much as a whimper from them."

Kate frowned down at him. "Hold on a minute. I think I missed something here. Amity Studios has a film option on *White Dove?* Why didn't you tell me that before?"

Matt shrugged. "I didn't think of it."

"A little detail like that just slipped your mind?" she asked with blatant disbelief.

Matt was surprised by her vehemence. "Kate, it's no big deal. Several of my books have been optioned by Hollywood producers, but nothing has ever come of it. I stopped getting my hopes up over things like this years ago."

Kate couldn't believe he would take something like this so lightly. "When did this happen? The option, I mean? The book was just released two weeks ago."

"That's right, but Bev and my publisher started shopping the manuscript around right after I completed it. I don't remember exactly when it was optioned, but it's been close to six months."

Dee laughed nervously in response to the sudden tension that had sprung up between her hosts. "I suppose there are a lot more books optioned than ever make it to the screen."

Matt looked at Dee gratefully, though he still couldn't imagine why this seemed to be so upsetting to Kate. Unless... "You wouldn't believe how many," he said amiably, then looked directly at Kate. "My chances of becoming rich and famous because of a movie option are virtually nonexistent."

Kate felt a wave of nausea roll over her. "Excuse me. I'll get the popcorn started," she said as she hurried out of the room.

Matt and Dee exchanged confused glances, but it was Matt who made it to his feet first. "Excuse me, too,

Collin. I'll see if Kate needs any help." He hurried into the kitchen and made sure the swinging door closed behind him. "Kate? What's wrong?" he asked when he found her fumbling with the cellophane wrapping on a bag of microwave popcorn.

She didn't bother looking at him. "What do you think is wrong? You drop a bombshell like that and expect me not to be upset by it?"

"What bombshell, Kate?" Matt asked incredulously. "A two-bit movie studio shelled out a few dollars for the right to *think* about turning my book into a movie. Nothing has ever come of these options before. I have no reason to think that it will this time, either."

She whirled to face him. "That's no excuse. You should have told me about it!"

"I had my appendix taken out when I was fourteen. Should I have told you about that, too?"

"This isn't the same thing."

"Yes, it is," he said heatedly, then made a supreme effort to calm himself. "Kate, you're behaving as though I deliberately withheld something from you, and that's just not true. I didn't tell you because I haven't even thought about the movie option in months."

"Oh, I'll bet," she said sarcastically.

"What does that mean?"

"You have a way of forgetting to tell me things, Matt. *Important* things, like movie contracts and your career as a romance writer and the fact that you'd been to L.A. before.... You even neglected to tell me your full name once, or have you *forgotten* about that, too?"

"Actually I had," he replied tersely. "But apparently you're never going to. Every time you need a convenient excuse to justify your distrust of me, you're going to latch on to that, aren't you?"

Kate stiffened. "I am not looking for reasons to distrust you."

"Yes, you are. You've got it fixed in your head that all men are deceitful slugs like Dan McBride, and you're going to do whatever it takes to convince yourself that I'm living up to your expectations."

"That's not true! I don't think you're like Dan."

"But you don't trust me yet." He didn't phrase it as a question. "If you did, you wouldn't feel so threatened by this movie option business."

"You're damned right I feel threatened," she retorted. "I've seen Hollywood make mincemeat of bigger men than you, Matt Gallagher and—" Her voice hitched as a frightened sob welled in her throat. By the time she conquered it her voice was soft and tears were brimming in her eyes. "And I don't want to lose you."

Matt's anger crumbled, too. "Oh, Kate...." It took only two long strides to cross the room and gather her into his arms. "You're not going to lose me to Hollywood," he said, pressing a kiss into her hair.

Kate rested her head on his shoulder, letting his warmth and strength wash away some of the absurd panic she was feeling. "I don't want you to be famous, Matt. I've seen what it does to people, and the people who love them."

Matt knew she was speaking in generalizations, but he couldn't rationalize what her words did to his heart. "Kate...Kate, look at me." He waited for her to look up, but when she didn't, he gently slipped his fingertips under her chin and lifted her face. "Do you love me?"

The intensity of his gaze was too much for her and Kate edged out of his arms. "You know what I meant."

"Yeah. I do." Matt swallowed his disappointment and leaned against the kitchen counter. He had known better than to press her, but he hadn't been able to help it. He was in love. Madly, passionately, hopelessly in love. But every time he even came close to declaring himself Kate seemed to sense it and would pull away from him. She was holding on to her emotional cushion as though it was a life preserver on the Titanic, and Matt wasn't sure how much more he could do to prove he wasn't going to let her drown.

He had to keep trying, though.

"All right. We'll leave that argument for another time," he told her.

"Matt, I don't want to argue. And I don't want to hurt you."

"I know," he said with an exaggerated fatalistic sigh. "You're just not ready to accept the fact that I'm the most wonderful man in the world and that your life would be utterly desolate without me."

He was back to the old familiar Matt who could make a joke out of anything—the Matt she felt comfortable and safe with. "My life would be desolate without you, Matt. If I didn't care very deeply about you, it wouldn't make the slightest bit of difference to me if every single one of your books was made into a movie."

Matt could have taken issue with that. If she really trusted him, nothing in the world would shake her as this had. He also could have pointed out the difference between "caring" about someone and "loving" him, but that would only back Kate into a corner and nothing in the world was going to force her into an admission she wasn't ready to make.

For now, he had to fight one battle at a time. "Tell me something," he said finally. "What does William Goldman look like?"

The question took Kate by surprise. "I don't know."

"How about John Grisham? Michael Crichton? Scott Turow? Robert—"

Kate smiled as she cut him off. "I get the point."

"Are you sure? How many times has Turow been married? Does he have any kids? Does he sleep in pajamas or in the nude? If he has a wife, has he ever been unfaithful to her? Does he—"

"All right, all right! I understand what you're saying," Kate said with a little laugh. "Those men are well-known, but the tabloids don't crucify them or their families."

"And not one of them to my knowledge uses a pseudonym, whereas I am shrouded behind the mystique of Andrea Mathers," he noted. "Face it, Kate, like it or not, you really are involved with a nobody."

He meant for her to laugh at that, but Kate couldn't. Now that the awful panic had subsided, guilt was taking its place. "I'm so sorry, Matt. This isn't fair to you. Having one of your books made into a movie would be an incredible career boost. You deserve someone who can be supportive and enthusiastic instead of a woman who panics at the first mention of success."

She had just raised an important issue, and Matt realized he couldn't gloss over it. "Kate, would it be so bad if one of my books did make it to film?"

She hesitated a moment, then told him, "I honestly don't know, Matt."

"Well, think about it, because there's an outside chance that it may happen someday," he warned her. "But think about this, too. Even if by some miracle a production company does buy a book, no one is going to care about Andrea Mathers, let alone Matt Gallagher. You can bet the farm that they wouldn't ask me to write the screenplay, let alone star in it. All it would do is boost the sales of Andrea Mathers's books. And believe me, a little extra income might make the IRS very happy, but it's not going to turn Matt Gallagher into a lying womanizer like Dan McBride."

Kate studied the face that had become so dear to her in such a short time. She wanted to believe him, but she had seen firsthand how seductive success could be. She had watched helplessly as Dan sank into the swirling mire of excesses that money and fame had put in his path.

But Matt was right about one thing. His own success would never lead to the kind of fame Dan had achieved. That had to make a difference—unless, as Matt had suggested, she was just looking for convenient excuses to keep from admitting to herself, and him, that she had fallen in love.

That was something Kate was going to have to think long and hard about, because Matt deserved better. And so did she. If she wasn't very careful, she could very easily sabotage the most wonderful relationship she'd ever had.

It all boiled down to a matter of trust, and Kate was going to have to decide soon just how trustworthy Matt Gallagher really was.

She finally summoned a smile for him. "All right. You win. You can go ahead and sell your next fifty books to Hollywood and I won't bat an eyelash."

Matt knew she didn't realize what she had just said, so he felt compelled to tell her. "Hmm. Let's see, now," he said, crossing his arms over his chest and stroking his beard thoughtfully. "I turn out about two books a year. Fifty books divided by two comes to about...twenty-five years," he concluded, then flashed her his devilish grin. "It's good to know you plan to stick around that long."

Kate fought back a smile. "Why don't we see if we can make it through this evening, first? Our guests are probably wondering what's happened to us."

Matt liked the sound of "our" guests more than he probably should have. "Let them wonder," he said as he gathered Kate into his arms for a long and thoroughly *un*satisfying kiss.

Chapter Eleven

"I think everyone preferred *Tentation,* don't you?" Matt asked as he shoved an armchair back into its usual position. Dee and Collin had just left and Matt was helping Kate put her living room back in order.

"Oh, I don't know," she replied, pointing to the end of the sofa she wanted him to help her move. "I think Collin was really getting into all that blood and gore."

"I could say the same about you," Matt countered.

She grinned at him as they lifted and pivoted with the sofa. "I admit it. I adore action/adventure."

"And you didn't like *Tentation?*"

They jockeyed the little love seat into position. "Not much."

"It was a great film!"

"I'm sure it was, but I just don't care much for foreign films," she confessed. "I know this isn't very elitist of me, but I prefer English language films. Movies are a visual art form and you miss so much texture while you're reading the subtitles."

Matt looked at her skeptically. "*Firepower* is your idea of art?"

"No, it's my idea of fun."

"Oh, I get it. You just prefer—" he threw his shoulders back, puffed out his chest and took three ground-swallowing strides across the room "—macho men."

Matt was suddenly towering over her with his hands on his hips like Superman.

"Not true," she replied, trying to convince herself that his macho impersonation looked more comical than sexy.

She failed completely when he grabbed her around the waist and pulled her roughly to him. "Don't give me that, lady. I know your type. You're more interested in a man's pecs than his IQ. We're just toys to a woman like you," he said with exaggerated and playful intensity.

Kate was having a little trouble breathing and it had nothing to do with the iron band of his arm that crushed her to Matt's chest. "Well, I do admit I have...fantasies," she replied coquettishly.

He smiled devilishly and quirked one eyebrow. "What kind?"

She raised her head defiantly. "If you know so much about women like me, then you should know the answer to that."

"I do know, you wicked wench," he said dramatically as he leaned forward, forcing Kate back until the only thing keeping her from falling was his arm at her waist. "You want to be branded with my kisses."

He'd gone one step too far, and Kate couldn't bite back a laugh. "Branded with kisses? Matt, that sounds like something out of a very bad romance."

His chest deflated and he released her so abruptly that Kate had to scramble to keep from falling. "When did you have time to read my first book?" he asked, looking like a little boy who'd just been told there was no Santa Claus.

"I didn't. Matt, you didn't write something like that, did you?" she asked, appalled.

"Of course I did."

"That's ridiculous."

"That's romantic," he countered.

"It's corny," she insisted.

"So is romance. What's wrong with a little corn, anyway? It's high in fiber."

She laughed. "We're talking about literary corn."

"No, we're talking about love," he replied, stepping close to her again, but this time the playfulness was gone. "Is it corny for me to tell you that you're beautiful? That you're wonderful? That I adore you? That I want to kiss you until you're so senseless that you forget you've ever been kissed by any other man? Is that corn?" he whispered.

Kate was breathless. "Yes."

"Is it bad?"

"No."

He slipped his hands around her waist and very gently pulled her close. "Wanna try it?"

Kate knew she should tell him no, but she couldn't have even if her life depended on it. "Yes."

His head dipped and his mouth covered hers, softly at first and then more insistently. His lips plied hers, but it took little encouragement for Kate to open to him. Their tongues mated, their breath mingled, their urgent sighs blended into one chorus of need and longing.

When Matt finally raised his head, his blue eyes had darkened to midnight. "Did it work?" he asked softly.

Kate ran her tongue over her lower lip, savoring the taste of him. "I seem to recall something about a boyfriend in the sixth grade who—"

He shut her up with another kiss, this one longer, deeper, more insistent, more thorough, and so incredibly arousing that Kate felt as though she was slowly catching on fire. The blaze started deep inside her and flared outward until her flesh burned everywhere Matt touched her.

By the time he finished, gasping for air and sanity as he released her and took a step back, Kate knew what it meant to be branded by a kiss.

There wasn't a bit of humor in his eyes this time. "I think I'd better go, Kate."

That certainly wasn't what she'd expected to hear. "What? You're leaving?"

"Yes," he said, but he didn't move.

"Why?"

"Because I'm just about past the point of being responsible for what happens if I stay."

She smiled. "Is that bad?"

He took a step toward her. "I'm serious, Kate," he said in the harshest tone Kate had ever heard him use. "I want you more than I have ever wanted any woman in my life. If that's corny, I'm sorry, but I'm reaching the end of my rope. I promised I wouldn't rush you, and I don't want to break that promise."

The ache inside Kate had been building for weeks. It was so deep that she knew it could never be satisfied, but she wanted desperately to try. "Matt, I release you from your promise."

He frowned. "What?"

"Stay," she said firmly. "As in, don't go, stop being a gentleman . . . rush me, already."

Matt took another step that closed the distance between them as he put his left hand on Kate's waist. "Are you sure?"

Kate reached up and lightly raked her fingernails through his beard. "You want a written invitation?"

Matt grinned, but his eyes were still dark with desire. "No, a verbal endorsement will do just fine."

She slid her arms around his neck. "Then what are you waiting for? A road map?"

Matt's answering laugh was also a half groan as he crushed Kate to him and smothered her lips with a searing kiss that went on and on and on, robbing her of thought and making her ache so badly that she thought she might die. His hands touched her everywhere, feeding the fire until she was almost too weak to stand.

Somehow, their clothes disappeared in the frenzy of the kiss that escalated to lovemaking in the blink of an eye. Kate wasn't really conscious of frantically fumbling with the buttons of Matt's shirt and she didn't remember raising her arms so that he could remove her sweater. She had no idea how he'd unfastened her jeans, but she vividly recalled unzipping his and feeling the heated ridge of muscle against her hand.

She strained to get closer to him, but there was only one way to do that and her bedroom seemed a million miles away. Matt apparently thought so, too, because suddenly he lifted her into his arms and took her only as far as the sofa.

"I should do this right," he murmured as he lowered his body onto hers and began pressing fevered kisses down her throat and across her breasts. "I should take you . . . to the bedroom."

Too spellbound to answer him, Kate wove her hands into Matt's hair as his lips and tongue nibbled at the hardening crest of one breast, then the other. She moaned as his mouth slowly worked magic on her, and when his hand brushed at the curls guarding her womanhood she gasped with pleasure. He stroked her intimately until she writhed beneath him and cried out as a ripple of pure sensation burst inside her.

Too frantic to think, she tugged at Matt's hair and urged his mouth toward hers. She wrapped her legs around him and arched up, but Matt suddenly pushed himself away from her, sliding off the sofa with a violent oath.

Bereft and breathless, Kate sat up. "What...what's wrong?"

"This, damn it," Matt swore as he reached for his jeans and tore into one pocket.

Kate was beyond blushing when she saw the foil package he finally came up with, but she couldn't believe she'd forgotten something so basic. But Matt hadn't forgotten even in his frenzy of need, and that act of tender consideration brought tears into Kate's eyes.

"Thank you," she whispered, pressing a fevered kiss to his lips.

"I won't ever put you in danger, Kate," he promised fervently. "I love you too much. I won't ever hurt you."

A sob burst out of Kate's throat, and before she realized what was happening, Matt was on his feet with her in his arms. He carried her swiftly into the bedroom and took Kate to a place she'd never been before.

KATE DRIFTED IN AND OUT of sleep, never fully regaining consciousness but never quite letting go of her hold on what had just happened. Or *had* it just happened? Was it minutes or hours that had passed since Matt had proven to her that fantasies could be real and magic was much more than an illusion?

Making love with Matt had been nothing short of magical. Kate hadn't known that such perfection existed. Dan McBride had been a clumsy, incompetent amateur who had made Kate feel as though there was something wrong with her. Matt had shown her just how right it could be between two people who were willing to give unselfishly.

Stretching like a contented kitten, Kate rolled over and nuzzled Matt, but when it finally dawned on her that she was snuggling up to nothing more than a pillow she forced herself to wakefulness. She sat up abruptly, shaking off a moment of disorientation. No, she wasn't crazy. Matt was gone.

Puzzled, she slid out of bed, grabbed her robe from the hook behind the door, and went in search of him. In their haste earlier, they had left lights on all over the apartment, but everything was dark now except for a sliver of light that bled through the crack of the barely open door to the spare bedroom Kate used as an office.

"Matt?" she questioned softly as she moved down the hall. When she didn't get a response, she pushed the door open and found him at her computer, of all places!

"Matt?"

He glanced up, but it was clear from the blank look on his face that it took a second for him to focus on her. Then, the confusion passed and a warm, welcoming smile lit his face. "Hi there, gorgeous."

Kate flushed all over again under the force of that smile. "Hi, yourself," she said, moving into the room. "What are you doing? Stealing another review?"

"I felt too good to sleep, so I thought I'd work for a while," he told her. He gestured to her computer. "Do you mind?"

"Of course not."

"I've been wrestling with this scene for the new book all week long, and the dam finally broke." When Kate approached the desk, he took her hand and guided her onto his lap. "You inspired me."

"Why, thank you. I've never been anyone's inspiration before," she said lightly, snuggling against his bare chest.

"Get used to it," he replied, then gave her a very tender and thorough kiss.

"Thank you for tonight," she whispered as she laid her head on his shoulder.

"Thank *you,*" he responded, hugging her close. "You were incredible."

Kate smiled. "So were you. It was—" She paused. Would Matt believe her if she told him that it had been the most unbelievable sexual experience of her life? Or would it just sound like a trite bit of ego stroking?

"What?" he prompted when she didn't go on.

"It was . . . nice."

"Nice?" he said playfully. "That's all? Just . . . nice? I'm going to have to work on my technique."

Kate blushed. "There's absolutely nothing wrong with your technique. It's perfect."

"Nothing is perfect, Kate, but with a little practice, I think we can make a few improvements here and there."

"Matt, if it gets any better than that, I may not survive."

"Now, that's more like it," he said with a grin. "Huh. Nice, indeed."

Kate splayed her fingers across his chest, weaving them into the soft matt of hair. "It was wonderful, magnificent, glorious, marvelous, splendiferous—" She suddenly ran out of adjectives and turned toward the computer. "Hang on a minute, I've got to check the thesaurus."

Matt chuckled as he pulled her back into his arms. "Don't bother. My ego is sated."

"Good," she said, then a strange, disturbing thought occurred to her. "Matt...the scene you were working on... It's not—I mean, you didn't...you're not writing about...what...us, are you?"

"God, I love it when you're articulate," he teased, then reached for the computer and scrolled the screen back to the beginning of the scene he had written. "Here. See for yourself. It's a scene between David and Molly, the hero and heroine."

Fearing that she was going to read every detail of her own intimate lovemaking with Matt, Kate turned on his lap without dislodging his arms from their snug position at her waist and began reading. A moment later, she looked at him over her shoulder and frowned. "This is a fight scene."

"That's right."

"You made love with me and were inspired to write an argument? Thanks a lot!"

Matt laughed. "If it's any consolation, it's a very sexy fight that ends with a steamy kiss."

Kate grew serious. "Like the one we shared in my living room?"

Matt sighed and propped his chin on her shoulder. "Kate, at one time or another everything in my life gets used in my novels. That doesn't mean that I'm going to dissect and analyze every move we make and put it in print. I couldn't do that. It's too personal and too private, for one thing. And for another, I don't remember half of what we did," he confessed. "It's all just a glorious blur of sensation and hunger.

"The best I could hope for," he continued, "would be to capture how you made me feel while we were making love, and I don't even think I could do that, because there just aren't any words for it."

She finally relaxed against him. "I'm being silly, aren't I?"

"No, you just want to protect our intimacy." He nuzzled her cheek. "So do I."

A self-satisfied grin worked its way to the surface. "Did I really inspire you?"

"Yes."

She hesitated a moment. "Wanna get inspired again?"

A rumble of laughter vibrated in Matt's chest. "I can always use a little inspiration. What did you have in mind?"

Kate turned on his lap, wrapped her arms around his neck and closed in for a kiss. She did it so well that it took only seconds for her to feel the pressure of his arousal against her hip.

Matt cleared his throat when she finally removed her mouth from his. "Yes, I am inspired. Shall we move this to the bedroom or would you like to be ravished right here in your office?"

As an answer, Kate slid off his lap and took his hand to help him to his feet. Matt stood, but when Kate moved around the desk, he didn't go with her. Instead he stood there holding her hand.

Kate looked at him questioningly. "What is it?"

"I love you, Kate."

Something melted inside her; something warm and oh, so wonderful. He'd said it earlier in the heat of passion, but this was different. "Why?" she asked because she had to know.

"Because we fit," he answered softly. "We're like two sides of the same coin. I've been in love before, Kate, but

I've never felt as though I found the other half of myself."

Kate had never wanted to believe anything as much as she needed to believe that, but his expression of love was almost too intense, too...perfect. She gave a nervous half laugh. "I think I need to read the rest of Andrea Mathers's books."

Whatever response Matt had expected, this obviously wasn't it. He frowned. "Why?"

"Because you're too good to be true. You seem to know exactly what a woman wants to hear."

"Is that bad?"

She held his stern gaze. "Not if it's the truth."

Matt's dark brows went up in irritation and he dropped her hand. "You think I'm conning you? That this is just...what? Slick seduction? Is that what you think?"

"I'm not sure what to think, Matt."

"Fine. Then read my books. I have to warn you, though, that I've used the phrase 'I love you' once or twice in print. I hope you won't hold that against me."

He was angry, and he had a right to be. She was at it again—finding reasons not to trust him just so she'd have a buffer against being hurt. But Matt had taken her beyond that point tonight. If their relationship failed now, nothing was going to keep Kate from being more devastated than she'd ever been in her life. She had to trust him. She didn't have a choice any longer. "I'm sorry, Matt."

The mood was definitely broken and he didn't seem inclined to be forgiving. "Fine. I'm sorry, too," he said tersely, turning back to the computer. "Now, if you don't mind, I'd like to work a little longer. I seem to have found some more inspiration for this fight scene."

He sat, planting his back to her, and Kate wasn't sure what do to next. She hadn't meant to hurt him, but obviously she had. She edged toward the door, then stopped and turned. "Matt?"

"What?" His voice was clipped and he didn't bother looking at her.

"I love you, too," she said softly. "So much that it scares me."

The tension in his back melted away and he swiveled the chair toward her. "Why?" he asked, capturing her gaze.

"Why does it scare me or why do I love you?"

"Both."

"I love you because you're everything I've ever wanted a man to be. I'm scared because this is just too perfect to last."

Matt came to his feet and moved to her. "Kate, this can last just as long as we want it to."

She wanted to believe that, too. "How long did you have in mind?" she asked seriously.

"Forever sounds pretty good to me," he said, cupping her face in his hands.

"Really?"

He nodded. "If I had a crystal ball and could see ten years into the future, you know what I'd like to find?"

"What?"

"Us. Together. Married. A couple of kids, two cars, a mortgage...maybe an argument now and then to keep things interesting. How do you feel about working toward something like that?"

"I feel—" Tears pooled in her eyes and her heart felt as though it might burst. She couldn't go on, particularly not after Matt gently kissed her tears away.

"Was that a yes?" he whispered against her cheek.

"Was that a proposal?"

He drew back and looked at her. "Let's just call it a statement of intent. When I propose, I'll do it dressed in a tuxedo on bended knee with a ring in my pocket and a bottle of champagne on ice." He grinned. "I might even go way overboard and ask your father's permission first."

Kate had to laugh. "Oh, he'd love that."

"But would he give me your hand in marriage? That's the important question."

"If I tell him I've finally found the right man, he'll even dance at the wedding."

"I don't care about that, so long as *you* save the first waltz for me."

"I'm all yours," she told him happily.

"Prove it," he demanded, and as soon as they reached the bedroom, she did.

Chapter Twelve

Matt tightened the belt of his terry-cloth bathrobe and took a quick inventory of the items he had laid out in his bedroom. His tuxedo, fresh from the dry cleaner, was hanging on the hook outside the closet door. All he had to do was remove the cleaner's tag.

Item One. Check.

Item Two, the small black velvet box was still on his dresser, and he looked inside again just to be sure the three carat marquise diamond engagement ring hadn't evaporated. Nope. It was still there.

Item Two. Check.

Item Three had two parts. One, the silver champagne bucket, was on his dresser right where it should have been; and unless gnomes were at work in his apartment, a bottle of champagne was chilling in his refrigerator. Matt resisted the urge to look in the refrigerator again and gave Item Three a half check.

And finally, Item Four—a small red velvet pillow for when he did the on-bended-knee business.

Check list complete. He had promised Kate the full treatment when he proposed to her, and that was exactly what he was going to give her. Tonight. At her place. She had told him she had something special planned for them this evening . . . and so did he.

Of course, *his* surprise was going to require some precision timing. He couldn't just show up at her door in his tux with a champagne bucket under his arm, but he had his plan in place. He would arrive in casual clothing carrying the tux in a suit bag. He'd tell Kate it was a change of clothes he needed for an interview he had to conduct tomorrow morning, and she wouldn't think anything of it. Then at the appropriate time, he'd slip away, put on the tux, and be ready to emerge at the stroke of nine when the champagne-on-ice was delivered.

Kate would be completely surprised—and delighted, he hoped. He had no reason to think that she wouldn't be. These past few weeks had been magical. Making love had been the turning point in their relationship; Kate wasn't holding back anymore. She had thrown herself into their relationship wholeheartedly, making every day count as something special and making Matt happier than he'd ever imagined he could be.

Finally, after years of waiting and searching, he had truly found the woman he was meant to spend the rest of his life with. He felt like a kid who'd been given the deed to a candy store.

He was also ridiculously nervous. That's why he had taken off work early and had showered a full three hours before he was due at Kate's. It also accounted for his repeated reviews of his check list, and it was why—when his phone rang—he nearly jumped out of his skin.

"Kate is not calling to cancel our date. Kate is not calling to cancel our date," he repeated over and over like a mantra against bad luck. Nothing was going to spoil his plans for tonight.

"Hello?"

"It's a go!"

Matt recognized his agent's voice, and assumed she was calling to congratulate him because *White Dove* had made it up to number one on the *New York Times* bestseller list this week. He'd never known her to start a conversation so strangely, though. "Who is this? Mission Control?" he asked gruffly.

Beverly Carter chuckled. "It's me, you fruitcake. The happiest agent in the world."

"Hello, Happy Agent," Matt said, checking his watch as he sat down on the bed. "You're working awfully late on a Friday. What's wrong, couldn't you get a date?"

"Don't give me any grief about my love life, Matt. If it weren't for you, I'd be sipping a martini at Sardi's with a very attractive investment banker."

"I'm sorry," he said unapologetically. "What, exactly, have I done that made you miss your date?"

"You wrote a bestseller that has producers in Hollywood scrambling like ants on a honeycomb."

He couldn't have heard her right. "What did you say?" Matt asked, coming to his feet.

"I said, *White Dove* is being made into a feature film. Amity Studios has made an offer."

Matt's mind wasn't accepting what his agent was telling him. "You mean they've asked for an extension on their option?"

"No, I mean we're going to contract on a film deal," Bev said with a measure of impatience. "What is wrong with you, Matt? Have you forgotten how to speak English?"

"Can the sarcasm, Bev, and tell me what the hell is going on."

"All right," she said tightly. "I found out today that Amity has been working on the preproduction details for months and now that they've got all their ducks in a row they're ready to commit. Of course, the fact that we've had several other producers express strong interest in the book this week may have forced them to move a little faster than they would have otherwise, but the deal is solid. All I have to do is work out the final details and we'll be set."

Matt sat down heavily. "I don't believe this," he muttered.

"Well, if you find that hard to believe, try this on for size..." She threw out a series of numbers that had dollar signs and a lot of zeros attached to them, but Matt was too stunned to absorb the news that he was about to become a rich man. All he could think of was what this news would do to Kate.

He glanced across the room at his tuxedo and felt a heavy weight settle in the pit of his stomach. So much for his well-planned proposal. *I love you, Kate. Will you marry me? And oh, by the way your worst fear is about to be realized.*

"Matt? Matt, are you still there?"

"What? Oh. Yes, Bev. I'm here," he said, pulling himself back into the conversation.

"Why do I get the feeling that you're not contemplating popping open a bottle of champagne?" she asked suspiciously.

Matt tried not to think of the bottle in his refrigerator. "I'm sorry, Bev, but the timing on this is very bad."

"What could be bad about a six figure movie deal?" she asked incredulously. "This is a writer's dream."

And Kate's worst nightmare. "I know that, Bev. But it's happened so fast and... frankly, I'm having second thoughts."

"About what? Selling the book?"

"Yes."

His agent laughed in disbelief. "Well, get rid of them, kiddo. As they say in Hollywood, this is a done deal. If you recall, you own only seventy-five percent of the movie rights. Granger Publishing holds the rest, and there's no way a shark like Russell Thatch is going to pass on an opportunity like this. Why should he? He's the happiest Editor in Chief in New York tonight. He's out dancing in the streets, and you should be, too. Now, what gives?"

Matt sighed heavily. "It's complicated, Bev. But... maybe it won't be so bad," he said more to himself than his agent.

"What won't be bad? Matt, you're not making a lick of sense."

"I'm sorry. I just need some time to digest this, Bev. Can I call you back on Monday?" he asked, his mind already racing ahead to how he was going to break this news to Kate. When they'd argued over this issue weeks ago, Kate had seemed to come to terms with the *possibility* that this might happen... someday. After they were married, had a child or two and had weathered some of the bumps and bruises that came with any relationship. Dealing with an issue like this would be a piece of cake then, but now? Was Kate ready to handle this?

Well, it would certainly be a test of their love.

"Did you hear me, Matt? Matt? Don't hang up!"

He had nearly forgotten the telephone in his hand. "What is it, Bev? Can't it wait until Monday? I've [illegible]t—"

"No, it can't wait. You haven't heard all the news yet," she said testily. "Look, I don't know what your problem is, but you'd better solve it quick because Russell has big plans for you."

Matt frowned. "What plans?"

"He's decided that it's no longer in the company's best interest to keep Andrea Mathers's identity a secret. He thinks that by coupling the announcement of the movie deal with a publicity tour he can get a lot of media mileage out of the man-writes-bestselling-romance-novel angle. You're going on tour."

Matt came to his feet again. "No," he said adamantly.

A stunned silence hummed on the lines between L.A. and New York. "No, what?" Bev finally asked.

"No, I am not going on tour. No, Russell Thatch is not going to reveal my identity," he said hotly.

"Matt, what is wrong with you? I don't understand why this is sending you into such a tailspin," Bev said. "I didn't think you cared whether the world knew you were Andrea Mathers."

"Damn it, Bev, that was before I fell in love!"

The pause was even longer this time. "You're in love?"

Matt stiffened and clutched the receiver more tightly in his fist. "What's wrong with that?"

"Nothing! I think it's wonderful," she told him. "It's just that in all the years I've known you I've never once heard you say that. You've had relationships that you called 'promising,' and you've dated women you really 'liked,' but you've never told me you were in love."

"That's because I hadn't met Kate yet. Believe it or not, I was planning to propose to her tonight—"

"That's wonderful! Now you have two occasions to celebrate."

"No, you don't get it. If Russell Thatch puts me on display like a prize pig at the county fair I can kiss Kate goodbye!"

"Why, for heaven's sake?"

Matt forced himself to calm down. He took two deep breaths, sat on the bed again and explained Kate's history with Dan McBride.

"Whew." Bev whistled softly when he finished.

"I think she can probably handle the movie deal, Bev, but as for the rest...she'll panic. You have no idea what she went through with McBride."

"I'm sorry, Matt, but I don't see any way out of this."

"I can refuse to do the tour and forbid Russell to release my identity."

"No, you can't," she told him. "You are contractually bound to help Granger Publishing promote this book. They are well within their rights to set up interviews and book signings, and they can use your name and photograph at will."

"Bev, how did you let that happen!"

"*Let* it happen? My God, Matt, there are hundreds of romance authors out there begging their publishers to give them a big publicity campaign, which you can bet Granger is going to do now. Get ready for it, because it's coming."

"And if I don't play along?"

"Then they'll sue," she replied. "We're talking about big bucks, Matt. *White Dove* has promoted you to the major leagues, and Granger is looking at millions in potential profit. *Millions*," she repeated for emphasis. "Now I may be able to negotiate you out of those types responsibilities in the future, but for now, you're stuck. And if you don't mind my saying so—your girlfriend Kate notwithstanding—it's a damned good situation to be stuck in!

"Remember, Matt, that a chunk of those *millions* are going into your pocket! Stop making an extraordinary career opportunity sound like a death sentence!"

Matt couldn't remember ever feeling more miserable. Bev was right. He should be jumping for joy. He should be popping the cork on that champagne bottle and toasting a bright and rosy future. This was the best news he'd ever had, careerwise. Personally, though, he knew it was a disaster in the making.

"All right, Bev. You win. I'll do the tour. I'll make the most of this opportunity, but I want a few concessions from Russell Thatch."

"Such as?"

"He doesn't do anything about introducing me to the press until I say so. I've got to find a way to break this to Kate so that it does the least amount of damage, and I don't want Russell mucking that up. And I want full approval of all press releases, media announcements and interviews. I'll play ball with Russell, but I'm not going to let him turn me into a three-ring circus. Is that understood?"

"I understand," Bev said cautiously, "but I'm not sure Russell will agree to those demands."

"Why not? They're not unreasonable. It's my life, and I have the right to say how it's managed."

"True enough, but Russell doesn't like giving up control of anything."

"I don't care what he likes," Matt said sternly. "You tell Russell that unless he wants Andrea Mathers's next book to be placed on auction to the highest bidder, he'll give me what I want."

"All right," Bev said doubtfully. "I'll get you the concessions. In the meantime, you find a way to break the news to Kate, because Russell won't agree to sit on this forever. There are a few final details to be worked out next week, and once the contracts are ready you'll have to drop by Amity Studios to sign them. After that's done, Russell will want to go public with the deal and your identity as soon as possible."

"Just so long as I have plenty of warning," Matt said. "That's all I care about."

"You'll have it," Bev promised.

"Thanks."

"Oh, and Matt... congratulations," she said glumly.

WHEN MATT ARRIVED at Kate's apartment building, he wasn't carrying the suit bag with his tuxedo, and no one was going to be ringing the doorbell with champagne at nine o'clock. After his depressing conversation with Bev, he'd thought about going ahead with his proposal and then later, maybe next week, telling her the "good" news.

He'd dismissed the idea almost instantly. He couldn't do that to Kate. It would be dishonest in the extreme. She had a right to be armed with all the facts about the upcoming changes in his life before she made the decision whether or not to marry him; but oh, how he wished that Bev's phone call had come sometime next week, after his ring was safely on Kate's finger. It might not have made a difference, but at this point Matt knew he could use every advantage he could get his hands on.

He had sweated bullets all afternoon about how to break the news to her. She supposedly had a surprise for him tonight, and he had one for her, too. It just wasn't [illegible] he'd originally planned.

Though he had his own keys to Kate's apartment now, he rang the doorbell just to give her some warning so that he wouldn't spoil her surprise. When the door opened, though, Matt realized he was the one who should have been warned. Every grim thought of the afternoon's revelations fled from his mind, replaced by a rush of pure, unadulterated lust.

Lit only by the golden glow of candlelight, Kate stood in the door wearing an Oriental-style dress that took Matt's breath away. Black, silky and slinky, it had a little mandarin collar and a split in the skirt that went all the way up her thigh. The dress clung like a second skin, outlining every luxurious curve.

With her hair loosely upswept so that a profusion of tendrils hung around her face and onto her throat, she was the most gorgeous thing Matt had ever seen.

"Hi there, sailor," she purred, assuming a seductive pose against the door.

Matt looked her over slowly from head to toe, then took a second gander just for the fun of it. "Excuse me, but am I in the right place? This is Madam Chong's Den of Iniquity, isn't it?"

"Yes, it is. But Madam Chong's is not for the faint-hearted. Are you sure you can handle this garden of earthly delights?"

"I'll risk it," he said with a grin.

"Don't say you weren't warned," Kate replied silkily, stepping back to admit him into the candlelit entry hall. "This way, please."

Matt swallowed the lump in his throat. "You look gorgeous," he said as he followed her.

"Thank you. Madam Chong chooses her hostesses very carefully."

"Does she allow hanky-panky?" he asked hopefully.

Kate turned to him with an inscrutable smile. "She encourages it."

"Glad to hear it," he said huskily as he gathered Kate into his arms for a kiss. She melted against him and it took all Matt's willpower to release her after just one steamy kiss.

Kate kept hold of Matt's hand as she led him into the living room where dozens of candles flickered with pinpoints of light that reminded Matt of dancing golden fireflies. "I hope you have the fire department on standby," he teased.

"You don't like the ambience of Madam Chong's?" she asked haughtily.

"Oh, no. It's wonderful. Very romantic."

"I'm glad you think so, because this is a celebration," she told him. She moved to the silver champagne bucket and filled two fluted glasses. "Tonight, the sky is the limit, sailor. Anything you want is yours." She handed him a glass and raised hers. "Here's to the continued and growing success of the number one bestseller in the nation—and its author."

Matt felt a guilty flush coming over him. So this was her surprise...a celebration of *White Dove*'s success. He was touched by her gesture, but if she had any idea how successful the book really was, she certainly wouldn't feel like celebrating. "Thank you, Kate," he said as warmly as he could.

He touched his glass to hers and took a sip of champagne. This was the opening he needed, he realized. It was the perfect opportunity to say, "Speaking of success..." but he just couldn't get the words out. Kate had [illegible] so much trouble and he didn't want to risk [illegible] the evening before it got started.

Instead they drank champagne by candlelight and ate dinner sitting on opposite sides of her coffee table, using oversize cushions for chairs.

Dinner consisted of Chinese takeout because Kate had worked late at the office, but Matt didn't seem to mind. In fact, halfway through the meal Kate realized that he was enjoying it a little too much. There was something forced about his conversation tonight, and his smile was strained.

Hoping he would tell her what was bothering him without prodding, she deliberately left a lot of long pauses in their conversation. It didn't work, and Matt was so distracted that he finished his meal without noticing the little white take-out box that hadn't been opened.

Finally, in frustration, Kate picked up her champagne glass, *accidentally* nudging the box in the process.

"What's that?" Matt asked. "Did we forget about the moo shoo pork?"

"No, it's the other half of your surprise," Kate replied.

"Other half?"

"Is there an echo in here?" She picked up the box and handed it to him. "Open it."

Matt shook the box. Something inside rattled lightly, but it was surprisingly light. He looked at Kate suspiciously. "Is it going to spring out at me?"

"That's for me to know and you to find out."

"Okay. Here goes." Matt gingerly flipped the four tabs and found a page of newsprint folded down to the size of a postage stamp. He unfolded it, studied the page and still didn't have a clue about his surprise. "A lingerie sale at Bryson's?"

Kate sighed with exasperation. "The other side, silly."

"Oh." Matt turned it over and smiled. "Well, what do you know. The Performance Repertory Ensemble in Ojai is opening their season with a production of *Madam Butterfly* next Friday. How nice for them."

"Would you like to go?" she asked him, placing as much significance on the words as she could.

Matt grinned at her. "Only if it means that I'm finally going to get to meet your parents."

"It does," Kate told him happily. "I talked to Mom and Dad yesterday and told them you've been bugging me for weeks to bring you up to meet them. This was Mom's suggestion, since they have season tickets to the Rep."

"I'd love to go, Kate."

"Good. It's all set then. I thought maybe we could get an early start Friday afternoon and have dinner with my parents before the play. Then Saturday, I was hoping we could sneak off to someplace romantic for the rest of the weekend. How does that sound?"

"Like heaven," Matt replied, knowing what a big step this was for Kate. She wouldn't want him to meet her family unless she was ready to commit to a relationship with all the trimmings. And that made him feel all the more guilty for not having told her his news yet.

His guilt must have shown, because Kate finally called him on it. "All right, Matt, out with it. What's wrong? You haven't been yourself all night."

Matt looked at her for a moment. She was so beautiful. He loved her so much. What was this news going to do to them?

He didn't want to find out. "Fortune cookie?" he asked, grabbing the little plate from the center of the table and holding it out to her.

"Matt..." She took one, sighing with exasperation. "Oh, all right. Since you're the honoree tonight, you go first."

Matt broke his cookie open and pulled out the white slip. "'*The star of riches is shining upon you,*'" he read, then grinned. "How did you arrange this?"

"I didn't. You should never question the wisdom of fortune cookies." She broke into hers and frowned. "Oh, great. You get shining riches, and I get this."

"What is it?"

"'*You have troubled times ahead.*'"

Matt froze for just a second, then held his paper out to her with a smile. "Wanna trade?"

"No, thanks. I'd rather you tell me what's bothering you," she said quietly.

Matt should have known he couldn't fool Kate. She was too sensitive and she knew him too well. "I have some news," he told her.

"Hmm. Since you're not acting like a man with *good* news, why don't you spill it before I leap to any distressing conclusions."

He took a deep breath before dropping the bombshell. "My agent called this afternoon to tell me that Amity Studios is buying the film rights to *White Dove.* They're already in preproduction and the contracts should be signed sometime next week."

Kate let the news sink in and though she was surprised, she wasn't startled. No stab of panic ripped through her. No bad memories came flashing back to haunt her or spoil the happiness she had found with Matt. In fact, only one thing disturbed her: the fact that Matt had been afraid to tell her the news.

"Matt, I think that's wonderful," she told him sincerely. "I'm very happy for you."

Matt couldn't have been more surprised if she had told him she was leaving on a space shuttle for the moon. "Really?"

"Of course."

"But last month—"

"We discussed the possibility and put it to rest," she said, cutting him off. "I made peace with this weeks ago."

"Are you sure?"

"Yes. I'm sure." Kate reached across the table and slipped her hand into his. "I'm sorry you were worried about telling me."

"Kate, I don't want anything to destroy what we have," he told her with an intensity that surprised them both.

"It won't," she promised him. "You made a believer out of me, Matt. A movie of Andrea Mathers's book isn't going to have an impact on Matt Gallagher's life—or our relationship. How could it?"

Tell her the rest. Now! a little voice commanded Matt. *There will never be a better time.*

But he couldn't do it. Kate was looking at him with such love and tenderness.... She had accepted the first part of his news, but he knew there wasn't a prayer that she'd feel the same way about the second half of his bombshell. He wanted to revel in her love as long as possible, because there was a very real possibility that he'd never see the same look in her eyes again after he told her.

Matt brought her hand to his lips and kissed it gently. "You're right, Kate. Nothing is ever going to change what I feel for you. As long as you believe that, we'll be fine."

"I do," she told him warmly. "I'm sorry if my stupid anxiety spoiled what should have been a triumphant moment for you. Are you sure you don't want to trade me in for a less paranoid girlfriend?"

"Not on your life," he said with a laugh. "Come here."

He tugged on her hand and Kate acquiesced to his desire for her to join him on the other side of the table. Smiling seductively, she knelt beside him and unfastened a few buttons on his shirt. "So now what, sailor? What can Madam Chong do to help you celebrate your newfound success?" she asked, running her fingernails lightly across his chest.

Matt sucked in a deep breath. "What would Madam Chong *like* to do?"

Kate bent until her lips were at his ear and described several intriguing possibilities in such intimate detail that Matt felt a hard tug of arousal. His eyes dark with desire, he ran one hand up Kate's thigh, which was bared by her daring dress, and when her eyes darkened, too, he smiled.

"I think we should put that suggestion into action," he told her. "But with a couple of slight modifications."

He outlined the changes he wanted to make, and Kate blushed so furiously that she had to wave her hand in front of her face to cool her cheeks. "Sailor, if you can do that, you'll be welcome at Madam Chong's anytime of the day or night."

"Can I get discount rates?" he asked with a grin.

"That depends."

"On what?"

Kate raised her leg and slid it seductively over Matt's thighs. It took only another simple movement to turn and straddle him completely. "On whether or not you satisfy the hostess."

Matt put his hands on Kate's waist and ran them lightly up her torso until they brushed against her breasts. "Oh, I think she'll be pleased with the results."

Kate wove her fingers into his hair. "Show me," she purred, and Matt was only too happy to accept the challenge.

Chapter Thirteen

Paul Griffith wasn't happy about letting Kate go early on Friday or giving her the whole weekend off, even though she had made the request early and had more than enough vacation time accumulated. He groused all week long and came up with a dozen excuses on Friday morning to keep her busy.

Kate stood her ground, though. There were no major theater openings this weekend and she had worked overtime during the week to be certain she had good features for the Saturday and Sunday papers. Griffith had no legitimate reason to complain, so she refused to let him make her feel guilty as she breezed out of the newsroom at noon on Friday.

She dashed home, did a little last-minute packing and was ready by the time Matt picked her up a little after one.

"Well, are you ready to brave the lion's den?" she asked as they loaded her bags into his car.

Matt slammed the trunk lid. "Is your father really going to be that tough?"

"I'm his youngest daughter. What do you think?"

"I think I should have packed a bulletproof vest."

They settled into the car and headed north for the Hollywood Freeway. "What have you heard from Bev about the Amity contract?" Kate asked. "Do we still have to drop by the studio this afternoon so you can sign the contracts?"

Matt tensed, but he was doing a better job of not showing it. After a long struggle with his conscience, he'd finally convinced himself that this weekend was the perfect time to tell Kate the news. After he met her parents he was whisking her away for a romantic retreat at the Casa del Aria resort in Carmel. He'd find a way to tell her there, in a place where Los Angeles seemed so far away that it couldn't possibly be a threat to them.

"Yes. The deal is all settled and the contract is ready to be signed. Finally," he told her. "It looked as though it was going to fall through for a while yesterday, but Bev told me this morning that this is the best deal we could possibly get. She arranged for me to have unlimited access to the set during the filming, but Amity wouldn't budge on creative input. They agreed to let me see a copy of the screenplay and they'll listen to any comments I have, but all final decisions rest with them."

He didn't add that on the other side of the continent, Russell Thatch had agreed to Matt's terms regarding the disclosure of his identity. So far, no plans of any type had been forwarded to him, which meant that he was still safely anonymous.

"Bev couldn't get you any casting approval?" Kate asked.

"Are you kidding?" Matt asked. "She dropped that demand on Monday right after the producer stopped laughing at the request."

"That's so unfair," Kate said, though she knew very well how the Hollywood system worked. The people on the creative end of the business were treated as little more than commodities to be bought and sold. "It's your book, your vision. You should have more say in what comes to the screen."

Matt reached over and squeezed her hand. "Thanks for coming to my defense, but it really doesn't matter. We're not talking about the movie version of *War and Peace*. If Amity screws up the book, the readers won't blame me. Much," he added as an afterthought.

Kate chuckled. "The readers won't blame you at all, because they have no idea you exist. That's the beauty of a pseudonym. Good old Andrea can take all the heat for you."

Matt forced a laugh. "I guess you're right. Anyway, the deal is out of my hands, so there's no point worrying about it. Frankly I'm a lot more concerned about making a good impression on your parents."

"Mom will love you," Kate promised him. "Dad, on the other hand..."

She left it hanging ominously, like the Sword of Damocles, and Matt grinned at her. "You're just doing this to torment me, aren't you? Actually he's going to roll out the red carpet, pat me on the back and hand me the keys to the kingdom, isn't he?"

Kate shrugged. "I guess anything is possible."

Matt thought it over. "What's the worst he could do to me?" he asked, then regretted it, because Kate gave him a vivid and detailed description of every indignity he had subjected her boyfriends to while she was growing up. By the time they reached Amity Studios in Burbank, Matt was making jokes about turning the car around and heading back home.

The studio was tiny compared to Universal and some of the other major players in Hollywood. It had no back lot and it boasted only one medium-size soundstage. There was no guard at the entrance to the parking lot, so they drove up unmolested.

"Listen, Kate. You don't have to come in with me if you don't want to," Matt told her as he shut off the engine and unbuckled his seat belt. "I know how you hate Hollywood types."

Kate thought it over. She didn't want to go in, but the California sunshine was already heating up the interior of the car. "I should be dutiful and stay at your side to witness this momentous occasion, but you're right. I've seen enough studio suits to last a lifetime. If it's all right with you, I think I'll just wait in the lobby."

"That's fine."

They crossed the parking lot together and when they entered the lobby, Kate stayed at Matt's side while he presented himself to the receptionist, a young, perky brunette who looked as though she was just killing time until one of the Amity producers discovered her.

"Matt Gallagher?" the young woman said, pursing her lips into a little pout as she looked over the list of actors, production people and guests who had been cleared to enter the facility. "I'm sorry, sir. I don't have a Matt Gallagher on my list. Who did you say you had an appointment with?"

"David Mercer."

She shook her head. "I'm sorry. Mr. Mercer is very busy right now. Perhaps if you called his secretary for an appointment—"

Matt sighed patiently. "I already have an appointment. I'm here to sign—" He stopped abruptly as he realized what the problem was. "Check your list again. This time, look for the name Andrea Mathers."

The receptionist's face lit up and she didn't have to bother with the list. "Oh, my goodness. You're Andrea Mathers!" she exclaimed happily. But she was looking directly at Kate.

"Uh, no," Kate said, shaking her head. She pointed to Matt. "*This* is Andrea Mathers."

The young woman smiled coquettishly and looked at Matt again. "She's kidding, right? Are you really Andrea Mathers?"

"'Fraid so."

"Oh, this is a hoot!" she exclaimed. "I loved your book. Everybody here did. I've been trying to convince Mr. Mercer's secretary that I'd be just perfect for the role of Callie. I'm from Oklahoma, too, and a lot of the things that happened to her happened to me when I first got to Hollywood."

"Is that so," Matt replied noncommittally, embarrassed by the young woman's gushing.

"My name is Marta Dearborne. I don't suppose you could put in a good word for me," she suggested, leaning forward just enough to give Matt a good view of the cleavage exposed by her low-cut sweater.

"I'm afraid I don't have any say over casting," he said apologetically, and made a mental note to thank Bev for dropping that particular demand. "Now, I think Mr. Mercer is waiting on me so we can sign the contracts, and I'm running a bit late. Where can I find him?"

The receptionist looked disappointed. "Through these double doors right here," she said, pointing across the corridor to her right. "He's waiting for you."

"Thanks," Matt said, stepping away from the desk.

Kate went with him only about halfway, then gestured to a sofa near the entrance. "I'll just wait over there," she told him.

"Fine. This shouldn't take—"

"Matt! We'd about given you up for lost!"

The unexpected voice caught Matt off guard and he wasn't able to contain his surprise when he turned and found Russell Thatch bearing down on him with an outstretched hand and a satisfied smile. "Russell? What are you doing in L.A.?"

Thatch grabbed Matt's hand and pumped it. "Somebody from Granger has to sign the contract, boy."

"But I thought you were doing that by express mail."

"Well, we were, but all things considered, I thought it would be better to put in a personal appearance."

"What things?" Matt asked suspiciously. "Russell, what's—"

The silver-haired publisher looked at Kate. "Hello. I'm Russell Thatch, Matt's publisher."

Kate extended her hand graciously. "Kate Franklyn."

Matt didn't believe what was happening. Kate still didn't know what Granger Publishing had in store for him. She wasn't prepared for that kind of news, but all Russell had to do was utter one thoughtless word and the truth would be out.

He couldn't let her find out like that. "Kate is a good friend, Russell," Matt said tersely. "And she was just leaving."

"Don't be silly. The party is just getting started."

"Party?" Kate questioned, looking expectantly from Matt to Thatch. There was an undercurrent that troubled her deeply. Obviously Matt was trying to protect her from something, but what? She couldn't imagine why he suddenly seemed so nervous.

"That's right," Granger replied, then looked at Matt. "I guess this has caught you by surprise. In all the rush yesterday I must have forgotten to have my secretary call Bev to tell you about the change in plans."

Matt didn't dare ask what plans he was referring to. "Excuse me a minute, Russell. Kate . . ."

"You go on. I'll wait here," she said, but Thatch had other ideas. He threw one arm around her shoulder and the other over Matt's.

"Nonsense," he said, drawing them toward the open doors a few feet away. "Come join the celebration."

"Damn it, Russell..." Matt shook off the man's arm, but it was already too late. Russell had left the doors open, and they had moved just close enough to see what waited for them inside.

The edges and corners of the huge room were bathed in shadows, but in the center rows of chairs had been arranged in front of a brightly lit dais that was garishly decorated with banners and huge enlargements of the cover of *White Dove.* A buffet table was set up on the opposite side of the room, and worst of all, a phalanx of reporters was milling around in the bright light, sampling hors d'oeuvres and talking among themselves. Two TV cameras were stationed behind the chairs, and the podium held a cluster of microphones worthy of a presidential press conference.

"Oh God, no," Kate murmured, feeling as though she'd just walked into an ambush. This little fête had taken planning; it wasn't just an impromptu thing. She spotted one of the entertainment reporters from the *Sentinel* and wondered angrily why Laurel Petty hadn't warned her about it or even mentioned it, but Kate quickly realized that she had no reason to. No one knew that the man she was dating was actually Andrea Mathers. That, apparently, was about to change in a hurry.

Kate felt sick.

"Wonderful, isn't it?" Russell said happily. "The studio is going to be introducing Matt to the press just as soon as the other principal gets here."

"Wait a minute." Matt ground out the words. "We had a deal, Russell. You can't do this without my approval."

Thatch shook his head. "Sorry, son, but you're wrong. It's being done even as we speak."

Matt frowned. "That wasn't our agreement, Russell."

"And I fully planned to honor it until Amity suggested the idea of combining all the announcements into one. They've signed a major box office draw to play the lead in *White Dove,* and they felt it would make for a much bigger splash of publicity. I had to agree with them."

Kate was having trouble taking it all in. "Matt? You knew about this?" she asked, aghast.

"No, Kate. I didn't. I swear."

"But you just said . . ." Kate wasn't exactly sure what he'd said. "What agreement were you talking about?"

Matt couldn't believe this was happening. It was a nightmare, and he didn't have a clue how to make it go away. "I was going to tell you this weekend," he said, cutting in front of Thatch to get closer to Kate.

"Tell me what?"

"That Granger Publishing wants to release my identity. But we had a deal," he said desperately, throwing a killing glance at Thatch. "I was supposed to have control of how it was done. I didn't know they were calling a press conference today."

Kate closed her eyes and crossed her arms over her waist. "Damn. . . ." she whispered, unable to take in all the implications at once. Matt reached out to her, but when she felt his hand on her shoulder, she jerked away. "Don't."

"Kate, please. Give me a chance to explain. If you really love me, you'll—"

"Russell! Is this our famous author?"

Kate heard the other voice and opened her eyes in time to see a well-tanned, thirty-something executive in an Armani suit slithering toward them.

Thatch turned to the newcomer. "He is, indeed. Matt Gallagher, this is our host, David Mercer, the CEO of Amity Studios. And this is Matt's friend, Kate Franklyn."

The studio exec greeted Matt effusively, then turned an appreciative eye on Kate. "Have we met before?" he asked.

"No, I don't think so," she replied stiffly.

"Really? I could swear I know you from somewhere. Are you an actress? Maybe I've seen your work."

Kate shook her head, praying he wouldn't remember that she had been a tabloid sensation less than a year ago. "No, I'm not an actress. I'm a theater critic for the *Sentinel.*"

"Oh, then you must know a lot of the entertainment reporters here. That's good. You'll be able to help Matt through the mine field. Listen, I hope you'll excuse us, but I need to get Matt up to the dais. The natives are getting restless for the show to start. Why don't you have a glass of champagne and make yourself comfortable, Kate? Matt, why don't you come with me?"

Mercer and Thatch started off, but Matt hung behind. "Kate, I'm sorry," he said softly, for her ears only. "You have to believe me. Thatch double-crossed me. I never would have let you walk into something like this unprepared."

That much, at least, Kate did believe. Matt was as stunned by the coming press conference as she was. But he had known that a scene similar to this one was only a matter of time, and he had kept it from her. For how long? A day? A week? Months? How long had he kept this secret, letting her grow to love him more and more each day?

"Play their game out, Matt. You don't have any choice now," she said flatly.

"I love you."

Kate didn't bother responding, and when Mercer called out to Matt, he had no choice but to go. She watched him walk away and be swallowed up by the crowd that included reporters she had worked with and those who had hounded her mercilessly during her relationship with Dan. The reporters were just yards away, and unlike David Mercer, who hadn't been able to remember where he'd seen Kate before, those men and women would remember her because it was their job to have very long memories.

Kate's instincts for self-preservation shouted flight instructions to her. She knew she should leave the room immediately and get as far away from this media event as possible. Her love for Matt wouldn't let her do it, though. She had told him she loved him. She had been ready to commit her life to him. She had sworn that she *trusted* him.

If that was really true, she had to give him the benefit of the doubt. Maybe he really did have an explanation that made sense. And maybe—please, God, just maybe—the revelation of his identity wouldn't have the devastating effect on their lives that she feared.

Kate was still standing just inside the door, trying to convince herself of that when the decision to stay or go was taken away from her.

"Kate! What are you doing here?" Laurel Petty called out, hurrying toward her. The heavyset *Sentinel* gossip columnist was carrying a glass of champagne in one hand and juggling a plate of hors d'oeuvres and her tape recorder in the other.

Laurel was a colleague, not a friend, so Kate didn't feel obliged to explain. During the worst of the press feeding frenzy with Dan, even the *Sentinel* had gotten in on the act, thanks to Laurel. Kate didn't resent her co-worker for doing her job, but she knew better than to say anything that she wouldn't want to see in print.

Instead of running for the door, Kate plastered on the friendly fake smile she had perfected when she was dating Dan. "I heard they were serving free champagne. You know I can't resist that."

Laurel didn't seem amused or charmed. "Griffith didn't tell me he was sending someone from your side of the room to cover this. It's just a tacky little press conference. Don't tell me they're getting some big Broadway muckamuck to star in the movie."

"Not that I know of," Kate replied. "I'm not here on business, Laurel."

The columnist glanced over her shoulder toward the dais. "Isn't that your new boyfriend? The one who made such a fool of himself coming into the newsroom a couple of months ago?"

Kate refused to argue with her assessment. "Yes. That's him."

"What's he doing up there with David Mercer? And who's the silver-haired gentleman with them?"

"I'm afraid you're going to have to wait for the announcement, Laurel."

The woman grinned slyly and shook a finger at Kate. She didn't seem to notice that the gesture made her champagne slosh over the side of the glass. "You're keeping something from me, Katie. Now, what gives?" She tucked her arm through Kate's possessively and began leading her toward the other reporters. "You come with me and tell Laurel all about it. If there's a big story here, I'm going to be very put out with you for not giving it to the *Sentinel* first."

Kate cringed, but she knew better than to pull away. Making a fuss or betraying her discomfort would only make matters worse. She was trapped now, and she would have to play the game, too. "There's no story here, Laurel. At least, there wasn't until Mercer decided to turn it into one."

Sensing that the press conference was about to begin, the reporters began taking their seats, but they weren't too preoccupied to notice the newcomer to their group. Several of them greeted Kate, asking the same questions Laurel had asked, but the columnist waved them off as though Kate was her own personal property.

Kate was about to make an excuse to avoid sitting with Laurel, but when she glanced around and saw her nemesis, Harry Townsend, on the other side of the aisle, she sat down quickly by her new best friend. Feeling the same sense of nausea she always felt when he was around, Kate tried to resist the temptation to look over her shoulder, but she couldn't. She glanced back and saw him moving toward her, rudely pushing his way through the crowd. She looked away, but the crawling sensation that snaked along her skin told her the minute he sat in the chair right behind hers.

Blessedly David Mercer stepped to the microphone before Townsend had a chance to say anything. The studio exec cast an anxious glance toward the door as though he was hoping someone might come through it, but finally he addressed the crowd.

"Ladies and gentlemen, thank you for joining us today. I know this press conference was called at short notice yesterday, but you won't be sorry you came. We have a couple of very exciting announcements to make today." He gestured toward the gigantic posters that sandwiched the podium. "As you've probably already guessed, Amity Studios has just acquired the rights to produce the hottest literary property of the year—*White Dove,* by Andrea Mathers."

There was a smattering of halfhearted applause. Reporters were notoriously hard to impress.

Mercer didn't seem fazed by the lack of enthusiasm. "What you probably don't know, though, is that we're going to introduce you to the author of that book and to the hottest star in Hollywood, who just yesterday signed on to play the hero of this phenomenal love story." He glanced over his shoulder, didn't see what he wanted to see and looked at the audience again. "And since our star seems to be a little late, let's start with Andrea Mathers. I'm sure you'll have a few questions you want to ask her—" his fake smile made him look like a carnival barker "—or should I say *him?*" he asked slyly.

A murmur rippled through the crowd and Mercer raised his voice dramatically as he gestured off to his right. "Ladies and gentlemen, I give you the best-kept secret in the publishing industry. Matt Gallagher, known to his legion of fans as Andrea Mathers!"

Kate's stomach turned over as a long swell of delighted laughter and applause accompanied Matt's ascent to the microphone. He smiled and bowed, waiting for the fuss to die down, but when it didn't he looked for all the world as though he was thoroughly enjoying the accolade.

As she watched him, Kate knew that she should be feeling pride and happiness; she couldn't muster either. She'd been down this road before. Her heart had nearly burst with pride the first time she'd watched Dan McBride at a press conference. Now, it was ready to burst for an entirely different reason as she watched Matt smile at the crowd.

But why shouldn't he be pleased? Kate asked herself bitterly. He was a celebrity now—or would be before the day was over. Who wouldn't be happy with that? Applause was a dangerous, addictive aphrodisiac, but it had serious side effects. Approval was a two-edged sword in this town. One side was sweet, the other was deadly.

A half-dozen questions were shouted at Matt as the applause died, but before he could sort through them and choose which one to answer, a commotion behind the dais brought David Mercer back to the microphone.

"Excuse me, Matt. I want our friends to ask all the questions they want, but our other star just arrived. Why don't we get him up here and let the press have a go at both of you?" Like a master M.C., Mercer gestured toward the shadowed figure moving across the room. "Ladies and gentlemen, the star of *White Dove,* Dan McBride!"

The applause swelled again, Dan McBride bounded onto the dais and something inside Kate died.

The nightmare was only beginning.

Chapter Fourteen

Kate refused to believe it. This wasn't happening. She saw Dan approach the microphones, but her mind denied that it was really him. She didn't really see him smile and wave at the reporters. Dan didn't look at Matt with narrowed eyes as they were introduced to each other. Neither of them pretended that this was their first meeting. They didn't stand at the podium looking like good buddies while the press shouted questions. Dan didn't really sulk because the reporters were more interested in how Matt Gallagher became a romance novelist.

It just wasn't real. It couldn't be. It was a nightmare and in a few minutes Kate would wake up and laugh shakily at her foolishness.

But that didn't happen. Instead she was jolted from her state of numbness when the man right behind her stood and asked a question designed to put her in the center of a feeding frenzy.

"Mr. Gallagher!" Harry Townsend called out. "Is it true that you're involved romantically with Dan McBride's former fiancée, Kate Franklyn?"

A collective gasp of delight echoed through the room, then everything became silent as the reporters waited for an answer.

Matt stiffened but tried to smile. "This press conference is about my professional life as Andrea Mathers," he said as affably as he could manage. "I'd rather keep my private life separate."

"But is it true?" someone else wanted to know. "Are you really seeing Kate Franklyn?"

"How do you feel about that, Dan?" another voice called out.

"Dan! Did you know you'd be working with Kate's new lover when you signed on to do this picture?"

The questions kept coming too fast to answer, and finally David Mercer had to step to the podium to restore order.

"Please, please . . . one at a time," he instructed, but order was all he called for. Kate could tell by the look on his face that he was delighted with this unexpected turn of events. Scandal was like money in the bank, and Mercer had just received a totally unexpected bonus. The studio would gladly play this for all it was worth.

Mercer pointed to Harry Townsend. "Now, what was that question again, Harry?"

"Are you involved with Kate Franklyn?" the tabloid photographer asked.

Matt's eyes met Kate's as he reluctantly admitted, "We've been dating."

"How do you feel about that, Dan?" someone else asked.

Kate wasn't sure when Dan had spotted her, but he was looking directly at her when he answered, "Kate and I stopped seeing each other months ago. What she does is her own business."

"Is there any chance that you two will reconcile?" the same reporter questioned.

Matt leaned toward the microphone and grinned. "Not if I have anything to say about it."

The reporters laughed and some of the tension seemed to break, particularly when McBride did his share by responding, "Kate and I are still good friends, and I'm all for anything that makes her happy."

There were a few more questions about the romantic triangle that had taken them all by surprise, but when it became clear that they weren't going to get anything more juicy than pat press-release answers the subject was dropped. If there was dirt to be dug up, they'd have to do it later.

Dan fielded a few questions about his other movie commitments, and Matt had to talk at greater length about what it was like being a man in a female dominated and oriented profession.

Eventually, though, the torture ended for the men at the podium. Unfortunately their reprieve signaled the beginning of Kate's persecution. The instant Mercer dismissed the official portion of the conference, inviting everyone to enjoy the buffet and talk informally with Amity's new stars, the press converged on Kate.

"Did you know that Dan was going to be doing this film?"

"What's it like to date a romance writer?"

"Are you the heroine in this book?"

"Are those steamy love scenes Gallagher writes indicative of your sexual relationship with him?"

The questions came at her like an avalanche, making it impossible to think or even breathe. Kate knew she ought to laugh it off. She should be charming and give her tormenters quotable one-liners and witty sound bites. The worst thing she could do was let them see that this was killing her, because once the sharks sensed that they'd drawn blood they would really close in for the kill.

But Kate couldn't come up with any one-liners. All she could think of was the hell her life had been eight months ago and the hell it was going to become again. Because of Matt Gallagher.

Feeling like a claustrophobic in a sealed coffin, she muttered a frantic string of "No comments" as she fought her way out of the crowd. A few of them, with Harry Townsend leading the pack, followed her to the door shouting questions, but when it became clear that she wasn't going to talk, they gave up and returned to the party.

Trembling and gasping for air, Kate hurried through the lobby and burst out the front door into the bright sunshine. The moment she realized she was alone, she had to stop because her knees grew too weak to support her. Stiffening her jaw against a rush of tears, she sagged against the wall and prayed that the shaking would stop soon.

"Kate?"

She whirled and saw Matt hurrying toward her. His face was lined with concern, but she didn't care. This was his fault. He had lied to her, in more ways than one. He had promised her that his career would never plunge her back into the glare of a media spotlight, and he had broken that promise with a vengeance.

"What are you doing?" she demanded harshly. "Did they follow you?"

"No, I slipped out by another door. It's all right." He tried to gather her into his arms, but she pushed him away.

"Don't! They'll find us. They'll take pictures." She had to dig her fingernails into her palms to fight the tears as she backed away from him. "Damn you! How could you keep this from me? How could you let that happen?"

"Kate, I'm so sorry. I didn't know."

"Oh, please. You really expect me to believe that?"

Matt stiffened. "I expect you to believe it because it's true. Come on. I'll get you out of here so we can talk," he said, taking her arm, but she jerked away from him again.

"Don't touch me."

"Kate—"

"You can't leave, Matt! Your publisher is here. The press is here. *Dan McBride is here!*"

"Kate, I swear to you I didn't know they had signed McBride!"

She glared at him, her eyes flashing white-hot anger and cold hatred at the same time. "Just like you didn't know your publisher wanted to release your identity?"

Matt clenched his fists in frustration. This was all his fault. If he'd told Kate the truth a week ago, this nightmare wouldn't be happening. Kate might have left him then, but she wouldn't hate him the way she obviously did now. "I was going to tell you about that this weekend."

"Sure you were. Tell me, Matt, just how long have you known?"

"A week," he admitted reluctantly. "Bev told me at the same time she laid out the movie deal."

That wasn't what Kate wanted to hear. She had been praying that he'd only known for a few hours. If he'd found out this morning, she could have forgiven him for the delay. But a week? For a full seven days he had lied to her.

Kate remembered all the comments she'd made about his anonymity and thought she might become physically ill. "I have to get out of here," she muttered, turning away from him.

"I'll take you home," Matt said, falling into step with her, but Kate whirled toward him.

"No, you won't," she said viciously. "You have to go back in there and show a little gratitude to your publisher. After all, he's made you a star!"

"Damn it, Kate. I didn't ask for any of this. You know that."

"Maybe not, but you got it, didn't you? And you dragged me into the middle of it!" She stalked off across the parking lot and Matt went after her.

"Kate, don't do this. Let me take you home."

"No! I'll find a pay phone and call a cab."

"I can't let you do that. I don't want you to be alone while you're this upset. We'll talk. It'll be okay. I promise!"

She turned on him. "Don't you get it, Matt? I don't want you to go with me! I don't want to see you. I don't want to be seen *with* you! Just let me go before you make it any worse!"

"Kate..." He reached for her one more time but she held up her hands to keep him at bay.

She froze that way, looking at his face. His eyes held such hurt, regret and so much love, that for an instant her love for him surfaced and nearly drowned out her agony. For a fraction of a second, she was tempted to throw herself into his arms and pretend that everything would be all right.

And she might have done it if the click of a camera hadn't awakened her to brutal reality. She turned and found Harry Townsend smiling happily.

"So Gallagher is just a nobody, eh, Kate?" he asked, hurrying forward. "Did you even know that he was Andrea Mathers? Come on, Kate, talk. What's the story? Why are you so upset? Is it because you're still in love with McBride?"

"Go to hell, Harry!" She rushed away without another glance at Matt.

Matt watched her go, torn between his need to make things right and his desire to protect her.

"Aren't you gonna go after her, Gallagher?" Townsend asked smugly.

Matt looked at the slimy little reporter and fought the urge to deck him. "Why? So you can follow us and get more pictures?"

Townsend grinned. "That's my job."

"Well, do it without involving Kate. You've caused her enough grief to last two lifetimes."

"Hey, she's public property again. That makes her fair game."

Matt took a menacing step toward him. "She is *not* public property! She's not *anyone's* property."

"She is as long as she's tied up with someone famous, and let's face it, you're famous now."

"Matt! There you are!" Russell Thatch exclaimed as he came out the front door. "We wondered where you'd disappeared to. John Winston, the anchor of a show called 'Hollywood Now,' wants an on-camera interview."

Matt gritted his teeth. He couldn't very well refuse with Harry Townsend looking on. "All right, Russell."

"Aren't you going to introduce us?" the photographer asked.

"Get lost, Townsend."

"Tsk, tsk, tsk. You have to learn to be nice to the press."

Thatch frowned. "What's going on here, Matt?"

"I'll explain later, Russell," he replied tersely as he moved back inside toward the soundstage. Thatch was right at his side with Townsend tagging along behind, but as soon as Matt could manage it, he ducked the photographer and pulled his publisher aside.

"This has gotten totally out of control, Russell. I don't want anything more to do with this circus you and Mercer have created."

"Don't blame us," Thatch said defensively. "We didn't know you were involved with Dan McBride's old girlfriend."

"Well, I am, and I'm not going to let you or anyone else destroy my relationship with Kate."

"Oh, come on. Grow up," he replied. "This is business. We couldn't buy this kind of publicity for a million dollars. *White Dove* sales are going to go through the roof."

"I don't care!" Matt exclaimed.

That wasn't what Thatch wanted to hear. His face hardened into lines that betrayed how many times he had played hardball with the big boys in a very tough business. "Well, that's too bad, Gallagher, because Granger Publishing cares very much about profits. We're going to get all the mileage out of this we can."

"Then you'll do it without me."

"No, we won't. You're a professional. You have obligations, and you're going to fulfill them."

"You had an obligation, too," Matt reminded him angrily. "You agreed to give me control of how and when my identity was released."

"That was never on paper, Matt, but as I said earlier, I did intend to honor the verbal agreement I made with Bev. But yesterday when David Mercer suggested combining the announcements I knew it was too good to pass up."

"And you didn't tell me because you were afraid I'd balk."

Thatch didn't bother denying it. Instead he softened his voice to something more conciliatory. "Matt, I think that when the shock wears off and you calm down you'll see just how valuable this publicity is going to be. Now, you come do the interview with Winston and we'll sit down this evening over dinner and discuss your publicity tour."

"I'm sorry, Russell, but I can't do that."

Thatch frowned again. "The interview or dinner?"

"Neither. I'm leaving, and I already have plans for tonight. From this point on, if you want to discuss anything regarding my work or my career, call my agent."

"Now, just a minute—" Thatch began, but Matt was already stalking out of the room.

IT WAS A MIRACLE, but Kate made it back to her apartment without shedding any tears. They were bottled up inside her, straining so hard to burst free that it hurt her physically to hold them in, but she managed. Once she was safely locked in her apartment, though, the tears couldn't be restrained. The implications of what had happened came crashing down on her, forcing her to her knees.

Anguished sobs racked her body and she slammed her fists again and again onto the carpeted floor. "Why?" she screamed, giving vent to the blind rage that overtook her. "It's not fair!" She had just found happiness again after years of uncertainty and misery with Dan. She had found the perfect man; someone wonderful and kind. Someone she could have joyfully built a life with.... Someone she couldn't trust any more than she'd been able to trust Dan McBride.

The pattern made Kate sick. Dan had seemed perfect in the beginning, too, before success overwhelmed him and turned him into a monster she hadn't been able to recognize, let alone love. And now it was happening all over.

Even if Matt hadn't deceived her, Kate knew she wouldn't be able to survive the hell their lives would become if they stayed together. Today had been nothing more than a dress rehearsal. Now that Kate, Dan and Matt had been linked together, Granger Publishing and Amity Studios would do everything in their power to fuel rumors of controversy just to keep the press interested in *White Dove*.

Stories filled with half-truths and innuendo would be written. Deceptive, unflattering pictures would be taken at private moments. Problems would be created where none existed. Kate's life would no longer be her own.

It was her worst nightmare coming back to life in Technicolor and stereophonic sound. Kate knew she had to escape it before it crushed her to death.

Fueled by anger at Matt for the pain and humiliation his deception had caused, Kate pulled herself together and hurried into her bedroom. Since her suitcase was in the trunk of Matt's car, she pulled out an overnight bag and began stuffing clothes into it.

"Kate?"

She heard the door close. Heard Matt calling to her. She didn't respond, and moments later, he appeared at the bedroom door.

"What are you doing?"

"Why is it that men ask the stupidest questions at times like these?" she muttered sarcastically. "What does it look like I'm doing?"

"Packing."

"That's right. But it's a little difficult, since most of my overnight things are in the trunk of your car. I don't suppose as one last act of kindness you'd consider bringing my bag up, would you? After that you can leave. For good."

If a look could have killed him, Matt would have been nothing but a chalk line on Kate's carpet. This wasn't going to be easy. But then, Matt knew he didn't deserve "easy." He deserved Kate's anger and her distrust, but he wasn't going to give her up without a fight. "Your bag is in the living room," he told her. "Under the circumstances I didn't think we'd be spending the night with your parents."

"I suppose I should give you credit for having a little insight, if nothing else," she said as she whisked past him. "Now, all you have to do is put your key on the coffee table and go."

Matt followed her into the living room. "Not until we've talked this through."

"I've said everything there is to say on the subject."

"Well, I haven't." He took her arm and spun her toward him. "Kate, I'm sorry. I left as soon as I could get away. I would have followed you immediately, no matter what you said, but I was afraid Townsend would just come after us. Protecting you from that was the least I could do."

She ignored what his touch did to her and jerked away. "Well, thank you for that, at least."

Matt didn't know how to fight her sarcasm or her anger. "Kate, I never wanted this to happen. I didn't ask for any of it."

"No, but you're in it now," she informed him hotly. "And once it starts, you can't stop it. The press won't forget about this because Granger Publishing and Amity Studios won't let them forget. You can't fight it, so accept it. Use it. Enjoy it."

"How can I enjoy something that's tearing us apart?"

Kate backed away from him in disbelief. "Don't try to put this off on publicity, Matt. *You* did this to us! You lied to me!"

"Kate, I didn't lie—"

"Oh, excuse me. What did you call it in the elevator that day—an error of omission? Well, I've got news for you, buster. Not telling me your full name the night we met might have been an innocent *omission,* but this isn't in quite the same category. You knew what Granger had planned and you didn't warn me. You knew what I went through because of Dan, but that didn't matter, did it? You let me walk into that press conference like a sheep being led to the slaughterhouse!"

"Damn it, I didn't know about the press conference!" Matt insisted hotly. "I was as much of a sheep as you were today. Russell Thatch promised me control—"

Kate slapped her thighs and turned away from him in disgust. "What planet have you been living on, Bo Peep? Promises in this town don't mean a thing, and anyone involved in the movie business who thinks he has any control over his life ought to be locked up for his own safety."

"Fine. Call me crazy. Call me naive. Just don't accuse me of deliberately trying to hurt you, Kate, because it's not true. The only reason I didn't tell you about Granger wanting to go public was because I was afraid of losing you."

Kate turned toward him. "Am I supposed to find that an acceptable excuse and throw myself into your arms?"

Matt prayed for patience and the words to convince Kate to forgive him. "I made you a promise, Kate. I swore that I would never let my career get in the way of our happiness. I knew that I could live up to that promise, no matter what Granger Publishing did. But what I didn't know was whether or not you loved me enough to believe that."

Kate glared at him stonily. "Well, now you know, don't you?"

"I know we can get through this if we try."

A tiny sliver of sympathy for him washed through Kate. He really did believe that there was hope for them. But that made him more of a fool than she'd been for trusting him in the first place, and she squashed her pity for him. "No, Matt. Read my lips. We can't survive this. I don't even plan to try. Even if I could forgive you for lying to me, I could never get past what happened today at that press conference. Did you hear that reporter ask me if you used our lovemaking as inspiration for scenes in your book?"

No, Matt hadn't heard the question. He had only seen what was happening and known that it was killing the woman he loved. "I'm so sorry, Kate."

"Will you stop saying that! It doesn't help. I know you're sorry. I know you'd make it go away if you could! But it doesn't matter now. The damage is done. It can't be undone."

"Then we'll find a way to get through it together," he said, reaching for her.

Kate didn't pull away when his hands cupped her shoulders, but she didn't move toward him, either. "No," she said softly. "I tried that with Dan, and it didn't work. I trusted him when every instinct I possessed screamed that he was lying to me. I stood by him. I smiled bravely for the cameras. I played the game. I said the right things and acted out the part of the dutiful girlfriend standing faithfully at the edge of the spotlight while her man accepted the applause that was due him." She shook her head. "I can't do that again, Matt."

Matt realized that Kate was slipping away from him. In fact, if he had let himself see the truth, he would have known that she was already gone. This was just the memorial service. "Kate, this is not the same as what happened with you and McBride."

She laughed harshly. "Really? It certainly feels the same. You kept the truth from me, Matt. Do you really think that your lies are any less painful than Dan's were?"

The comparison to McBride infuriated Matt. "Kate, you can't equate having endless affairs with what I did."

"Yes, I can," she retorted hotly. "You have systematically deceived me from the moment we met. How do you honestly expect me to trust *anything* you say to me? For all I know, you probably knew that Dan had been signed to star in the film."

"I didn't, Kate," he swore. "I never would have kept that from you."

She shook her head. "Sorry. I don't believe you."

"Damn it, Kate, you love me."

She shook her head. "No, Matt. I loved an illusion. I loved the Matt Gallagher you wanted me to see and fall in love with. I don't think the man I loved ever existed."

Matt's hands fell away from her as though he'd been burned. "You know better than that, Kate," he said, stiffening his jaw against the pain of her accusation and a rush of anger. "I was wrong to delay telling you the truth. I admit that. But you can't imagine how I felt last week when Bev told me what Granger was planning. I was going to propose to you that night. I had the tux, the champagne. . ." Matt dug into his pocket and removed the velvet box he had been carrying around for a week. "I even had the ring."

Kate looked at the box in his hand and a wave of sorrow for all the things that could never be washed over her. She had to dig her fingernails into her palm to keep from crying. "Why are you telling me this now, Matt? Is it supposed to make some kind of a difference?"

"Yes. It should," he told her. "If I'm really such a deceitful lout, why didn't I go ahead and propose?"

"I don't know. Why didn't you?"

"Because I love you too much to be dishonest with you!"

"Then why didn't you tell me the whole truth last week?" she cried.

"I was going to, but you looked at me with so much love that I thought my heart was going to burst. I couldn't bear the thought of seeing that light go out of your eyes. I wanted to hold on to it for as long as I could."

Kate just stared at him. "Funny, isn't it? You preached trust to me for two months, but when push came to shove, you didn't trust me, either, did you?"

"No," Matt said sadly. "I guess I didn't."

"And you were right not to, Matt," she told him as a tug of sadness crept back into the empty space where her heart used to be. "I can't live with what your life is about to become."

"I won't accept that, Kate," he told her flatly.

"I'm not giving you a choice, Matt."

"Kate—"

"Enough! I don't want to hear any more! It's over. Don't you understand that? It's over, and if you really love me as much as you say you do, you'll accept it."

"I can't do that."

Kate wasn't sure how much more strength she had to fight him. She turned away and moved across the room, searching desperately for some way to make him accept the truth. It was a long moment before she faced him again with a measure of calm. "After what I went through today because of you, I'd say you owe me at least one favor, wouldn't you?"

"I'll do anything but give you up, Kate," he swore.

She let the promise pass. "Here's what I want, Matt. You go home and leave me alone for one full week. Consider it a cooling off period, if you like. Convince yourself that if you give me some time I'll have a change of heart, if you have to, but just stay away from me for a week."

Matt thought it over. They certainly weren't getting anywhere now. Maybe some time apart would be best, but he really didn't think so. Kate was leading up to something, and he was pretty sure he wasn't going to like it.

It didn't seem that he had much choice but to accede to her request, though. "All right. But next Friday—"

"Next Friday, I want you to take a good hard look at your life, Matt, because you're going to find out the hard way what I already know." She moved toward him purposefully. "In seven days, you won't be the same man, and nothing in your life will be the same, either. If you really love me as much as you claim to, you won't be able to come back next week, because no man would put a woman he loved through the kind of hell you're facing."

Matt realized he'd allowed himself to be painted into a tidy little corner, and it infuriated him. From this point on, anything he did would be wrong.

He nodded to her. "Very neatly done, Kate. If I come back, I'm a selfish lout. If I don't come back, I lose the only woman I've ever loved."

Kate was beyond being moved by his words. "You know where the door is, Matt. Use it."

There was a stone cold deadness in her eyes that chilled Matt to the bone, and he finally realized that whatever she had felt for him—whether it was love, or only the illusion of love—had died. There was nothing left to fight for. "All right, Kate. I'm going."

He started to turn, but when he became aware of the black box that was being crushed in his clenched fist, he stopped. "Here. Catch," he said, tossing the engagement ring across the room.

Kate caught it out of reflex, and the warmth of the box spread through her hand as surely as if Matt had touched her himself. "I don't want this, Matt."

"Keep it anyway. As a souvenir. Put it in a box with your Mickey Mouse ears, our miniature golf trophy and Tweety. Next time you get lonely, pull it out and remind yourself of what you threw away today."

Kate fought back another surge of tears. "All I'm giving up is an illusion, Matt."

"Haven't you heard? This is Hollywood. This is the place where illusions become realities—if you're not afraid to make them happen."

He pulled open the door and let it slam behind him when he left. The reverberation went through Kate like a shot, and she sank to the floor as a flood of tears coursed down her cheeks.

Chapter Fifteen

For Kate, the next two weeks were like a carnival fun house—without the fun. Laurel Petty hounded her daily, trying to convince her to give the *Sentinel* the scoop on her relationship with Matt. Somehow Harry Townsend learned her schedule and followed her to two theater premieres, shouting questions at her and taking pictures. Another tabloid reporter was caught one night in the entertainment section newsroom rifling through Kate's desk.

Everywhere she went, even if reporters weren't in attendance, someone recognized Kate. They asked for her autograph or demanded that she tell them what Matt Gallagher and Dan McBride were really like. She lost count of the number of times she was asked which man was the better lover.

Kate tried to avoid reading the tabloids, newspapers and gossip columns, but they were like a train wreck—horrible to behold, but impossible to look away from. One headline screamed Romance Novelist and Actor Embroiled in Love Triangle.... One paper ran an old photo of Kate and Dan arguing; next to it, was the picture Harry Townsend had taken of Matt and Kate outside the Music Center two months ago....

One paper rehashed her scandal-ridden breakup with Dan . . . another ran details of Matt's outlandish courtship of Kate along with the picture Townsend had taken outside Amity Studios with Kate holding her hands up to ward Matt off. . . .

It was every bit the nightmare Kate had known it would be. She encased herself in a shell of granite, played the game with a pasted-on smile and used every new indignity inflicted upon her to reinforce her anger at Matt.

On the Friday that ended their agreed-upon week, Kate didn't hear from Matt. She really hadn't expected to, but she also knew that he couldn't have gotten in touch with her even if he'd wanted to because he was booked for autograph parties all over the city that day and evening. And he didn't call the next day. Or the next. Or the next.

Kate knew why, of course. He was experiencing the same publicity nightmare that she was. The only difference was, of course, that he couldn't get by with a string of "no comments." Granger Publishing's public relations staff had booked him on every TV and radio talk show in L.A. He gave print interviews and posed for pictures. One article even gave his itinerary for an eight-day, eleven-city book tour.

Through it all, he smiled as though he was enjoying himself. He deftly sidestepped questions about his relationship with Kate and cracked endless jokes that made him the darling of the media. Everyone was charmed by him, and Kate was probably the only person in the city who could see the effects of the strain he was under. Makeup could hide the circles under his eyes, but not the weariness in them. He was quick-witted enough to fool interviewers and audience alike into believing he was having a good time, but Kate knew the difference between the relaxed, easygoing, fun-loving Matt Gallagher and the forced carbon copy she was seeing on TV.

Despite herself, despite her anger, she felt sorry for him. He was a babe in the woods . . . a lamb being fed to the lions. . . . The press was eating him alive and he was handling it all alone. There was no one in the wings to bolster his spirits when the pressure got to be too much. There was no one to yell at when he needed to scream but didn't dare curse at the press. There was no one waiting at the end of the day to listen to all the crazy things that had happened.

He was alone and besieged, just as Kate had known he would be when she extracted that promise from him. As it turned out, though, the promise was a double-edged sword, because Matt wasn't staying away from her just because he was busy. He loved her and he didn't want her to suffer with him.

Instead she was suffering alone and feeling a mounting sense of guilt. A stronger woman would have put her own fears aside and helped guide the man she loved through the publicity mine field. She would have been at his side warning him where not to step and telling him where the booby traps were located.

But Kate wasn't that woman, she reminded herself endlessly, doing everything she could to fight her growing sympathy...and her love. This was Matt's fault. He had lied to her.

Of course, if she was to take his word for it, he'd deceived her only because he didn't believe that her love for him was strong enough. Obviously he'd been right.

Kate found that knowledge galling, but it didn't make her cave in, not even when the media pressure on her finally started to ease up.

Matt deserved what he was getting.

As long as she could remain convinced of that, she was safe.

THE BEVERLY CENTER was a madhouse. Hundreds of fans were pushing and shoving their way around the central court stage where "Andrea Mathers" and Dan McBride were autographing copies of *White Dove.* Scheduling the event on Saturday had guaranteed record crowds, and it was everything the security guards could do to keep that crowd from mobbing the stage. Instead the fans had to be content with filtering one at a time in a steady stream past the celebrities.

It was an awesome spectacle; particularly for the men at the center of the straining mob.

"I feel like a goldfish in the shark tank at Marineland," Matt muttered beneath his breath as one fan moved off with her autographed book and another gushed toward him.

"What did you say?" Dan asked as he reached for a book being shoved at him. They were sitting side by side, and while Matt's smile was strained, Dan's was genuine. Though the actor had undoubtedly played this same scene out hundreds of times, it was obvious that he was thoroughly enjoying himself. Matt didn't understand how that was possible.

"I said I feel like a goldfish in a shark tank," he repeated as he scrawled a nearly illegible signature.

"Get used to it," Dan advised him.

"Excuse me, but could you sign that 'To Candy, with all my love'?"

It was an effort for Matt to focus on the teenager in front of him, but he managed a smile. "Why, Candy, I hardly know you."

She leaned against the table. "That could change," she said coquettishly.

Dan chuckled. "You walked right into that one, buddy."

Matt felt a genuine sense of revulsion—both at Dan for calling him "buddy" and for the flirtatious child—but he tried not to show it. Instead, he modified the inscription to read *To Candy, Best regards,* and handed her the book. She looked at it and shot Matt a perturbed glance, then sidled down the table to Dan.

The girl flirted with him outrageously, and though Matt didn't see what Dan finally wrote, Candy was a lot happier when she saw his autograph. Muttering something about giving Dan her autograph in exchange, she shoved a piece of paper at him before a guard hustled her along.

Dan looked at the slip. "Another phone number," he said, holding it out to Matt. "You want it?"

"No, thanks. I've got a collection of my own," he said, glancing down at a box beneath the table that was serving as a trash can.

To his credit, Dan had been using the box almost as often as Matt. He crumpled this one up, too, and dropped it in.

They'd been at this for nearly four hours, and Matt was afraid that if it didn't end soon he'd go stark-raving mad. These past two weeks had been nothing short of hell. Book signings, public appearances, short jaunts out of town to bookstores in San Diego, Bakersfield and Modesto, and always—everywhere—the media...

And now this. The ultimate indignity. Four hours of pretending to be bosom buddies with Dan McBride. It was just too much.

"How much longer is this supposed to go on?" Matt asked his "partner" when there was a lull in the procession a few moments later. Two women were gumming up the line with an argument about who was there first, and the guards were having to break up the shoving match that ensued. Matt was beyond caring who won, and Dan was too seasoned to pay any attention.

Dan checked his watch. "Fifteen minutes."

"Thank God."

Dan shot him a curious glance. "You don't like this much, do you?"

Matt shrugged. "As torture goes, it's not so bad. Granger hasn't brought out the boiling oil or asked me to walk over burning coals, yet."

Dan chuckled. "You'll get used to it."

"I'd rather not have to."

"That attitude is only going to make it harder," Dan warned him with a touch of condescension.

Matt gritted his teeth and shot McBride a killing glance, but he kept his mouth shut. If not for Dan, Matt might very well have been able to enjoy what was happening to him. Or at the very least, he would have been able to endure it more easily because Kate would have been at his side. Together they would have found the humor in incidents that now just seemed stupid, sordid and exhausting. The very center of his life had been ripped away, and Dan McBride was directly to blame.

Not that Matt had let himself off the hook for all responsibility. He knew exactly what his delay in telling Kate had cost him: she would never be able to forgive him for putting her through that scene at the press conference or for what she saw as his betrayal of her.

But Matt also knew that in the final analysis it really wouldn't have made any difference if he had told her the truth the night he learned it. Even if she had agreed then to try to withstand the pressures they were about to be subjected to, she would have run away the moment she learned that Dan McBride was doing the film. He was the wild card that had turned a ho-hum revelation of Matt's identity into a sordid love triangle that had sent the press into a feeding frenzy. Dan's betrayal of Kate had made her terrified of publicity and distrustful of any hint of success.

But since making that kind of accusation in public was tantamount to suicide, Matt swallowed his resentment. Pam McFadden, the Granger Publishing PR representative who had arranged the autographing and all Matt's other engagements, finally brought the altercation at the stairway under control and got the line moving again. The combatants were escorted away by security men, and another woman with a book moved up the stairs onto the stage. The line of fans resumed, but at exactly four o'clock, Matt signaled Pam.

"Yes, Matt?"

"It's four, Pam. I'm out of here. Where's that escape route you said you'd have ready for us?"

The publicity expert was young, pretty and she looked incredibly fragile, but one of the first things Matt had learned about her when she took over his life ten days ago was that she had a core of iron. "Matt, please. Look at that line. Not all your fans have had a chance to buy your book yet. Won't you stay another hour?"

"Sorry, Pam. We advertised four hours, and that's all I'm giving you." Matt stood and slipped into the suit jacket he had hung over the back of his chair. "You can start selling the books we signed earlier for the bookstores."

"I have other plans, too," Dan said as he stood and stretched. "Why don't you just let us wave goodbye and then get those security guards up here to escort us out the back way."

"All right," Pam agreed reluctantly, then moved off to the microphone.

While Matt and Dan smiled and waved at the crowd, Pam thanked them all for coming and announced that autographed copies of the book would be on sale at both mall bookstores. The security guards gathered around, and the crowd pressed in as Matt and Dan were spirited toward a door marked Private, No Admittance. The guards helped them through and remained behind to keep the crowd at bay.

"Is the car waiting?" Matt asked as soon as the door was closed and locked, giving him the first moment of peace and quiet he'd had in four hours.

"Certainly," Pam replied as though he had offended her by insinuating that she wasn't doing her duty. She checked her clipboard as the three of them moved down a wide corridor. "I know you're tired, Matt, but I have some details here that we need to go over about the tour."

"Forget it, Pam," Matt replied. "I'm sick to death of this tour already and it hasn't even started."

"But it's important you be prepared before we leave on Monday. We'll be doing eleven cities in eight days and that takes—"

"I don't care what it takes," Matt snapped. "Russell Thatch is paying you to handle the details, so you just do your job. I'll go where you tell me whenever you say to be there, but beyond that, I don't owe you or Russell anything."

"All right," she said tersely. "In that case, I'll leave you two here and see if I can do anything to assist the bookstores. I'm sure they're being mobbed already." She stopped and when Dan came to a halt with her, Matt reluctantly turned as well. "The limos are waiting for you at the exit and there are guards at the end of this corridor to cover your escape. Mr. McBride, we really appreciate your cooperation."

Dan accepted her firm, no-nonsense handshake. "It was my pleasure, Ms. McFadden."

She looked at Matt. "I'll see you at the airport Monday at nine."

"I'll be there," he told her.

She nodded brusquely and headed back down the hall.

"That's a tough lady, but you're not making her job any easier," Dan commented lightly.

Matt had taken about all the advice he could stomach for one day. "Look, McBride, I had to smile and be pals with you out there, but there are no fans and no reporters back here, so let's get something straight. I know what you did to Kate and I think you're a lowlife slug. You screwed up, but I'm the one who's paying for it."

Matt was stunned that Dan accepted the condemnation without showing the slightest sign of anger. Instead he looked almost as sad and haunted as Matt felt. "You're right, Gallagher. I did screw up, but you're wrong if you think I didn't pay for it. I know what I did and what it cost me."

For the first time since the night he'd met the movie star at the Music Center Matt felt genuinely sorry for him. Whatever his faults, he had loved Kate—and still did. Matt softened his tone without really being aware of doing so. "You nearly destroyed her, McBride. She may never get rid of the scars."

"I know. If I had it to do over..." He sighed and shook his head. "Aw, forget it. It's too late for that now." He turned and they started down the corridor again. "You know, I make it a point never to believe anything I read in the tabloids, but apparently the rumors are true this time. You and Kate broke up?"

Matt didn't want to get into this with McBride but since he had raised the subject himself, he felt compelled to answer. "Yes."

"Was it serious? Your relationship, I mean?"

Matt gritted his teeth. "Yes."

McBride paused a moment. "I wish I could say I'm sorry you two have split, but I'm not."

Matt saw red and came to a stop again. After what McBride had put Kate through, the least he could do was hope she'd find someone else who could make her happy and give her things he hadn't been able to. "You selfish son of a bitch. I think we'd better part company here," Matt growled. "I'm about two seconds away from ramming those perfect teeth down your throat, and you don't have a stunt double here to take the punch for you."

The threat brought out the brawler in Dan. He threw his shoulders back and stiffened his spine but even with that movement he was still a few inches shorter than Matt. "If you think you can do it, take your best shot."

Matt clenched one fist, but managed to restrain himself. Instead of venting his anger and frustration, he laughed humorlessly. "No, thanks. This isn't a jousting match and the winner isn't going to win the hand of the fair lady. Besides, I don't think you want to see Action Hero Pulverized By Romance Author in tomorrow's headlines."

Dan took the insult to heart. "Oh, really? You think you're that good, huh?"

Matt couldn't believe it. The idiot was actually ready to fight. "Oh, hell. Grow up, McBride."

He turned away in disgust, but Dan grabbed his arm and spun him around. Matt jerked away so violently that he went careening into the wall, and that was all it took to snap what little self-control he had left.

Too angry to see straight, Matt pushed away from the wall and took his best shot.

Chapter Sixteen

"Kate, I need the terminal. Aren't you finished with that piece yet?"

Kate shot an exasperated glance at Tom Fielding, the entertainment reporter she shared her desk with. "I would have been finished fifteen minutes ago if I hadn't had you hovering over my shoulder asking when I'll be finished." She inserted a disk, saved the article and popped it out of the driver. "There. All yours."

"Thank you," Fielding said with exaggerated courtesy, slipping into Kate's chair as she slid out of it. Kate nearly tripped over him getting out from behind the desk.

She called for the copy boy to pick up the disk, and waited as he fought his way through the Saturday afternoon madness.

"Kate! Katie!"

If there had been a ladies' room close by, Kate would have ducked into it, but that wouldn't have helped. Laurel Petty would only have followed her. Kate tossed her disk at the copy boy, then turned to face the gossip columnist who was bearing down on her. "Yes, Laurel, what is it?"

When Laurel finally reached the desk, Kate didn't know which was more comical, the woman's out-of-breath huffing and puffing or the phony solicitous look on her face. "Oh, dear. You haven't heard, have you, Katie?"

Kate was in no mood to play games. "Heard what, Laurel?"

There was nothing a gossip columnist liked more than having someone beg them for the latest juicy tidbit, but Laurel seemed to be enjoying this more than usual. "I just got a phone call from my source at Mercy General. Matt Gallagher was just rushed into the emergency room."

Kate felt all the blood drain from her face. "What happened to him?" she asked frantically.

"I don't know, dear. Honestly. Though a car wreck might be a possibility. My source says they called a plastic surgeon and scheduled an operating room moments after he was wheeled in."

"Oh, God...." Kate couldn't breathe. She couldn't think. She only knew she had to get to Matt. "Thank you, Laurel," she said as she snatched up her purse and began fighting her way across the room.

"Don't thank me. I'm coming with you," the plump columnist replied as she chugged along behind her, but trying to keep up with Kate was a waste of time. Laurel was only halfway across the newsroom when Kate hit the door at a dead run.

WHEN KATE ARRIVED at Mercy General, the emergency room looked like a war zone, but it had nothing to do with bombings, knifings, car crashes, or any of the other medical emergencies that could turn an ER upside down. This afternoon, the media was responsible for the chaos.

The parking lot was filled with news vans from every TV station in town. Just inside the door of the ambulance entrance, spotlights were glaring and reporters were tripping over each other. Microphones were being shoved into the faces of anyone who moved, but as near as Kate could tell as she quickly assessed the situation, the only man in a white uniform doing any talking was a brash young orderly who seemed to be enjoying his moment in the sun.

Kate didn't waste any time on trying to hear what he was saying. She pushed rudely through the crowd, not caring who noticed her, but when someone finally did, she found the lights being shone on her and the microphones being shoved in her own face.

"Kate, who are you here to see?"

"Have you heard a prognosis yet? Will there be permanent scarring?"

"Is it true they were fighting over you?"

"Where were you when you heard the news?"

The questions didn't even register on Kate. She was totally focused on reaching the swinging doors to the treatment area in front of her. Finally, though, someone shoved one microphone too many at her, and Kate rudely pushed the black wand away. "Get that damned thing out of my face and get out of my way," she ordered.

Her unexpected reaction caused enough of a shock to allow her to break free of them, and she sprinted through the doors into a room of cubicles defined only by white curtains. She had left the press behind, but she now had a nurse hot on her heels.

"Wait a minute. You're not allowed in here!" the nurse shouted at her. "Get back out there with the rest of the barracudas."

Kate whirled toward her. "I'm the next of kin," she told her, not caring that it was a lie. She had to see Matt. She had to know that he was all right.

"Oh. Well. That's different," the nurse said, calming herself somewhat. "You still can't be back here, but I can put you someplace a little quieter than that zoo cage out there. Just whose next of kin are you?"

"Matt Gallagher's. Where is he? Is he going to be all right?"

The nurse looked perturbed. "That depends on whether or not he can keep that handsome face of his away from—"

"Kate? Is that you, Kate?"

Kate pivoted and found Matt standing in the white V of the curtain he was holding back. His blue shirt was stained with blood, he had a butterfly bandage over his swollen left eye, and he was scowling at her, but he was also standing on his own two feet and he had never looked better to Kate.

"Thank God," she breathed, rushing toward him.

"What the hell are you doing here?" he demanded, stopping Kate in her tracks.

How could he possibly talk to her like that after what she'd just gone through to get to him? "Laurel Petty heard that you'd been in a car wreck. That they were taking you into surgery."

"A car wreck? Jeez.... You'd think a reporter might bother with little details like getting her facts straight." He dropped the curtain, cutting himself off from Kate, and returned to the examining table.

Kate threw back the white sheet and followed him in. "You weren't in a car wreck? Is that what you're telling me?"

"No, I was not in a car wreck," he said testily, rubbing his jaw. "Though I do feel a bit like I was hit by a bus. Fortunately, McBride looks like he was run over by a train."

Kate took a second to digest that. "Dan is here?"

"Yes."

The reporters' questions Kate had ignored earlier finally reached her consciousness. "You and Dan had a fight. Over me."

"Don't flatter yourself, Kate. Dan and I had a fight because he's a childish bully."

"Who started it?" she demanded.

"Does it matter?"

Kate took a step back to distance herself from Matt and the confusing emotions that were washing over her. She didn't need details about the fight because she knew Dan well enough to envision exactly what had happened. They had exchanged a few words, and since Dan was always looking for a reason to start a brawl, he had probably goaded Matt into taking the first swing. "No. I don't guess it does matter," she replied.

Matt eased gingerly onto the examining table, and the pain in his ribs took some of the sting out of his words. "Kate, why did you come here?" he asked plaintively. "Don't you know what you've done? The press was easing up on you. If—"

"How do you know that?"

Matt sighed wearily. "Thanks to the press, I'm not able to do my job as a critic anymore, but I still have friends at the *Enterprise*. I know all about Townsend following you...and the other stuff. But when the piranhas saw that you weren't having any contact with me, they did finally let up, didn't they?"

"Yes," she admitted, realizing for the first time that not one of the reporters who had hounded her was from the *Enterprise*. Matt must have called in a few favors to get them to leave her alone.

"Then I ask you again," he repeated wearily. "Why did you come here? Don't you know that it's going to start all over now?"

Kate hadn't given that any thought, and she didn't want to. Not yet. "I came because I heard you were hurt. I thought you might need me, and I wanted to be with you." She suddenly felt like crying, and to keep the tears at bay, she summoned a little self-righteous anger. "Of course, I didn't realize you and Dan were just cooking up a little publicity stunt."

"You know better than that, Kate," Matt said sternly. "Aren't you even a little curious how he is?"

"I couldn't care less."

Matt told her anyway. "He took a punch that split his lip. It required stitches, so he asked that a plastic surgeon be brought in. I think he's up in the OR now because he wouldn't let them do the stitches with a local anesthetic."

"That's Dan. He'll do anything to avoid paying the price of his own stupidity." Kate finally noticed that Matt was holding his side. "What about you? Is that cut above your eye the only damage?"

"I don't know," he replied. "I'm waiting for someone to read the X rays and tell me whether or not I've got a cracked rib."

"Nothing more serious than that?"

"Nope."

"Well, good.... I guess I'm not needed here anymore. Not that I ever was, apparently."

Kate knew she should let that be her exit line, but she found herself rooted to the spot. She had expected Matt to at least be grateful for her concern, but that didn't seem to be the case. She'd been such an emotional basket case when she came in that he could have very easily used that to his advantage, but he didn't seem interested in doing that, either. He just seemed tired and beat-up, and irritated with her for running the gauntlet of reporters on his behalf.

Fine. If that's the way he wanted it, she wasn't going to beg him to tell her he was grateful for her concern or that he loved her...or that he wanted her back more than he wanted air to breathe.

She didn't want to hear any of those things anyway.

And pigs could fly.

"Well...I guess I'll be seeing you, Matt." She turned and started searching for the opening in the curtain.

"Kate..."

She whirled around expectantly. "Yes?"

"Thank you for coming. For caring. After what I put you through, it's more than I had a right to expect."

He seemed so impossibly sad that it nearly broke her heart. "Matt, you don't stop loving someone overnight," she told him gently.

He straightened his shoulders. "That's not what you said the last time we were together."

"I was angry."

"But you're not anymore?"

Kate noted that the question wasn't phrased with any hope attached to it. Just curiosity. "Of course, I'm still angry. You deceived me. No matter what your motives were, it was still wrong."

"I know that. And I also know that you were right to ask me to leave you alone for a week so that I could experience this nightmare for myself. You wanted to make a believer out of me, and it worked. I hadn't even made it through that first weekend before I realized that I could never subject you to this kind of torture."

"And that's why you haven't called?"

Matt's face turned to stone. "That's why I never will, Kate."

It was the gesture of self-sacrifice Kate had set him up for two weeks ago. It was what she had counted on. Prayed for. It was what she knew without question was in her best interests...and it was also the last thing in the world she truly wanted. For all his faults, she loved this man. The fact that he would give her up only proved that he loved her, too.

"Well, I guess this finally proves it," Kate said with a touch of grandiosity. "Matt Gallagher really is a liar."

A dark storm cloud began gathering over Matt's handsome face. "What does that mean?"

"You promised me *more* than once that you'd *never* give up on me," she reminded him.

Matt came off the examining table. "Damn it, Kate. Don't play with me. You wanted me out of your life because you couldn't handle the changes in mine. Are you trying to tell me you've changed your mind?"

Kate frowned in confusion. "I don't know, Matt. Maybe I have. I've been miserable without you," she admitted. "How much worse could it be if we were handling this together?"

Matt didn't believe what he was hearing. It had taken every ounce of strength he possessed to keep from gathering Kate into his arms the moment he saw her. He wanted to hold her. Kiss her. Prove to her how much he still loved her. But he knew that the only way he could really do that was to let her go.

She had frantically rushed to his side when she thought he was seriously injured, and it was obvious those emotions were still clinging to her. Once she had to cope with the realities of what her dash past the press had cost her, though, she would sing a different tune. She'd push him away as she had before, and Matt knew he couldn't survive losing Kate twice.

Once was already more than he could bear.

"I'm sorry, Kate, but there's no point even discussing it. You were right when you said it was over. We have to chalk this one up to a lost cause and get on with our lives."

Kate was stunned. She'd practically gotten down on her knees and groveled, and all Matt could say was "Sorry, kid. Take a hike"?

"Fine," she said tersely. "If you think I'm going to beg you to let me forgive you, you can just think again. Have a nice life, Matt." She turned on her heel and stormed out.

It would have been a stunning exit if it hadn't taken her three tries to find the gap in the curtain.

Chapter Seventeen

While Matt chatted with Phil, crossed swords with Geraldo and charmed Oprah on national television that next week, Kate stewed over his rejection of her peace overture. She tried to convince herself that she was glad Matt hadn't taken advantage of her moment of weakness. She tried to tell herself she was still furious with him for deceiving her. She tried to make herself believe that she couldn't bear spending the rest of her life on a publicity merry-go-round.

None of it worked. No matter what argument she used, one incontrovertible fact remained: She loved Matt Gallagher more than she had thought it was possible to love anyone. She devoured his TV appearances like a starving woman at a Weight Watchers banquet—the morsels weren't satisfying, but she was so hungry for Matt that she would take anything she could get.

But she didn't know what to do about it. Nothing had really changed. Those desperate minutes when she'd thought he might be dead or dying had chiseled away all her defenses, but he was still living under the glare of a media spotlight and probably would be for the rest of his life. Every time Kate convinced herself she could cope with that, memories of her nightmare with Dan and the recent publicity onslaught sent her spinning back into a mire of confusion.

By Friday night, as she watched Matt smile through a fifteen-minute segment with Karen Lane on the prime-time news magazine "Up Close and Personal," Kate wasn't sure how much more she could take. But she was equally unsure what to do about it.

When her doorbell rang, the last thing Kate wanted was company, but she switched off the TV and went to see who it was. She looked through the peephole, and when she saw Dan she was so shocked that she opened the door without thinking.

"What do you want?" she demanded gracelessly.

"Hello, Kate." He looked incredibly handsome in the studied California-casual style he had perfected, and the delicate stitches in his lip were barely visible. He didn't look nearly as bad as she had expected. Unfortunately. "Is this a bad time?" he asked with just the slightest hint of hesitancy, as though he thought maybe there was just the tiniest possibility that Kate might not welcome him.

"For you, *anytime* would be bad, Dan."

He looked at her patiently. "Let me come in, Kate. Please. I thought it was time we talked, and I'm sure you don't want your neighbors eavesdropping. You never know who might be anxious to earn a few dollars selling a new story to the *Enquirer.*"

"There is no story as far as we're concerned, Dan," she told him flatly, but she stepped aside to admit him anyway because she knew he was right.

"Thanks." He moved through the foyer into the living room as though he owned the place. "Nice apartment."

He had been here only once before, shortly after Kate had vacated the Benedict Canyon home they had shared.

When he had appeared at her door that time, she hadn't let him cross the threshold. Hopefully she wouldn't live to regret her moment of weakness this time.

She followed him into the living room but didn't move far from the foyer entrance because she expected to show him out momentarily. "What do you want, Dan?"

"Like I said, to talk."

"About what?"

"Us."

"There is no 'us,' so I don't see that we have anything to talk about. And frankly, I'm not in the mood for any of your games tonight."

"This is no game, Kate," he said with the sincere intensity that had earned him a million female fans. "I know that you ended things with Gallagher, and I know why."

"Dan, I don't care what you know or *think* you know. I'm not going to discuss Matt with you."

He approached her, but Kate wasn't even moved enough by his nearness to feel the necessity of edging away from him. "You have to answer one question for me, Kate," he said quietly. "I *have* to know. Would you have broken off with Gallagher if I hadn't shown up at that press conference three weeks ago?"

Kate had asked herself that question a million times, and the answer usually came up "no." If Tom Cruise, Alec Baldwin, or any other popular heartthrob had been cast in *White Dove,* the press wouldn't have had a story to sensationalize. Kate would have eventually forgiven Matt for keeping the bad news from her, and they would have dealt with the moderate amount of media attention together.

But it hadn't happened that way. "No, Dan. I probably wouldn't have stopped seeing him."

He gave her his million-dollar smile. "That's what I thought."

Kate wasn't moved by the sexy smile. In fact, when she realized what he was getting at, she was furious. "Wait a minute. Are you insinuating that I broke up with Matt because I realized that I was still in love with you?"

"Of course."

He was so obnoxiously egotistical that Kate nearly slapped him, but instead, she took two angry strides away from him and counted to ten. It didn't help.

"You are so arrogant!" she finally exclaimed when she couldn't hold it in any longer. "You slept with at least four other women that I know of while we were engaged, and because of your infidelity I was subjected to the most humiliating public degradation anyone could possibly endure. And you think I could possibly love you after that?"

"I made mistakes, Kate. I know that," he said gravely. "But I still love you and I want to spend the rest of my life making it up to you."

She just looked at him. "Who wrote that sparkling piece of dialogue, Dan? Did you pay a script doctor or did you just invent it yourself?"

"It's true," he insisted, coming toward her.

"Oh, really? Tell me, when did you come to the startling conclusion that I still love you?"

"At the autographing. Once Gallagher confirmed the rumors that you two had broken up, I knew why."

"And it's taken you a week to get around to approaching me?" she asked, holding her anger in admirably.

If he had answered that it had taken him this long to find the right words or get up the nerve to come see her, Kate might have given him credit for at least having enough intelligence to tell a semibelievable lie. But that's not what he told her.

"I wanted to come before, but I've been busy," he replied. "I've been in the recording studio all week dubbing lines for that movie I did in the Yucatán."

Kate shook her head and laughed wearily. "Which loosely translated means you couldn't find a date tonight, so you thought you'd give old Kate a try."

"That's not true," he insisted. "Kate, why won't you believe that I still love you?"

This time his voice held a ring of sincerity, at least. Kate didn't doubt that he had feelings for her, but she was miles beyond caring. "Dan, you don't know how to love anyone but yourself. I feel sorry for you, but I *don't* love you anymore. The best I can manage is pity."

Dan frowned. "That's not what I want from you, Kate."

"But it's all you're going to get," she said firmly.

He knew her well enough to realize that he had completely misinterpreted her breakup with Gallagher. But instead of beating an embarrassed retreat, he moved to her sofa and collapsed heavily on the soft cushions. "You don't understand, Kate," he said sadly, like a petulant child who had just been told he couldn't have ice cream for dinner. "I need you. Sometimes I just feel so overwhelmed that I don't know what to do. I have no one I can trust. There's no one who knows me and loves me for who I really am...."

If Kate had wanted to drive a nail into the coffin she could have told him it was unlikely he'd ever find a person who could know him and still love him. A year ago she might have said it, but tonight she didn't. Dan McBride was nothing more than a pathetic child in a man's body. More than anything, Kate felt embarrassed that she had ever loved him, and for the life of her, she couldn't figure out why she had.

For a moment, she almost took pity on him. Some old motherly, protective feelings welled up in her and she almost sat beside him, ready to encourage him to talk about his problems.

But when she realized the trap she had almost fallen into, she felt nothing but disgust. "Dan, I'm really sorry you're having a rough time, but you brought it on yourself. You always do. What is it this time? Did a girlfriend dump you? Did you get a bad review? Did *Entertainment Weekly* publish an unflattering picture?"

"Nothing like that," he assured her, then recanted. "Well, sort of. I've been seeing this actress..."

"And she told you to get lost?" Kate asked when he let the sentence hang.

"We had a fight," he admitted. "She was upset because I'd gotten into a fistfight over you. We were arguing...I'd had a little too much to drink, and I said some things that she didn't like."

"That's typical," she muttered.

He looked at her beseechingly. "Kate, the real problem with every woman I've dated is that they're not *you.*"

"No, Dan. The problem is that you're self-centered, thoughtless and careless with other people's feelings. And when you realize you've gone too far you drag out all your boyish charm and say 'I'm sorry,' as though that's going to make everything all right. There's nothing special about me except that I was stupid enough to forgive you more often than anyone else you've ever dated."

"I'm sorry, Kate, but I don't know how to be any other way. This constant grind of public attention and media pressure—"

"Oh, stop making excuses," she snapped, unwilling to be manipulated. "You were always that way, Dan, even before your first big hit. Fame just brought out your faults and put them under a spotlight. Stardom didn't change you—your own weaknesses did," she told him, then stopped dead still, not even breathing as she realized the importance of what she had said.

In one heated sentence, Kate had peeled away all the layers of her problem with Matt and hit the core. She wasn't afraid of the everyday grind of publicity, and her anger at his "lie" had been just another excuse to push him away and protect herself from her real fear—that success would turn him into another Dan McBride. And *that* was something that could never happen in a million years.

Dan McBride was a charming, boyish man who couldn't stand up to the temptations of fame because he was weak, immature and insecure. Matt Gallagher was boyishly charming, too, but there was nothing weak or immature about him and he didn't have an insecure bone in his body.

The impact of that revelation stunned Kate because it was so simple and so obvious. She stood in the middle of her living room looking at the man who had betrayed her and fought the urge to kiss him. His visit was exactly what she had needed—an up-close reminder of what he was really like. And how different he was from Matt.

"How could you be so stupid?" she muttered furiously, hitting herself in the forehead.

Dan sat up, shocked. "What? Kate, are you all right?"

"No, I'm not," she told him. "I'm an idiot. I'm a blind, stupid idiot."

Dan came to his feet. "What are you talking about?"

"None of your business," she told him, grabbing hold of his arm to drag him toward the door. "Just go. Out. Find another shoulder to cry on next time you're feeling blue. Mine's not available."

"But Kate—"

She stopped and faced him squarely. "Look at me, Dan. Read my lips. I am madly, passionately, hopelessly in love with another man, and in a way, I have you and Harry Townsend to thank for that. If Harry hadn't caught you with Sandra Berringer, I might have married you and never would have met Matt Gallagher." She took his arm again and herded him toward the door. "So thank you for being a cad, Dan. Thank you for being an unfaithful, weak-willed, insensitive lout." She opened the door and shoved him through it.

Dan turned and looked at her as though she had gone stark-raving mad. "You're welcome," he deadpanned.

His timing was so perfect Kate had to laugh. "Here's one last piece of advice, Dan. Take a cue from Schwarzenegger and try comedy. You'll be a natural. As for me, I'm getting married."

Dan opened his mouth just as Kate slammed the door in his face. She was in love and she had things to do.

WALKING AIMLESSLY through San Francisco's Golden Gate Park made Matt feel like a kid playing hooky from school, but he was too miserable to enjoy the first taste of freedom he'd had in three weeks. He couldn't stop thinking about Kate. The interviews and autographings were wearing him down, and it didn't seem to matter that he only had two more days of the book tour to go. When he returned to L.A., he still wouldn't be able to go to Kate and it was a sure bet that good old Pam McFadden would have another media blitz waiting for him.

He was so miserable he'd been surly and uncooperative all week, but apparently being a pain-in-the-rear did have some rewards, because right after his last book signing this afternoon, Pam had told him to get lost.

They had been in the limo headed for the hotel when Pam had emphatically decided she'd had enough of Matt's bad mood. She told their driver to take a detour through the park and when they reached Overlook Drive, she made him pull over.

"All right. Out," she had ordered sternly.

Not even fully aware of where they were, Matt had looked around, then looked at Pam. "What?"

"I said get out of the car," his keeper had replied. "I can't stand this moping a minute longer. Take a walk in the park. Soak up some sunshine. Do anything it takes to get a new outlook on life, but do it quick. There are still two days of this tour left and I don't need a walking zombie on my hands."

Matt still hadn't comprehended what she wanted. "I thought we had another interview this afternoon."

"I'm canceling it," she told him. "You're no good to yourself or Granger Publishing like this, and I don't trust you to give a decent interview."

Matt hadn't needed another invitation. Grateful for the reprieve, he had climbed out of the car. Pam had offered to pick him up in an hour, but Matt had refused and walked away from the limo without another glance. He'd take a cab back to the hotel—if he decided to return at all; five minutes in the lush green park was enough to make him consider an all-out revolt. He had played the good little marionette, dancing at the end of Russell Thatch's strings for nearly three weeks. Were two more days of publicity so important?

Not to Matt, certainly. He hadn't wanted any of this in the first place, and a continuing spot on the *New York Times* Bestseller list wasn't worth a fraction of what it had cost him.

"I beg your pardon, sir, but aren't you Matt Gallagher?"

It was a gorgeous spring day and there were people everywhere in the park, but Matt hadn't been aware of any of them, not even the grave-looking, impeccably dressed elderly gentleman with the British accent who had just approached him. Though Matt didn't want to smile for another fan, he took the man's age into consideration and remembered the manners his mother had taught him. "Yes, sir, I am. What can I do for you?"

"You may come this way, sir." The old man made a broad gesture toward a green hillside overlooking the ocean, and waited expectantly for Matt to comply.

"I beg your pardon?"

"Forgive me for being unclear, sir. I wish you to accompany me to that spot up there on the hill. It has one of the loveliest views of the ocean that you'll find anywhere in the entire city. The fog will be rolling in soon, and it makes quite an impressive sight."

For a second, Matt had the feeling he had dropped down the Mad Hatter's rabbit hole into a formal drawing room complete with British butler. "I'm sure it does, but—"

"Just follow me, sir."

The butler started up the hill, but Matt stood his ground. "Is this a mugging?"

The old man turned. "Certainly not, sir. Do I look like a common highwayman?"

"No, but—"

"Forgive me for being impertinent, sir, but you must cooperate. My employer has gone to a great deal of trouble on your behalf."

Matt groaned. *Russell Thatch strikes again,* he thought irritably. This was some half-baked publicity stunt, and Matt wanted no part of it. He should have known that Pam McFadden was just setting him up for the kill when she'd let him out of jail so unexpectedly.

Though his first impulse was to refuse to take part in whatever scheme Thatch had planned, Matt didn't have the heart to protest. Nothing mattered anymore. He might as well go along for the ride. At least this was something different from the usual publicity grind.

"Very well, Jeeves," he said finally. "Carry on."

The old man gave him a grandfatherly smile. "This way, sir."

They climbed the steep hill, and Matt was a little surprised that his escort didn't have to stop even once to catch his breath. The old man was in shape, Matt had to give him that. But what he found at the top of the hill was even more surprising. A catering van was parked a short distance away, and two young women in short frilly skirts and starched white aprons were in the process of setting up a small banquet on a white wrought-iron table.

When the old man saw them, he shook his head and clicked his tongue. "Forgive me, sir, but I must ask you to wait here a moment. These girls are impossibly slow." He leaned toward Matt and lowered his voice confidentially. "You know how hard it is to get good help. I shall return in a moment."

The butler—for he could be described as nothing else—bustled off, and Matt watched in amazement as he and the housemaids made trip after trip to the van, transforming the hill into a romantic country garden, complete with a vine-covered arbor, flowering plants and an elegantly laid champagne buffet.

"We're ready for you now, sir," the butler said when he had everything arranged to his satisfaction. He escorted Matt to a cushion-covered wrought-iron bench. "Please help yourself to the hors d'oeuvres, sir. Your host will arrive momentarily. Oh, and do take a few moments to enjoy the view," he said, gesturing toward the open expanse of sky over the ocean. "I am assured that you won't be disappointed if you do."

With that, he snapped his fingers and his staff fell in behind him as he made his way back to the van.

What on earth...? Matt was mystified. Was this Russell Thatch's way of paying him back for having done his duty these past three weeks? If so, a simple thank-you, I'm sorry and a promise never to subject him to this kind of torture again would have sufficed.

Not knowing what else to do, Matt took a finger sandwich off the table beside him and leaned back to enjoy the view. Below him kites were flying, and in the distance the fog was, indeed, beginning to roll in toward the bay. The only thing that could have made it more perfect would have been a view of the Golden Gate Bridge within the panoramic scene—that, and of course, sharing it with Kate.

Matt shoved the thought aside and watched the horizon. A helicopter flew almost directly overhead, but he ignored the buzzing and concentrated on the patterns being made by the fog in the distance. The helicopter went over again, and Matt wondered what was keeping his mysterious host. A bottle of champagne was being chilled in a silver bucket beside the table, but he wasn't tempted to sample it. He wasn't in a celebratory mood.

The helicopter buzzed overhead a third time, and Matt glanced over his shoulder at the catering van. It was still there, but there was no sign of Jeeves or the Bobbsey Twins.

What was going on? What was he waiting for?

The helicopter skimmed the trees a fourth time, and Matt finally glanced up in irritation. With his luck, it was probably a police chopper getting ready for riot control. What he found instead was a brightly colored helicopter trailing an advertising banner like the ones he had seen so often in L.A. that usually said something like Listen to Radio KRLA.

Only this one wasn't hyping a radio station. This one was for him and no one else, because it read *Surrender Matthew.*

Not really believing his eyes, Matt came to his feet and laughed out loud. He wasn't mistaken. The helicopter flew on with the banner waving like a brilliant serpent's tail, and Matt ran after it. "Wait! Come back!" he shouted, waving his arms like a lunatic as it disappeared over the trees. He stopped and waited, and a few moments later the copter circled back one last time.

"Well, it certainly took you long enough to get the message. Do you surrender?"

Matt whirled around and found Kate standing under the vine-covered arbor. She moved forward a few steps to the table and began pouring champagne as Matt stood looking at her like an idiot, praying he hadn't gone insane, though it seemed highly likely that he was hallucinating. Kate was dressed in a man's tuxedo, complete with boutonniere, spats and a top hat covering her upswept hair.

"Kate?" He took a few hesitant steps toward her.

"Who were you expecting? The Wicked Witch of the West?" She smiled and held out a glass of champagne. "Here. Drink this and sit down, Dorothy. We have a ceremony to perform."

Matt finally accepted what his eyes were telling him and what his heart wanted to believe. Kate was really here. The renewed publicity that had resulted from her dash to the hospital hadn't forced her into another change of heart. And best of all, she was giving him a look that said, "I love you, you idiot."

It was everything he could do to keep from snatching her into his arms, but he resisted that overpowering temptation and sat as she directed. He also took the champagne. "Kate, what's going on?" he asked.

"What does it look like? It's a proposal, of course," she said as she removed her hat and knelt beside him. "It took a lot of fast talking to convince Ms. McFadden to play along, so don't spoil it, okay?"

He bit back a stunned, joyful laugh. "A proposal?"

"Don't you remember?" she asked, leaning toward him, her eyes filled with love. "You were going to propose to me, and do it right. In a tuxedo on bended knee with champagne on ice and—" she reached into her jacket and withdrew the ring box he had left with her "—a ring in your pocket. By the way, I called your mother this morning and she said it was okay with her."

"Oh, God, Kate..." He dropped the champagne glass onto the grass and cupped her face in his hands. "I shouldn't let you do this. I should send you away for your own protection."

"Don't go all noble on me again, Gallagher," she warned him lovingly as she turned her head and kissed the palm of his hand. "You don't wear martyrdom very well and I can't possibly live without you. If you send me away, I'll just come back again and again because I'm not giving up on you."

Matt didn't need any more convincing than that. She was here. She had come after him. She had made a spectacle of herself in a public park, and she wasn't going to let him get away. Matt couldn't have refused her proposal if his life had depended on it.

"I love you," he said as his lips closed impatiently over hers for a long, frantic and wholly satisfying kiss.

Kate clung to him, savoring his urgency and the love that he poured into the kiss. By the time it ended, they were both breathless, but Kate somehow found enough air to ask, "Does that mean you'll marry me?"

Matt's answering smile brought out his dimples and erased the lines of exhaustion and misery that had marred his handsome face. "Are you sure you want to spend the rest of your life with a famous author?"

"No, I want to spend it with you. But if I can't have one without the other, then I'll just have to smile for the cameras and enjoy the ride."

"I promise you it will never be dull," he whispered.

"Just promise me it will last forever. That's all I need."

"I'll give you forever on a silver platter, Kate. I love you."

A feeling of perfect contentment washed over Kate and she handed him the velvet-covered box. "Here. Let's make this official."

He opened the ring box and found only a scrap of brown paper. "What's this?"

"It's your engagement ring, of course," she told him as she took the scrap, unfolded the silly looking cigar band and slipped it onto his finger. "What were you expecting? Diamonds?" she asked, wiggling her left hand in front of his face. Her ring finger sparkled with the brilliant cut marquis he had bought for her.

Matt gathered her into his arms with a joyous laugh, and from out of nowhere a huge round of applause and catcalls filled the air. Startled, they looked around and when Kate saw the enormous audience that had gathered, she stood quickly, pulled Matt to his feet and took a deep bow.

"Thank you, ladies and gentlemen, for your kind attention. The next floor show will begin in fifteen minutes!" she announced, then threw herself into Matt's arms for another kiss and another round of applause.

You asked for it...you've got it. More MEN!

We're thrilled to bring you another special edition of the popular MORE THAN MEN series.

Like those who have come before him, Chase Quinn is more than tall, dark and handsome. All of these men have extraordinary powers that make them "more than men." But whether they are able to grant you three wishes or live forever, make no mistake—their greatest, most extraordinary power is of seduction.

So make a date in October with Chase Quinn in

#554 THE INVISIBLE GROOM
by Barbara Bretton

SUPH6

A NEW STAR COMES OUT TO SHINE....

American Romance continues to search the heavens for the best new talent... the best new stories.

Join us next month when a new star appears in the American Romance constellation:

Kim Hansen
#548 TIME RAMBLER
August 1994

Even in the shade of a broad-rimmed Stetson, Eagle River's lanky sheriff had the bluest eyes Katie Shannon had ever seen. But why was he *in the ghost town—a man who was killed in a shoot-out one hundred years ago?*

RISING STAR

Be sure to Catch a "Rising Star"!

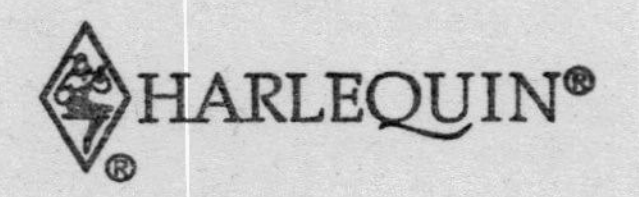
HARLEQUIN®

HARLEQUIN®

Don't miss these Harlequin favorites by some of our most distinguished authors!
And now you can receive a discount by ordering two or more titles!

HT #25525	THE PERFECT HUSBAND by Kristine Rolofson	$2.99	☐
HT #25554	LOVERS' SECRETS by Glenda Sanders	$2.99	☐
HP #11577	THE STONE PRINCESS by Robyn Donald	$2.99	☐
HP #11554	SECRET ADMIRER by Susan Napier	$2.99	☐
HR #03277	THE LADY AND THE TOMCAT by Bethany Campbell	$2.99	☐
HR #03283	FOREIGN AFFAIR by Eva Rutland	$2.99	☐
HS #70529	KEEPING CHRISTMAS by Marisa Carroll	$3.39	☐
HS #70578	THE LAST BUCCANEER by Lynn Erickson	$3.50	☐
HI #22256	THRICE FAMILIAR by Caroline Burnes	$2.99	☐
HI #22238	PRESUMED GUILTY by Tess Gerritsen	$2.99	☐
HAR #16496	OH, YOU BEAUTIFUL DOLL by Judith Arnold	$3.50	☐
HAR #16510	WED AGAIN by Elda Minger	$3.50	☐
HH #28719	RACHEL by Lynda Trent	$3.99	☐
HH #28795	PIECES OF SKY by Marianne Willman	$3.99	☐

Harlequin Promotional Titles

#97122	LINGERING SHADOWS by Penny Jordan	$5.99	☐

(limited quantities available on certain titles)

	AMOUNT	**$**
DEDUCT:	**10% DISCOUNT FOR 2+ BOOKS**	**$**
	POSTAGE & HANDLING	**$**
	($1.00 for one book, 50¢ for each additional)	
	APPLICABLE TAXES*	**$**__________
	TOTAL PAYABLE	**$**__________
	(check or money order—please do not send cash)	

To order, complete this form and send it, along with a check or money order for the total above, payable to Harlequin Books, to: **In the U.S.:** 3010 Walden Avenue, P.O. Box 9047, Buffalo, NY 14269-9047; **In Canada:** P.O. Box 613, Fort Erie, Ontario, L2A 5X3.

Name: ______________________________

Address: __________________ City: ________________

State/Prov.: ________________ Zip/Postal Code: ________________

*New York residents remit applicable sales taxes.
Canadian residents remit applicable GST and provincial taxes..

HBACK-JS